The Lights Below

Also by Carl MacDougall

The One Legged Tap Dancer

Elvis is Dead

Stone Over Water*

The Devil & the Giro (ed.)

Behind the Lines (ed.)

**available from Minerva*

Carl MacDougall
The Lights Below

Minerva

A Minerva Paperback

THE LIGHTS BELOW

First published in Great Britain 1993
by Martin Secker & Warburg Ltd
This Minerva edition published 1994
by Mandarin Paperbacks
an imprint of Reed Consumer Books Limited
Michelin House, 81 Fulham Road, London SW3 6RB
and Auckland, Melbourne, Singapore and Toronto

Reprinted 1994

A CIP catalogue record for this title
is available from the British Library
ISBN 0 7493 9714 4

Printed and bound in Great Britain
by Cox & Wyman Ltd, Reading, Berkshire

For the Monday Night Woodlands Road Group.
Did I ever say thanks?

Life is but a day at most.
Robert Burns

I would like to thank the English Departments of Glasgow and Strathclyde Universities and the Scottish Arts Council. This novel was mostly written between October 1990 and March 1991 when I had a fellowship at both universities, jointly funded by the Scottish Arts Council.

It is often safer to be in chains than to be free.

The Trial Franz Kafka

At the back when they opened the door, he rocked himself forward, back and forward on his feet, trying to empty his mind.

Just me, he was thinking. Only me.

He imagined this moment: lying in bed and awake with the snoring; as heating moved along the pipes, he pictured himself at the front by the door. The light would dazzle, cut through the air and land around him, changing colour as if it had been filtered through a glass geometry.

He imagined being released from Dungavel, into the country and the open air, where he sometimes caught the smell of pine, working in the garden. Wind slapped the flagpoles, missed the wires, hummed like a generator or the sound of a seashell, murmuring between the poles and the razorwire fencing.

'Best no to think about it,' said Charlie Sloan, whose pipe made a clucking sound when he drew on it. Charlie had murdered his wife. He looked like a fat man who'd shrunk, as though he had too much skin.

'I've got too much blood,' he said. 'Always have had. Any time I go to give some, they always take it. Here comes the blood man, they say. That's what they call me, the blood man.' Charlie never spoke of his wife and did not want released.

Andy dreamed of catching his breath as his feet crunched the gravel; but this was Barlinnie. Andy Paterson was back in Glasgow and about to be freed into rain, transferred because it was easier to release the Glasgow prisoners from Barlinnie, Edinburgh men from Saughton and stuff like that. He was at the back because there were things to check, money, clothes and bureaucracy. He imagined being released alone, his release and no one else.

'Right then, straighten up.' This was the warder with the Brylcreemed hair. 'Intae a line and straighten up. My shift finishes at three o'clock and yous're no oot yet.' The warder had watery eyes. He blinked a lot and used a cream for conjunctivitis. The cream made the rims of his eyes shiny.

There were eight of them, mostly with ski jackets, jeans and trainers, fading sports jackets of imitation tweed, synthetic trousers that never creased, tieless shirts and unpolished shoes. They stood with their shoulders hunched, hands in their pockets, moving sideways from foot to foot. They looked as if they needed their hair washed and everyone carried a brown paper parcel.

'Fucksake. Look at the state of yous. Right then. Hold on.' The phone was ringing.

Andy was wearing the Crombie he'd bought at Oxfam, the black Crombie coat with the velvet collar, double-breasted, single-buttoned, cost a fiver, best of gear.

The warder stopped talking, he had been rearranging shifts; he stopped talking, left the phone on the table and opened the door. There was a breath of wind. The man at the front said, 'Jesus suffering,' blew on his hands and stepped through the door within a door, the small door that was part of the bigger gate, through the door, over the stile and out of jail.

*

He did not know the form. There would be a form. He had never been released from jail and was anxious to survive the etiquette. There was a small cinematic moment when the door closed with a click, never an echoing slam. The others were standing around in bunches. Some turned and looked towards him; he turned to look at the door.

An older man looked at the two boys, hands outstretched, and counted their money. 'How much have yous got?' he asked. They raised their hands towards his face. 'We've enough,' he said. 'Who's in?'

'I'm away hame for my nookie. I tellt her tae get us a carry-oot in wi a video and a wee pizza, so I'm fucken sure I'm no staunin here,. drinking with you lot in the pouring rain.' The young man pulled his ski jacket collar around his neck and ran towards the bus-stop. Two others moved in different directions without a word.

'What about you, sir? A small refreshment?'

'No thanks,' said Andy. 'I'll give it a miss.'

'You couldnae gie us a wee half quid then?'

Andy shook his head.

'Very wise,' said another wee man. 'Drink's a curse.'

'Are you in?'

'I wouldnae mind, but you know what it's like yoursel. I'm a wee bit stuck, embarrassed.'

'Here.' One of the younger men handed a crumpled pound note. 'That's you in, auld yin.'

'God bless you, son. I'm an alcoholic by the way, know what I mean; got the jail for nothing.'

They moved down the hill towards the off-licence, opened at half seven because there was business at that time of the morning.

Andy walked towards the bus-stop. Four people were waiting, one had been released with him. He nodded. 'I didnae think you'd've been joinin the early morning drinkers,' he said. 'That lot'll be begging along Sauchiehall Street by dinnertime and back in the garage the night.'

'Suppose so.'

'Been in long?'

'Two year. Yourself?'

'Couple of months. This your bus?'

'I don't know.'

'It goes intae toon.'

'How much is it?'

'Forty pence, I think.' He shouted in the bus to the driver, 'Still forty pence to town?' The driver nodded.

They went upstairs, sat at the front and introduced themselves. Jimmy Wilson's tobacco tin was decorated with used matches and JW burned into the wood. He lit a thin roll-up.

'I've never smoked,' said Andy Paterson. 'Don't know why. Never fancied it, I suppose.'

'Must have saved you a right few quid inside.'

'Suppose so. You never think how much you save no doing something.'

'That's a bit too deep for me.'

Jimmy drew on his fag and coughed. Andy caught a lump of smoke, Old Holborn, and smelled the tobacco. He moved towards the smoke again but this time there was nothing. Jail smelled like a hot butcher's shop. Prisoners lost their sense of smell in what they said was the mixture of sweat and piss. For the visitor, there was something more, the smell of jail rather than its ingredients. Andy smiled. Jimmy Wilson had been talking. 'This is me,' he said. 'Alexandra Parade.'

The rain was heavier. Andy watched it roll and gather across the pane as the bus moved to town. A young girl sat beside him, reading a magazine which trembled with the bus. Andy tried to smell her perfume. Nothing. Maybe she wasn't wearing any.

The bus took him to George Square and a train from Queen Street took him to Milngavie where Eileen lived on the edge of Drumchapel.

Eileen was his next of kin. She lived in what she called a maisonette, with a burglar alarm and a small car. She looked and dressed like her mother. Her daughter, Tracy, looked like her.

Eileen married Joe Sweeney when she was nineteen, had a daughter and stayed at home.

Their father died when Andy was eight. Eileen was four. Andy remembered his father as a tall, slim man who liked cats and walked like a dancer, standing with his feet splayed. There were four cats in the house. Eileen hated cats: 'They're creepy,' she said.

Daddy went to a casino where he won a lot of money and was murdered on his way home. Murders are now a daily occurrence, no longer mysteries, except for sexual murders, which increase newspaper circulations. Andy and Eileen's father was murdered at a time when the event alone sold newspapers.

POLICE HUNT KILLER

said the newspaper headlines. Andy's father's death was a public memory. Death now made his father exceptional. There was a lengthy trial, during which the public absorbed obsessive details of airy wins and fulminous losses. Details strangers should never have known were told to people who did not care, family secrets were shared in death.

They surfaced like lost whales. He was christened Jacob on the whim of his mother who heard the name on a radio programme about sheep. He took a size seven shoe, preferably brown, had eight teeth missing, consistently used a word of his own devising, *indentification* instead of the state of being identified, took tea without sugar, smoked an average of forty Players Weights a day, never backed horses and used milk in his hair.

'I swear to God,' said Malky MacKenzie with eyes like oysters. 'On my mother's life, we met just the once and that was it. On the night of his death I was seeing my sister.'

'I repeat,' said the counsel, 'this court has heard testimony. You and the deceased were together on the night of his death. You were heard to threaten the deceased. You lost at cards, owed him money and was the last person in whose company he was seen alive.'

The case against Malky was Not Proven.

Andy Paterson can never remember; even now he cannot remember Malky MacKenzie visiting his house, or hearing his name as much as mentioned. Malky's story was sold to the papers.

I KILLED FOR LOVE, SAYS GAMBLER'S MURDERER

with a picture of Malky and Andy's mother wanting peace in their life together. 'I want to set the record straight,' the papers quoted Malky as saying. 'I'm doing this for Rose's sake. She deserves to know the truth.'

'My life with Jacob was never happy,' Andy's mother told the press. 'I've forgiven Malky. I know that he can make me happy.'

WIFE MARRIES KILLER

said the newspaper headlines. 'She'll roast in hell,' said Andy's granny; and Grandpa asked her, 'Where's my tea?'

Malky moved from Govan to Scotstoun, bought a house for

the mother and daughter, opened a shop and bought a car. Andy went to live with his granny. Malky was done for tax evasion. 'Same as Al Capone,' said Granny. 'Worse,' said Grandpa.

'My wee Jake was fine till he met her,' Granny said if anyone asked. 'It was her that did it. Her and hotels. Kip shops, full of whores and comic singers. Jacob got in with the wrong crowd. Gallivanting. Once that starts everything's dull. Your faither met her and she made him marry her. She knew he would, he was that sort of man. And look at her now. How she can hold her head up high I'll never know. I'll say this for him, your faither was the smartest wee waiter I've ever seen. And references; he never worked in a place that didnae want him back.'

Andy became a waiter by accident. Only when they threatened to remove his benefit if he did not appear for another interview did he agree to go. He got a start, surprisingly liked the work and never told Granny. She thought he worked in an office, doing the books.

He became a waiter when the city was poised on the edge of consumerism, when we were still a source of manufacture and the differences were more clearly defined than at any time since. He could see the life of his father. The head waiter dictated your wages by making you serve unpopular tables, in a draught by the door, away from the band, close to the kitchen, or by giving you an extra couple of tables which meant everyone had to wait for their food, though good tippers got his special attention. He would also give you customers who consistently complained, fussy people who were never pleased or folk who had never been to the restaurant before.

When Andy started the head waiter told him: 'This is not a job. This is a career. You are never seen and never heard. My customers do not care what you think or if you think. They care that you serve their food correctly and remove their plates when they have finished eating. They care that you give them a clean ashtray. They never want to hear the sound of your voice, unless they speak to you. Do you understand?'

'Yes, sir.'

'Now why did you want a career as a waiter?'

'My father was a waiter.'

'And is your father still a waiter?'

'No sir.'

'Why not?'

'He's dead.'

'Did he work here?'

'No, sir.'

'Good.'

Andy learned to fold the napkins and lay the tables. He polished the silver and glasses, was told not to fraternise with other staff. The waiters wore morning coats, boiled shirt fronts, white bow ties and comfortable shoes. Waiters have bad feet; corns, bunions, and verrucas are common and they always wear their oldest shoes. No one looks at a waiter's feet. The head waiter wore a dinner suit and a black bow tie, with polished shoes. All the waiters had two voices, one for their customers and one for themselves. It was said they gambled and were prone to drink. The head waiter gave himself a foreign name and accent, but waiters had no names. Some had known Andy's father and always asked for Andy's Granny. 'She's some turn, Jake's maw. Is she still making soup?'

Granny never slept. She dozed by the fire and went to work every night, selling cardboard to down and outs who used it to sleep in; fifty pence a box, newspapers were extra. She collected the boxes from rubbish skips and supermarkets, pushed them around in a pram with the papers, going to doorways and alleys, lanes and closes, sometimes the parks. Along with the boxes she sold soup made from vegetables she found in the street or begged from greengrocers, and the butchers' useless meat and bones. The house always smelled of soup.

Andy lost his first job when he was caught in bed with a girl from the Islands. She said she would like to teach him Gaelic. Andy had gambled most of his wages. At four in the morning he was barred from the table.

Morag was making toast and tea when Andy came into the kitchen and sat at a table, counting his money.

The housekeeper came to Morag's room when she did not appear for her shift.

'Out of my dining room and never come back.' The head waiter left for a haircut when Andy appeared to prepare for lunch. He and Morag met in the office and said Cheerio at the staff door.

'Of all the things I thought you'd do, I never thought you'd end up the same as your faither.' Andy's granny was by the fire. He did not tell her why he was sacked, nor that he was going to London to work the season.

'Now you can help me look eftir him, that auld bastard ben there, Sir Winston Churchill.' Andy's granny hated Churchill. 'If there's a hell at all, that man is in it,' she said.

When he'd had his soup around seven o'clock, Andy's grandfather went to the pub. At half past ten she laid his pyjamas across the bed.

Every night he undressed in the dark. When she heard the snoring, Andy's granny went to work.

She went in with his tea and found him dead. The minister spoke of a race well run. Andy's granny did not go to the service. There was a reception, tea and scones in a small hotel.

'Hello, Andrew,' said his mother. 'This is your sister, Eileen.'

'I know.'

'How are you getting on?'

'Fine.'

'Malcolm. Why don't you take Andrew for a refreshment.'

Malky swallowed his whisky whole and shook the dreeps in his tumbler of beer.

'Your mother wants you to come and visit. If you ever need anything, let us know.'

'What does she drink?' asked Andy. He ordered a half for Malky, vodka for his mother and Eileen with a tonic between them. He paid the barman, went to the lavatory and left the hotel.

'What kept you?' Granny never mentioned the funeral, asked who was there or what had happened.

His mother and sister came to visit, usually on a Saturday afternoon. The three of them went to the Art Galleries or the Museum of Transport, had tea and cakes and were back by five. The visits stopped because Granny got angry.

They met again when Eileen married. Joe Sweeney said Andy should come to the house and this was how he met his sister. Joe had visited him in jail and insisted he stay when he was released.

'You can't stay here,' Eileen said when she opened the door.

'This is my address,' he said. 'They could come here to check up on me.'

'Don't stand there talking about stuff like that. Come inside.'

'I'll take a cup of tea,' said Andy.

'I don't want you here,' she said. 'You're a pal to Joe, no brother to me, though why he puts up with you God alone knows. You never came to our Tracy's wedding.'

'I was in the jail.'

'You never even sent a present. And now you've got the cheek to come back here, giving us a showing up.'

'How's your mother?'

'Our mother's fine. No thanks to you. She was worried sick, so she was. The shame nearly killed her.'

'And Malky'll be fine as well.'

'My daddy has cancer.'

'Your daddy is dead.'

'You can leave right now if you're going to bring that up again.'

'Your faither's name was Jacob Paterson.'

'The court passed a verdict of Not Proven.'

'And you believe what you hear in court?'

'You were found Guilty.'

'Jesus Christ, Malky said he did it.'

'There's no need for blasphemy. Just as well you weren't at our Tracy's wedding if that's the kind of language you use, not very nice I must say.'

He met Joe coming home from work. They hugged in the street. 'Christ,' said Joe. 'It's great to see you. Let me look at you. God Almighty. It's great to see you.'

They went to the pub. Joe phoned Eileen. 'Please,' he said, coming back with a round, 'stay for a day or two, till you're on your feet. Tell you what: I've taped some games. I knew you'd want to see them.'

They sat for four hours, drinking beer and watching football. Eileen was in bed. Andy's room was warmed, his clothes unpacked. They shook hands and hugged at the top of the stairs.

'That was some goal McStay scored.'

'Cracker.'

'Listen, it's great to have you back in the land of the living.'

Lying in bed, in the dwam before sleep, he remembered his grandfather gave him a hammering for playing football. Granny tried to intervene. 'Is the boy not supposed to play football?' she asked.

'Not in sandshoes.'

'Then buy him football boots.'

'Who has money to waste on that?'

'That's all you're good for, lifting your hands for anything but work.'

Granny only made it worse. His grandfather held his hair and hit him with a stick. 'Stand still, you little bastard,' he said. 'Stand still, or it'll be worse for you.'

Granny washed his back, put cream on the wounds and sat beside him till he went to sleep. Grandpa went to the pub.

He did not hear his grandfather come home, but Granny woke him during the night. 'Come away ben here,' she said.

His grandfather was sleeping on his back, snoring loudly, teeth out and his cheeks quivering. The room smelled of stale whisky.

'Hammer him,' she said.

'Eh?'

'You can punch the auld bastard as much as you like.'

'He'll waken.'

'He's never wakened when I've done it.'

Andy climbed onto the bed, sat on the blankets and punched his grandfather across the face. The old man snored.

'Again,' she said. 'I'll tell you when to stop.'

The room was dark. A yellow light shone through from the kitchen and lit the wall behind the bed, beside the dresser and the trellised wallpaper with honeysuckle and roses climbing the wall.

'Give him a doing.'

He pummelled the old man's face and chest, lashing out,

hitting the pillow and crying with rage. Grandpa never wakened. Granny lifted him down from the bed, exhausted and crying.

'Here.' She gave him a dishtowel to blow his nose. He washed his face under the tap, went back to bed and she tucked him in.

The old man never said a word in the morning.

Just like Eileen.

At the end of his sleep, Andy wondered if the noise would go when he opened his eyes.

A vacuum cleaner; the head of the suction thing tapped against the skirting board. The tapping sound, banging the board at irregular intervals, wakened him. There was the droning and the suction and the added anxiety of metal against wood.

To waken in jail is to be made aware of how little you slept, waking with a headache from the heating and the noise. No matter how you sleep, how deeply or how long, it is always the sleep of a sickly child, aware of what was going on, the shouts and the sobbing. To be in jail is all the time to want to sleep somewhere else.

Half past nine and now awake in his sister's house with sunshine on the curtains as she hoovered the stairs. Andy had the jail headache; not so heavy, getting better.

'Worms,' the doctor told him. 'Everybody gets them in here, it's the bacon and pork. Take this, twice a day and keep a look out, small white and wriggly things, look like pudding.'

The doctor was a pasty man who smoked too much. His breath smelled of burning rubber. 'Stubborn little buggers,' he said a fortnight later.

'The headache's worse than ever.'

'Tapeworm. They can be anything, six, seven feet long. Have you been hungrier than usual?'

'No.'

'Sure?'

'I eat the same as anyone else.'

'That's not saying much. I'd imagine there's more than one tapeworm in this place, perfect conditions, right diet, low activity, consistent warm temperature. If you've got a tapeworm, it's there for keeps. There's no point in trying to shift it; bloody thing breaks up. So keep a watch, tell us how you're doing. If there's an increase in your hunger, sudden weight loss, anything like that, let us know and we'll arrange a fluoroscope, shoot some dye in you, see where he is and what's his size.' He stretched his arms above his head and stared out the window to Wardlaw Hill. 'I think tapeworms are coming back. They were very common when I was training. Hardly ever hear of them now, except in South America, Africa, places like that.'

He knew about the worm. Since childhood he had wondered about a living thing thriving inside him; sometimes sure he could feel it turn, change direction. When he was hungry he imagined he was feeding the worm rather than himself; indigestion or heartburn meant the worm disliked what he had eaten.

Now he sat on the edge of the bed, feeling the ache of comfort. Prison life seems based on the army and also has a logic of its own. They use sheets, blankets and horsehair mattresses; all the clothes they issue are blue, except for the pullovers, which are brown.

He stared at himself in his civvy suit, folded the downie and, fully clothed with the Paisley patterned tie, brushed his teeth.

'Why do you dress before you wash?'

'I think it has to do with the cold.'

'This house is centrally heated.'

'Granny's wasn't.'

The bathroom had been scrubbed and perfumed. Bright and carpeted, lilac and blue, the walls had tasteful Victorian prints, fat urchins and cheery folk warming their hands on a brazier, ice skating or languidly dancing at a military ball. Bevelled glass shelves caught and spun the dissected light; there were soaps and mirrors, bath salts, talcum, toners and creams; there were coloured cotton-wool balls in a glass jar, shampoo, aftershave, tissues and conditioner; the make-up was separated from the male requisites; there were two mirrored cabinets which could have been locked and the spare toilet roll was covered with a pink and orange woollen crocheted dog with red buttoned eyes; there were other things too silly to mention. Andy slopped away his presence, wiped round the sink and used the air freshener, knowing his sister would do it later, when he had gone.

Eileen listened to Radio One. She was wiping the sink: 'There's your coffee and I've made some toast.'

The coffee was instant. A slice of margarined toast lay beside it. He held his hand beneath his face to catch the crumbs. The house had no smell.

'You can't stay.'

A car horn sounded in the street outside; insistent, two or three urgent raps. 'The fish man,' said Eileen. She spoke staring out the window, towards the patch of garden, her back to Andy.

'It's different. I thought it would be all right. If I knew it would be like this I'd've said no. Joe said it would be okay, so I went ahead. Having you here brings it all back.'

'Brings what back, Eileen?'

'Everything. When you have a brother you never see, it's better to keep it that way. Otherwise you get caught up imagining what things'd be like.'

'I always thought it was all right for you; you were with my mother and her man, the wee Malky.'

'I call him Daddy.'

'Your father's dead.'

'You're just out the jail and in no position to talk.'

'I thought if we could get together we could try to have a proper family. I thought about it a lot in jail and imagined all we had to do was talk. Now it seems we've nothing to talk about.'

'You had a wife, that was your family.'

'You can't recreate what you've never had; if you've never known a proper family, no matter what that's like, no matter what the reality's like, if you've never had it yourself you can't make it for someone else.'

'Still the philosopher.'

'Is it because I've been to jail? Is that why you don't want me here?'

'Mum was okay, she tried and Daddy did his best. I don't mean he wasn't like a proper father, he was.'

'How the fuck do you know what a proper father's like?'

'Do not swear in this house. If you must use language like that then please do it outside these walls.'

'Is that because you consider it offensive? Is it rough and crude, same as your background; it's everything you should have been, except you became the most insidious of all creations, the working-class child with bourgeois pretensions, middle-class values on working-class money.'

'What do you know about my life? First there was Mummy and then there was Joe. What life have I had? First a daughter then a wife. You were spoiled rotten. I'd've gone to live with Granny any time.'

'How often were you in the house?'

'I wasn't allowed to go. Remember?'

'Do you know what she did?'

'You didn't go short.'

'You ought to find out what things were like before you start resenting them.'

'Shut up, Andrew. Just shut up. I don't want you here. You're Joe's friend and nothing to do with me. Away you go.'

He slammed the door, was in the road a block and a half away before he realised he neither knew the time nor where he was going.

The Department of Social Security is a stink and a hassle and a way of life. There is no alternative.

Shiny and slippery red plastic benches, scattered rolled-up dowts, cans of superlager, the *Daily Record*, *The Sun* and *The Star*, the small paper slips and numbers collected from a machine which tells whose turn it is to go forward to the cubicle. The noise is constant. Everyone talks loudly, as though they were in the dark.

Because it had lately started to rain, Andy was wet when he arrived in the office. He'd walked from Milngavie to Maryhill. The shoes he had worn indoors were leaking, steam came from his jacket and trousers. When his number was called, three and a half hours later, he was still wet, damp and uncomfortable. There had been two rows and a fight, because of dogs. The police were called. They took fifteen minutes to arrive from their office less than a hundred yards away on the same side of the street. The arguments started when men refused to move because their dogs were fighting, small and angry mongrel dogs that sniffed each other and growled like a headache. The fight was between a man and a woman; she punched him then started screaming.

'Can I help you?' The woman behind the glass wore a wide flowery skirt and a pink T-shirt.

'I got out the jail yesterday.'

'Do you have an address?'

'I was staying with my sister.'

'A payment will have been sent there.'

'Nothing was sent.'

'Is this your local office?'

'I don't know. My sister lives in Milngavie.'

'Then you'll need to go there.'

'But I'm not staying with my sister.'

'If that is the address you gave, a payment will have been sent and if that payment has not arrived you will need to consult your local office, that is the office nearest to the address you gave. It's all in this form, please take it and study it carefully.'

He phoned Eileen. 'A letter came this morning,' she said. 'You were in such a rush to leave I forgot to tell you. If you're coming to collect it you'd better get here within the hour. I've a hairdresser's appointment, a cancellation. I was lucky to get it.'

The bus journey took half an hour, back along the way he'd walked. The bus was a one-person-operated vehicle. Andy wondered why you couldn't buy a ticket before you got on the bus; other countries do it, why not here. There were adverts for a Transcard. He missed his stop.

'There's been a problem.' Eileen had changed her clothes and was sitting in the living room as though expecting visitors. 'I've phoned Joe and I think he's coming home. There's been an awful bother. Hooligans. The roughs from Drumchapel come down here and cause trouble.'

'Have you got my letter?'

The cheque was intact: £70 for two weeks. Enough to get a room.

By the time Joe arrived, Andy and Eileen were having tea. 'Actually, Andrew came back, so it's not as bad as it could have been; and he's decided to find a place of his own. We had a wee discussion and I agree it would be better in the long run, after all, it has to happen sooner or later, he can't stay here for ever.'

In the car, Joe said, 'I'm sorry.'

'It's not your fault.'

'Every time that arsehole next door gets into trouble, she sends for me. I know she's your sister and I know how things are between you, but honest to God, I don't think I can take much more of this fucken nonsense. Kids come down here and screw the houses; drugs I suppose. Some come round a day or two later and try to sell you the stuff they've knocked. The kids down here whose houses get screwed go cruising in motors looking for kids from Drumchapel to give them a doing. They do it in threes and fours. The Drum kids are not at all daft and if three guys in a motor beat you up with a stick you tend to remember them. So Jason, that's his name, honest to Christ; he was walking home last night when four Drum boys jumped him, kicked six colours of shite out of him, because Jason and his pals did it to them. Jason's father phoned the polis who know the score, of course, but they've had a complaint and they have to investigate; not the sort of complaint they get in Drumchapel. And how does Eileen come into all this? Well may you ask. She gets frightened. Where will I drop you?'

'Charing Cross.'

'You'll be happy to know it's got nothing to do with the politicians. It isn't their fault. It's either a new evil, that's what they said, or else it's the weather. Honest to God, the biggest crime figures this century and they blame the weather. We're worse. We listen to that shite. Some of us even take them seriously. They tell us it's got nothing to do with deprivation. After all, we've had deprivation for years and this has never happened before. Must be the fairies. Well seen they don't have to live with it. Listen, son; promise me you'll keep in touch.'

'Cross my heart and hope to die.'

'Here.' Joe gave him thirty quid, six blue fivers.

'I'll pay you back.'

'Don't bother. Joe Sweeney's imperial reserve; only opened in cases of emergency. All I ask is you don't do anything daft.'

'I'm gonnae get myself settled in. Don't look at me like that. I promise. The only one I want to see is Fenian McGuire.'

'He's still around.'

'You seen him?'

'His name crops up from time to time. He's still a lawyer, still getting by. I don't move in these circles any more. I havnae been to the casino in years.'

'Nae wonder you've money.'

The room was advertised in a post office window:

Single gentleman
ROOM TO LET
SS welcome
Pay in advance
Nice house
West End Park Street
Phone 332 3742

The landlord took the money, sixty quid, a week in advance. The house was on the ground floor and the room faced the street. The air was musty. There was a bundle of newspapers and books on the mantelshelf, *Redgauntlet* by Sir Walter Scott, *The Story of San Michelle* by Axel Munthe, Keats' and Burns' Poetical Works, *Labour in Ireland* by James Connelly, with damp and curling pages, lying beside paperbacks with no covers. The room had a ten pence meter, a Baby Belling, a bed and a chair, a reading lamp and a small table, sheets and blankets, stripy maroon and grey wallpaper, dark and heavy curtains, brown linoleum and a patterned rug. The fireplace was cast-iron, painted white, and above the mantelpiece was a picture of Loch Lomond.

The rules of the house came with the key: no cooking smells or overnight guests and a breakfast contract which would be signed when ready. The contract raised the rent from thirty to fifty quid a week and a breakfast was provided, tea and toast, except the landlord was busy and sometimes forgot. The Social would pay. Breakfast contract tenants agreed to a week's notice. The landlord was Polish: 'Don't fuck about,' he said. 'If you want a bath put your name on the list.' The telephone was in the hall.

Andy bought bread and jam, milk, coffee and cheese, found the library on St George's Road, remembered his address and filled in the card. His books were fiction; two Elmore Leonard, a Graham Greene, Kurt Vonnegut, Jnr, and George Mackay Brown.

Back in the room, with a bar of the electric fire working, he ate bread and jam and made some coffee, then went to bed and lay awake reading, occasionally disturbed by the noise from the street, car horns, the shouts and the chatter when the pub came out, now and then wondering where the money was coming from, thinking he would like a transistor and Radio Three while reading about the lost and the lonely.

*

Andy Paterson got the jail for nothing.

In the garden or the hothouse, tying tomato plants to their canes or digging in the seed beds, he tried to piece it all together, tried to make a memory of imprisonment, the way he remembered his grandfather's blindness or the way he remembered his wife.

Grandpa would shout and Granny argued, taunting him by standing her ground: 'Go ahead, hit me. Do it. Do it now, in front of the wean so's he can see what kind of a man you are.'

'He knows what kind of man I am, provoked and demented.'

Grandpa was blinded by glaucoma. 'Bloody drink,' said Granny. 'That's what did it.'

The doctor sent him to an optician, who sent him back to the doctor for a hospital appointment. The appointment came nine months later.

'Sorry,' said the surgeon. 'Not much we can do. It can be treated if it's caught early enough. You should have come sooner.'

'He'll need a guide dug tae take him tae the pub.'

There was a truce for a while, never an actual reconciliation. The arguments became less violent. His grandfather became pathetic, hopeless and lost, sensitive to light and sound, sitting in his chair listening to the wireless.

'I think I preferred it when you were disappearin for days at a time, coming in drunk with nae money, looking for food and giein me a doing,' she told him. 'I could handle that. I knew it wouldnae last for ever. Why don't you go for a pint?'

'I cannae see.'

'Andrew'll take you.'

He left his grandfather at the pub door, afraid to move forward, shouting for someone to come out and get him. Two hours later they heard him as usual at the foot of the stairs, giving his money to the other children: 'Yous're aa good weans to your mammies and grannies, helping a poor auld blind man up the stair.'

His clothes were laid out and he went to bed without a word, same as usual.

Next night he asked if Andrew could take him to the pub. 'Go yoursel,' said Granny. 'He's no gonnae turn oot like you. If you go, you go on your ain and I hope you fall and break your neck.'

Two years after the blindness, he died, never having been out the house for six months or more. No one came to see him and nobody asked. He became worse, throwing food around the place, shouting and lunging if anyone came near him.

One day Andy came in from work.

'Who's that?' the old man shouted. His Granny put her right forefinger to her mouth. Andy neither moved nor spoke.

'I know you're there. Who is it? By Christ, if it's either one of you, I'll fucken kill yous.'

Granny tiptoed behind his chair and moved her head around making a buzzing sound like a fly. Watching the old man flail his arms, she stuck a pin in him then watched as he hit himself on the face and head.

Later she did that twice a day and encouraged Andrew to do the same. She moved the furniture around while the old man was sleeping, hid the soap and toilet paper, put vinegar in the jam and disinfectant in the milk.

The February before he died, Andy found his grandfather sitting in front of a dead fire. There was snow on the ground. The old man was wearing his bunnet, overcoat and scarf.

'Make us a cup of tea, son,' he said.

Andy had promised he would not help. 'Winston Churchill can get one of his servants to do it,' Granny said.

'Make us a cup of tea, son. I'm freezing. I cannae see tae light the fire, aa the matches in the box are duds.'

'Where's Granny?'

'She told me to tell you she'd gone out in a hurry.'

He drank the tea and smashed the cup.

'Do you want me to tell her how it broke,' he said. 'After aa I've done for you, taken you in when naeb'dy wanted you, gied you a home and a bed. You'll be sorry when I'm gone and it won't be long now.'

Three weeks later the old man died. He caught a chill and took to his bed. 'Bronchial pneumonia,' the doctor said. 'The old man's friend.'

'Mine too,' said Granny.

After the funeral she cleared the house. 'I've been saving up for this,' she said. 'Wait till you see.'

The changes came gradually, room by room. The furniture was sold in bundles of sticks for firewood, bed linen, rugs, carpets and curtains were sold from her pram in the Briggait. 'This stuff came fae a doctor's hoose,' she told customers.

The front door was painted black with a chromium letter-box, bell and handle. She put spotlights in the hall and painted the kitchen yellow. She lowered the ceilings in the living room, installed window-boxes, plastic flowers and spotlights by the fireplace. Only the bedroom remained unfurnished. The place where his grandfather slept was the first room cleared, left with the waxcloth bare on the floor; it and the chair she slept in were all that remained when the house was finished. Her cats made their home in Grandpa's bedroom. 'Winston Churchill hated cats,' she said. 'They gave him hay fever. I used to bring them in at night when he was sleeping.'

Strays were given milk and food, fishmongers' scraps and butchers' meat. Children brought cats to the door. She named them and could remember them individually, even when she did not see them for months at a time. Her favourites, who were around for most of the time, were called Elizabeth, Margaret, Diana and the Princess Royal. She put a picture of the Queen above the fireplace and the Queen Mother in the hall. The Duchess of Windsor's picture was in the lavatory.

Then came Orlando. 'This is my home,' she said.

'It's lovely,' he said. 'Wonderful.'

'Orlando's my business partner,' she told Andy. 'He's going to get the boxes and I'll take them round. He's a poor soul who needs something to do, a bowl of soup now and then, a hot pie in winter.'

Orlando was full of advice. 'Never have a bet if you meet a cock-eyed man or a bowly-legged woman, never drink with a woman and don't feed cats. You should never boil cabbage and green is not a lucky colour.'

'God love him,' said Granny. 'He's the same as your grandfather. He was never the same since a polisman hit him with his baton.'

'When did the polisman hit my grandpa?'

'He was a fine strapping man, your grandpa, working at his trade. It was a strike for nothing, a strike in the yards, not one of the big ones, just a wee strike, about a bonus or something like that. It was inconvenient. The order needed finishing, so a bit of trouble was manufactured, the polis charged the men and your grandpa got hit on the head with a baton.

'At first he was okay. He lost some blood and went back to work when everyone else went back. Then the headaches came, sudden lights before the eyes and blackouts. Terrible. He never knew when they were coming. I think he lived with that all his days. It was the sort of thing you get fed up talking about so you just put up with it.'

Orlando said he knew a blind man who could hear electric light working.

'Away and get your boxes,' Granny said and away he went.

'I'll tell you something else about your grandpa, he came through the war. He fought in the desert, then in Sicily and Italy with the 45th Highland Division of the Black Watch, the D-Day Dodgers, Lady Astor called them. God roast her and rest him; silly bitch. Headaches and all, it didnae matter, he came through the war. That changed him too, he was never the same after the war. These two things finished him, the polisman's baton and the Second World War.'

Despite the changes in Granny's surroundings, she went to work, same as before. She sold boxes, soup and papers. Flies alone could make her swear. She carried a dishcloth and slapped it onto any surface. 'Dirty buggers,' she said, 'Pishing and shiting on folks' food.'

Neither did she go to bed. She left every evening around ten o'clock, pushing her pram and doing the rounds of the lanes and closes, the back courts, alleyways and derelict buildings. Orlando went round the supermarkets, especially the bigger electrical goods suppliers, those who sold refrigerators, washing-machines, dishwashers and the like, gathering boxes of all sizes, gathering newspapers. The newspapers were given free to anyone who bought a big box, and smaller boxes were priced according to size.

Orlando advised on the warmest protection, by wrapping themselves in newspaper, finding small boxes they could fit themselves into, before fitting into the bigger box, which they shut at the top.

Granny came back alone, made a cup of tea and sat in the chair. She came home around three in the morning. Orlando came round every day at nine o'clock and stayed until he was told to go. Andy pieced his granny's life from her conversations with Orlando.

'He took me to Ayr for our honeymoon. We booked into the Station Hotel and went to the races. He won £6, ate a fish supper and we got the train home. We only had the one night. We couldnae afford more than that. The rest of the honeymoon was spent going round factors' offices, looking for a house. Our first house was a single end in Partick, nice and near his work, he just got the ferry over in the mornings. Then we got a wee room and kitchen in Whiteinch; handy for the work again. But as sure as I am sitting here and God's my judge, that was never a lucky house. There was a curse on it, or somebody died there who didnae want to die. You didnae know at first, it was the sort of bad luck that creeps up on you, wee things, nothing noticeable. One Friday he came home and said he'd lost his wages. I lost a baby in that house and that was where the incident occurred with the polisman's baton.'

'Bad luck always comes in threes,' Orlando told her. 'This is a well-known fact. It is also a fact that it is unlucky for a black cat to walk in front of you, to spill salt or see a single magpie, except in Scotland where two magpies are unlucky; it is unlucky to look at a new moon without silver in your hand, to first foot with an empty hand, to cut your nails on a Friday or see your reflection in a hearse; if you walk backwards your parents will go to hell; horseshoes hanging the wrong way round bring perpetual bad luck, May is a bad month to get married, it is unlucky to bring catkins and lilac into the house, if a bride hears her banns read her children will be born deaf and dumb and if a corpse doesn't stiffen there'll be another death within the year. If your left hand is itchy it means you're going to get money, itchy feet means you'll walk on strange ground, seeing a black cat which does not walk in front of you is lucky, white heather is lucky, so is a rainbow, a chanty with salt, a wren and a chimney sweep.'

'God love him,' Granny said behind his back. 'He talks a rare load of shite, but it keeps him happy.'

Orlando brought the same surprise every day, a small bar of Galaxy chocolate. 'I buy it for the name,' he said. 'Galaxy. Chocolate called after a band of stars, just as the nine of diamonds is the Curse of Scotland.'

'You'd better go and see to the boxes.'

Her memories softened. 'Your husband was a wonderful man,' Orlando said, as if he had known him.

'It was me that made him the way he was. And everybody knows he was never the same since the polisman hit him with his six-foot baton.'

Andy's granny died sitting in her chair, singing hymns and seeing light. 'I can see the angels,' she said. Orlando told Andy that was what she said.

Andy left because of Orlando. He felt in the way. It embarrassed him to know this.

No one knew where Orlando stayed. 'Here and there,' he said. 'I have a sister; other friends and acquaintances are always glad to see me. My belongings are scattered here, there and everywhere, but I don't actually stay anywhere as you would understand the term, seeing as you stay here; no, the son of man has no place to lay his head.' When Andy left he stayed with Granny.

Granny moved from Partick to Govan to a house in Grant Street, near St George's Cross, part of the square where Andy came to live, with the Woodlands Hill at the top and St George's Cross at the bottom, bounded on one side by the Inner Ring Motorway's concrete swathe and gridded as far as Park Road, with West End Park Street in the middle, north to south, and West Princes Street running the other way, east to west, like a crucifix.

From Grant Street Granny moved to Bardowie Street in Possilpark, arriving at the end of the war. A Pakistani family had come to Grant Street. 'I've put up with whores, whoremaisters and comic singers,' she said. 'I've nothing against them, it's the smell of their cooking. That's not food they cook, God alone knows what it is, but it isnae what I'd call cooking. And they're very stand-offish.'

The man in the housing department said she was lucky, her husband was a soldier and she had a son who needed fresh air and good schools. Possilpark was just the place. 'Not too many stairs,' she said. 'My man doesnae like climbing stairs.'

Top flat, right, in a concrete block tenement with a glossy maroon dado, cream emulsion walls in the close and stairs, houses like them all across the city. Bardowie Street is treeless.

Granny and Grandpa watched the last of St Cuthbert's School being built in Auckland Street; from planning to completion it took twenty years, interrupted, like everything else, by the Second World War, a central block with long wings. 'It'll do Jake,' she said, till she found out the school's name. 'Don't tell me this is a Catholic street,' she said. 'Catholics arenae lucky. Too many weans and nothing but debt.'

Their first caller was the minister from Rockvilla Church, a small and stocky man with a black moustache.

'Will you be coming to church?' he asked.

'Only for the Christmas Watchnight Service.'

'There are services every Sunday.'

'I should bloody well hope so,' said Granny. 'My man's drunk every Saturday and it would take whatever Jesus did to the dead folk to get him oot his bed, never mind intae church. Do you know you have to cross two roads to get to your church?

Sunday morning's the only peace I get. He's as sick as a barrel of tripe, full of drink and party tunes on Saturday night and full of remorse on the Sunday. Sunday's the best day of the week, so it is, a day of rest, as God intended.'

'This is a nice house,' the minister said, placing his empty tea cup on the sideboard. 'I'll call again some time.'

'Have you ever lived in Grant Street?'

'I don't think so.'

'Whores and whoremaisters, comic singers and goings on.'

There was a previous tenant, now deceased. Granny said it felt like a nice house. On the day they moved in, folk gave them tea and sugar, milk and bread; others came to sell the usual, carpets, furniture, radios, butcher meat, groceries, a three-bar electric fire, a gas cooker and an electric kettle.

'Belonged to my sister,' the wee man said, looking back down the stair. 'She doesnae need it, never oot the wrapper; you know what it's like yoursel.'

Bardowie Street men and women worked in Macfarlane's or the Possilpark depot, driving, conducting, washing, maintaining or cleaning tram cars. Some women worked in the Askit factory or the Vogue cinema and the blind men worked in the blind asylum. One or two men travelled to Springburn to work on the railway or in the loco building sheds; a few worked in town.

Macfarlane's ironworks became world famous, second only to Carron in Falkirk, which, like the steam engine, has entered history through mythology; some historians have given the lighting of the Carron furnace fires on 1 January 1760 as the start of the Industrial Revolution. Other industries, potteries and chemicals, came to Possil to feed from Macfarlane's trough and in the first of the city's housebuilding programmes, austere corporation tenements supplanted the nineteenth-century city village.

When the factory workers came home, the noise of their work was replaced with a kind of deafness. They looked at the fire in silence, or stared out the window, watching back court life, before speaking. The whistles went at a quarter past or half past five; three quarters of an hour or an hour later, the silence lifted and workers spoke in their homes.

Grandpa worked in Macfarlane's, a storeman who not only knew the foundry catalogue, but where everything was kept. 'If your boy wants to serve his time as a moulder let us know; we could maybe get him into the drawing office, if he's good enough,' the manager said. But Jake was Jake: up, away and married by the time they closed the gates.

There were the rumours. News of closures crossed the city. Some said they were going to close the engine works in Springburn, the shipyards as well. There was even talk of Beardmore's going, but that was ridiculous. The Parkhead Forge was the biggest in the country, making what industry needed. The only work was in demolition, roadmaking or the building trade. 'We'll be okay,' said the folk at Macfarlane's. 'We'll be okay. Everybody wants iron railings. You cannae have plastic railings. It's iron railings or nothing; so we'll be okay.'

When the factory closed and a security firm took over the site, there were men in Possil, grown men and working men, men who got up at the usual time, dressed and walked to their work, who stood at the factory gates talking to their mates for an hour or two, then every day discovering the gates would never open, they went home to where their wives were waiting.

Tradesmen faced the possibility that their skills would never be used. If no one did their work what work would be done, they said. They were skilled men. Skill was never out of fashion. Even in recession, there is room for skill. If work returned, things would be different. We've been through this before, the old men said. The Thirties were like this. No one believed their present tense. Now the older trades suffered more. Precast concrete instead of sandstone, chipboard replaced wood.

The yards and engine sheds, the factories and foundries were compact with skills known only to them. People saw the results where skill was hidden. Knowledge was passed by word of mouth. Apprentices learned by watching. It had nothing to do with the range or type of work. It had everything to do with practicality, things unimportant outside their context: the best way to heat a rivet or mix varnish, how to use a spanner or lift a bag of cement, ways of doing things were passed in a series of secret codes and messages, signs and symbols; a union.

The first change was silence. The familiar noises, the factory noises, the morning, dinnertime and evening horns, the pulse of the hammers, all shut down. When the factories closed, a new smell crossed the city. The usual smells of smoke and rain, of heat and metal, electricity and dust, the smell of tar and stones, the smell of building, busy smells were replaced by a stillness and the small smell of cooking, rib dinners, cabbage, barley broth and stews, the early morning smell of baking bread.

The rivers smelled of oil and making, loading and unloading, boats and the smell of boats. Now the rivers smelled of neglect. The ferries went and the yards were closed, bits at a time, here and there redeployments and redundancies, with no one keeping score, nobody noting down the numbers. People said they were sorry, times were changing, the good times would be back, nothing to do but wait. This was Glasgow, Second City of the Empire; we had always survived. We were a manufacturing city with an entrepreneurial base; other folk said something else. Divisions were drawn, the war was with each other, with the enemy at the door; and the city smelled of diesel.

Then came mysterious illnesses and deaths. Folk would suddenly take no well, go to the doctor with a lost appetite, unable to sleep, with pains and headaches, a sore back. Doctors gave their patients pills and told them to come back a week or two later. The deaths were unexplained and sudden. People gave up. They sat in the house and smoked too much, coughed and went to the doctor. Sometimes they could not wait for death. Sometimes they could not live with the winter rain, the anger or the night, the things no one ever talked about, the things they lived with every day.

Suicides happened one way or another, sometimes disguised as something else, even arriving on a slant of light like simple death, a lack of life, a loss of the will to live.

People watched television advertising things they could not afford, things they did not know they wanted. From the streets, the solution appeared; standing on the corner like a memory. You go up and ask, leave your name and address. You make an agreement, borrow a fiver and pay back six a week from today. And so it goes with the threat of more threats hanging around. They come to tell you what will happen and already you know what happened to others, either you do it or they will. A lot of people jumped out the window.

The community began to fray at the edges, noticeable now it was going. Shops closed, changed hands and function. The butcher sold cheaper cuts of meat, hamburgers and frozen chickens. Betting shops opened and the co-op closed. Off-licences sold cheap drink, strong wines and lagers. Women came round the doors, asking if anyone would like to join their wee menage. Then the clothes shop closed. There were a lot of sales and shops with names like Pricecutter and the Mini Market. Eventually, the video rental shops arrived; others took to renting videos. Horror films, love stories, violence and revenge were very popular, war films and adult videos, take out two for the price of one.

The church hall was called a community centre. There was a community project with community workers, a neighbourhood project, a befriending project, murals depicted an industrial past. There was a welfare rights office, a health centre and a drug dependency unit. There were the doo fliers sending out pouters, hoping they would bring another one back. There were the doo flying championships and an open market on a piece of waste ground where the chemical plant used to be.

Social workers talked of a drug and alcohol epidemic. Possil attracted neither small businesses, wool shops nor craft centres. The district council gave up, the school was closed and houses transferred to the residents' association. Anybody who wanted a house in Possil could get one. No one bought their council house. Youngsters dealt in dope, pills or heroin, whatever was available. They shared needles and went on raiding parties, shoplifting, housebreaking; the girls worked in town. The garden-party team were drunk by ten in the morning, sitting on the benches left by the community landscaping project. They pooled their money and shared their drink. Dole payments were staggered throughout the week. The addicts despised the garden-party team and the young women pushing prams walked around with the cans in their hands, or joined the garden party, smoking, drinking their Carlies.

And always there were those who were trying to survive, trying to deal with it, listening to politicians who spoke about issues so remote they seemed of little or no concern.

Granny found out by watching television. They said the streets were home to the homeless, folk like that all over the country, Glasgow as well. She thought at first she ought to join them, nothing to do, nowhere to go, only him coming and going, only this, better off in a convoy of homeless, better off around a fire on a derelict site with people to talk to, keeping warm; then she'd come back and look after him.

Andy's grandpa had the horrors. Every night he'd shout in his sleep. There were snakes and rats, there was fire and drowning, falling from the sky; there was choking. Sometimes he wakened with his hands at his throat, pulling his skin till he was told to be quiet. That was the worst. He never went back to sleep after that, but sat up in bed, smoking with the light on, staring at the wall. The horrors lasted five or ten minutes and always came two hours after he had gone to sleep. When they were over, she left the house and walked around Possil, strangely quiet in the night.

She might have expected noises of some sort, shouting, taxis, a bus or two, people. Alone at night, Granny saw more than during the day. She could see what folk were trying to do, trying to make the community work, holding on because there was nothing else.

She was touched by their lives. There was something warm and tragically spiritual, even their means of expression was lost. Rituals were adopted to obscure living; the ritual of the husband, the wife, the hard man, the hard woman. The ritual of not giving a fuck and needing to belong. Sometimes it is better not to know, better to assume you don't want to know. Occasionally the sight of a wean's head, and the awful sweep rises to meet us. There are time bombs, lying around all over the place, waiting to be detonated, waiting to explode.

When Granny was a girl and the family went on holiday, lying in the strange place, the first night on a camp bed, she could not sleep thinking how wonderful it all had been and was going to be, looking into pools and scrambling round the rocks, salty water, looking at the fishes with their silvery eyes, eating breakfast every morning, salt on a boiled egg, tea and toast.

Sometime during the following day, a Sunday when the shops were shut, after lunch when they went for a walk, her older sister Annie took her aside. 'I don't know what you're so happy about,' she said. 'My Mammy adopted you.' Granny remembered nothing more of the holiday.

The following year, she would be ten or eleven, standing by the door, ready to march into church with the other girls in the Sunday school to receive their prizes, same as school, for General Excellence, Good Attendance; a book with a label stuck near the front. The label had a twined border of pink and pale blue vine leaves and written in golden letters, *This Book Awarded To: For: On: Signed.* The spaces would be written in blue-black ink with the superintendent's signature across the bottom. The minister smiled as the girls came forward and the congregation sat along wooden rows. The minister spoke in a nice voice. He had fair, wavy hair and purple-blue eyes she had looked into once and knew she could never do it again, never in a million years. His wife was young. The minister smiled: 'You're a credit to your family,' he said. 'They must be very proud of you.'

She did not know why she had cried. Her recollection was two separate parts of the same thing, like an apple being halved down the middle and joined again with a line separating the two parts that should have been whole. She was standing, slightly nervous because everyone was looking, shaking hands with the minister, her new book that would smell nice when she opened it, *Robinson Crusoe*, in her left hand. She started crying when the minister spoke. He looked into the congregation, smiled, held onto her hand and she liked him even more. He could easily have let her hand go, moved to the next girl, her sister Annie who was waiting for her book.

The minister gave her a white linen handkerchief, folded into a tight little square. She blew her nose and cried even louder, embarrassed now because she did not want to cry and knew she ought to be able to stop, embarrassed because of the mess she made of the nice clean handkerchief. He put the handkerchief back in his pocket and touched her head, just on the top; he rested his hands and she stopped crying long enough to say, 'I haven't got a family,' in a voice everyone could hear.

Her mother and father stared straight ahead, walking from church, a child on each hand. Granny was crying.

Mother closed the door. Father said, 'Explain yourself,' and Granny told him what Annie had said when they went to Kirn and had the high tea in a Dunoon hotel, with scones and jam and pancakes with raisins, when they stayed with the landlady who made funny noises in the bathroom and had the cat with one eye and half a tail.

Daddy looked at Annie: 'Is this true?'

'She told me on the first day we got there, on the Sunday afternoon when we went for a walk.'

'Quiet. I asked you girl, is this true?'

Annie stuck her chin out and stared at her father. 'Prepare yourself,' he said.

He took the black belt from the back of the door. 'You can't,' said Granny's mother. 'It's her time.'

Father shut the bedroom door. There were twelve lashes. Annie did not cry.

'Apologise,' their father said.

Annie said, 'Sorry.'

When Annie was sixteen she left the house to go to work and did not come home. The police were called and after two days they asked Granny's mother to search the clothes. Some were missing. Two years later, when Mrs Robertson up the next close's daughter Joan went to Canada and came home again because she was pregnant to the Jamieson boy (his father had to buy the ticket), she told them she had met Annie in Toronto, working in a shop, the only news they ever heard.

Granny wondered how Annie was doing. She wanted to share her sister's life, to meet her boyfriend, be a bridesmaid and near for the birth of her children. Somehow she knew Annie was still alive. She assumed she would know when Annie died. She wanted Annie to know about her.

She never cried. Often at night she could hear her mother sobbing, but Granny believed she would see her again, at first resolved to go and find her. When that was no longer possible she believed Annie would get homesick like Scots people do and looked for her in the street, ready to see her and take her home. Perhaps she didn't go to Canada. She could be living in the next street. Maybe as she was walking now, her sister Annie was behind that building walking down the street, missing her, wondering how she was and sorry for what she'd done. If Granny had kept her mouth shut Annie would still be home.

And older, after Grandpa died and before Orlando, alone in Possil on the street at night, for the first time since standing in the church with Annie beside her, she let it slip and it all came out.

Somewhere around Saracen Cross, at the junction of Saracen Street and Balmore Road, she could keep herself to herself no more and fluttered like a birch tree. She had sometimes thought it was an absence of colour or that she was a room locked and bolted, a damp room without a fire, curtains drawn, lights extinguished, open the gates, but the water stayed still at the heart of the well and the only sound was it dripping inside her. She told herself there were diseases worse than she had known and terrible things had happened to others. There were aches that did not ache the soul. She had dreams more real than life and imagined ailments worse than her pains. Things she knew did not exist were real to her and these were the things that lingered like clouds on a hill, these were the things that stayed. It began to be the start of colour in a chilly tint where the black was thinning.

Afterwards she was suddenly tired, as if the sky forgot to rain. The following night she went looking for the homeless. The night after that she took a torch. She did not know where to look. All she found were drunks in the shelters, lovers on park benches.

A policeman stopped her; young and weary he looked as if he had seen it all and did not want whatever was happening to be happening now. She told him she was looking for homeless people.

'Try the Square,' he said. 'Get down about the back of ten. There's a soup run.'

On the southern edge, between Moore of Corunna and Sir Colin Campbell, the man who led the Thin Red Line, a small green van left an urn at half past ten.

A young man with a blond moustache smiled at Granny and offered her soup, barley broth and peppery peas.

A tall man stood near her and asked if all was well.

'Are you homeless?'

'Not really. I have a sister I sometimes go to and there are other people who seem pleased enough to see me, though my belongings are scattered here, there and everywhere.'

He left school at thirteen, was a Weekender in the Thirties, leaving Glasgow on a Friday, walking and tramping for a day or two till he landed in Dumfries and was married when the war broke out in 1939. Served in the war and since then had worked all over the place; construction, Loch Sloy, Shira, roads and motorways. His days were spent in the library. At night he went to the Square to talk with folk.

The van was gone. Granny was holding a gospel tract.

'I wonder if you'd help me? I don't know what to do, but there has to be something.'

They parted at Saracen Cross, arranged to meet the following night.

'Is Orlando your real name?'

'Mother stayed at home and father went away. America, I believe; everyone goes to America. He was a sailor who sent my mother a photograph of himself standing beneath a tree covered with dollar bills. That was the last she heard of him.'

Granny later found it strange how readily he talked about himself and his background. He never did so again; having told her once, she ought to know.

They moved through places where Granny could not go alone, through the pens and closes, vacant ground and derelict buildings. There were huddles, men and women sharing a bottle or a fire. When Granny gave them the boxes to sleep in, they offered her money. If they had none, she gave them the boxes anyway and they promised to pay later.

Within a week the drunks and the young mothers who sat around Possil offered her money to buy stuff for the soup and she was invited to sit with the garden-party team.

Andy worked seasons in various hotels, London, Brighton, Aberdeen, Edinburgh, Blackpool and Perth.

'Same as your faither,' Granny said. 'And take a look at what happened to him.'

The rooms were small and cramped, away from the hotel, in

outhouses or round the back. The bathroom and lavatory were the only communal facilities. The rooms were places to sleep in, impersonal, a place to keep your clothes, rooms to lock. The card school was held in one room, another took in drinkers. Sometimes these were the same room.

Andy did not know how to come back to Glasgow and not stay with Granny. He did not like the way the Glasgow staff talked about the great days, when there was no running water in St Enoch's Hotel and you were damned lucky to get a job, when chambermaids carried jugs and basins. Elderly waiters talked about the Grosvenor, Ferraris, Guys, Rogano, the One-O-One and the Ca'doro, days before Indian restaurants, pizzerias and diners, when there were restaurants, tearooms and cafés, when a cup of tea cost a penny and you sometimes got a bun as well.

It was a theatrical setting. Waiters came in an hour and a half before lunches. They washed, shaved, scrubbed their fingernails, pressed their trousers and made themselves ready for the performance, lined up for inspection five minutes before the customers arrived. The patrons came into a room of sparkling glass and light, with the cast assembled.

There was a silent cameraderie. They were thrown into each other's company and forced to get on, marooned together, dependent upon each other for favours, often sharing jobs and the ways of working, except for the demarcation of the kitchen.

He came back to Glasgow to be nearer home. The reasons for staying away were gone. He'd as well be here as anyplace else. He stayed in the hotel, drank with the waiters and the kitchen staff, socialised with the chambermaids, barmaids and ate in cafés. He loved their menus, their milky coffees, sweets, ice-creams and the women who served, the young girls who loved to talk, who chattered for hours and later had you wondering what the conversation was about, films usually. There was a gradual shift from Italians to Asians, but still he loved their casual ways, the McCallums and wafers, iced drinks and oysters, the double nougats with raspberry.

Cathie was properly called Catherine, after the saint from Sienna who had a mystical marriage with Christ.

Everyone called her Catherine but Andy called her Cathie. One night in bed, he said, 'Give us the matches, Cathie,' after wondering what she would do if he changed her name. She passed the matches without comment, kissing the box before she handed it to Andy, giggling at the Freak Brothers comic, *Fat Freddy's Cat*. She was stoned.

He was twenty-one, she was thirty. They met in the hotel, though she did not know him. Andy recognised her. Waiters come to recognise their customers.

Her father used the restaurant regularly. She came with her parents, with her father, her boyfriend, her husband and later she came with her daughter, a well-behaved child with formal table manners, a child who did not speak unless she had been spoken to.

Andy wandered in the afternoon. He saw her in Fraser's. 'Hi,' she said, stopping suddenly.

'You don't know me, do you?'

'I know your face.'

'I served you dinner last night.'

'Of course.'

She had never looked at his face before and now was embarrassed. She had taken him for granted and now she was facing him, smiling and thinking of something to say.

'I was going to have some coffee.' She said the first thing that came into her head, faltering slightly: 'I was thinking of having some coffee and wondered if you'd join me.'

And he said, 'Sure.'

He liked cafés because you could see the kitchens. You could smell the food and, more often than not, watch it being cooked. You could also see the ingredients and how they were stored.

This was important to someone who knew hotel kitchens. Customers saw the finished products, waiters saw how they were made.

The first of the kitchen staff chased the rats, who lived in the walls and emerged at night. The common supposition that they came from underground or the same level was entirely wrong. Kitchen staff know the habits of rats; they travel from the top, come down the rone pipes and move between floors, down the walls, eating through the brick, wood and plaster, through electric wires and cables to a safe place where they can emerge. They know it is safe by the sound and the smell. This is done in the early light, when they are hungry. They take enough food to last through the day. Some kitchens leave out scraps for the rats, the sort of stuff you would give a dog; that way the good food gets left alone.

The first of the kitchen jobs is to chase the rats; the second job is to remove their teeth marks from the stored food. Rats piss on their own food and survive. The first smell in a kitchen is the smell of rats' piss.

The other thing Andy liked about cafés was that customers saw how the food was served. Restaurant patrons always looked at the food rather than the plate and never looked below the surface. If a waiter felt the customer deserved it, the commonest thing is to spit on the food, serve it with a smile and fill the wine glasses, watching while the customer ate the first few mouthfuls, and, if he or she was anxious to impress, sent their compliments to the chef. Spitting was the start; things could get worse, especially in coffee pots.

*

The first joy was to walk around, looking. Gradually his sense of smell returned, coming and going at first, teasing with something significant and pungent, something remembered, bacon frying, a curry shop doorway, petrol fumes or a flower shop, cut grass, a fruiterer's tray or the night-time smell of the malt and barley mash from a whisky bond.

Andy Paterson's sense of smell came back in a café. Reading a newspaper, a different one every day, sometimes two or three, doing the crossword by a café window, drinking coffee was a joy for a while. He sometimes worked on his Open University essays, read a little or revised. Sitting in a café not far from Charing Cross he smelled his bacon roll before it came. The waitress, whose head was shaved at the sides, asked if he was all right.

He almost asked her out, almost said something like, he wasn't sure what, maybe something like, Would you like to go to the pictures? He would have done, he was sure; he would have done it, but he didn't know what he wanted. Since coming out of jail knowing what he wanted had become very important.

Was it her or was he lonely? It had nothing to do with sex. Jail had dealt with that, one way or another. It could have been the company, it could have been the warmth, it could have been the possibilities.

Walking back towards Kelvingrove Park, it occurred he would like to discover what the possibilities were: showing someone his room, taking someone back and saying, This is it; this is where I live.

Where would she sit? On the chair or the edge of the bed? What would she think of his radio tuned to Radio Three? Would she say he had a lot of books? And would she ask for the curtains to be opened?

For now, he had no money, hardly enough to take himself to the pictures far less anyone else. The Giro arrived on Saturday morning; he would ask, ask her then, casually, not at all anxious: You don't fancy coming to the pictures? Or was that too casual? Talk to her. That was it, get a conversation going. That way it would seem a natural extension to something that had gone before. She was friendly enough. They had spoken, had a conversation, or maybe she was like that with all her customers. How could he tell?

It was difficult to know the things he took for granted.

He got a table for the side of his bed, put the bedside lamp on it and now was able to read in bed. He bought four linen place-mats with flowers embroidered around the edges. He put one underneath the lamp, the large one on top of the sideboard, the other two in a drawer.

He found the table in a skip; that started him wandering. Often at night, he thought of his granny as he walked around from skip to skip.

Within a fortnight he had a reading lamp, another table which sat by the window and would do as a desk, a piano stool, two rugs, a small shaving mirror and a birdcage.

He bought finches from a pet shop in Maryhill Road, opened his heavy curtains and bought a net curtain remnant which hung from the top of the window. He put the finches' cage on the table and kept their seed in a single-door bathroom cabinet he found in a derelict house. The bottom of the bird cage was lined with newspaper.

The finches had mossy backs and eyes like tiny beams. They sang a melancholy song. After a week he wanted to release them, but knew they would not survive the city's sparrow-hawks. He covered their cage with a blanket at night, or during the day when their song became a memory, as though they were singing for something they'd forgotten. They scratched the newspaper and hopped around the tiny cage in the dark beneath the blanket.

The finches cost £3 each, which left him broke for that week. He knew he now would have to save, to budget without extravagant buying. For the first time in his life he knew exactly how much money he had in his pocket at any one time. Granny taught him to make soup, which became the main meal of the day, usually in the evening between six and seven o'clock, just before the evening concert on Radio Three.

He always had a sturdy breakfast, running to the shop every morning for a newspaper, two pints of milk, two well-fired and two soft rolls. He had cereal, rolls and coffee for breakfast, with bacon at the weekend, occasionally a boiled egg, while he read the paper or did the crossword, listening to the morning concert.

He was out of the house by eleven o'clock, usually to the library, shopping, the park. Sometimes in the wet or cold weather he stayed in the library reading-room, working on his Open University course. He liked the library and was delighted to discover it was Glasgow's grandest branch library, the most classical of half a dozen designed by James Rhind, between 1902 and 1906; small deceptive buildings, inside and out. The fluted Ionic columns were an obvious bluff; so was the segmental pediment where the Muses inspired us to do better, one appealing, two reclining. Above the main entrance, against the sky, a mother is reading to her children. Every time Andy looked at the sculpture and turned towards St George's Cross, he thought, Daddy would have liked that. They walked together every Sunday, looking at buildings.

'Glasgow is one of the finest stone-built cities anywhere,' his father said. 'Lift your eyes, look up and see it.'

If Andy came back from the library around lunchtime he lay on the bed, and stared at the ceiling till it was time to go out for the afternoon. He came back between five and six o'clock, had his evening meal, listened to radio, read, made hot chocolate and lay in bed reading until he fell asleep.

He bought a couple of posters for the walls: a painting by Joseph Crawhill, *The Flower Shop*, a sturdy black horse and a red cart with the flower shop window in the background. The other, from a Third Eye Centre exhibition, was a small architectural detail from a building designed by Alexander Thomson, the demolished Cairney Building in Bath Street, a buff poster with black and red lettering. There were lots of cards in lines and bunches, groups of images around the walls. Every week he bought some flowers.

Paperback books cost ten pence each in second-hand shops, five pence in jumble sales. He was careful to buy what he would want to reread: *The Iliad*, *Ulysses*, *Don Quixote*, *The Grapes of Wrath*, the sort of book he had read before.

It took four weeks to save for the black radio cassette he saw in a pawnshop window. He was broke and knew he would be in trouble if the Giro was late, but he didn't care. Only when he was back in the room, talking to himself with anticipation, talking to the radio, bidding it welcome, he realised he did not have a plug. He went out to steal one from Woolworths; if he was caught he'd go back to jail. He took the plug from a lamp and bought a new one for forty-five pence at the end of the week. At first he put the radio on top of the mantelpiece, but when the books began to cover the shelf, the radio was moved to the wee table by the side of the bed, a larger linen place-mat beneath it.

Every time he came in the room, he locked the door.

To be in jail is to be alone, even in a crowded cell.

Sharing a cell with two other men was part of the humiliation. Prisoners went to church to be alone. Most coped by being noisy, in the cells and communal places. Silence was often seen as weakness and caused occasional problems of adjustment. There was the usual pecking order nonsense to be sorted out, but Andy sought to keep himself to himself, challenging no one and no one challenged him. He did enough to survive, had responded to confrontation and survived. There were a couple of flurries, small challenges which were easily handled. Waiters can usually deal with people. Small men who pouted in the restaurant were left alone for fifteen minutes, by which time they had either mellowed or were inarticulate with anger. People who need to assert themselves are precisely the same in jails or restaurants; animals do it all the time, stare at each other until one eventually moves.

'Go in with the intention of coming out,' Orlando told him.

Granny smiled and shook her head: 'This is something that has to be tholed.'

By the time he had been challenged for his bed, his pudding, his tobacco and his library books, by the time his posters and pin-ups were torn, his soap removed and his jam eaten, four weeks after he went into Barlinnie he was moved to Dungavel for the rest of his sentence.

There the similarities and differences were subtler. It was a smaller prison, fewer folk to deal with and prisoners slept in dormitories. Dungavel, being a converted stately home, was like a public school, or how he imagined a public school would be. Once you were locked in for the night you ignored the others or carried on with the games which were never too rumbustious. Of course, people fell in the showers, but that did not happen very often. There was access to pay-phones; little wooden kiosks in the same room as the billiard tables.

There were writing classes, painting classes, computers or gardening; ways of diverting emotion, something for which the prisoners' backgrounds rendered them entirely unsuitable, things they would hardly pursue outside.

He got through it, mainly by dreaming of the stately home, imagining the rooms in their previous incarnation, with himself as a servant wandering from the kitchen to the dining room, from the lounge to the library, sometimes a valet or a butler, stable boy or chauffeur, never the master.

There was a flurry of activity when the family were coming, everyone getting ready for the hunt, the chase, the meals in the evening and the entertainments. Sometimes he and a girl, another servant, exchanged shy glances, becoming friendlier when they worked together. He helped her when she served the table; she looked at him, conveying everything with her eyes. Going downstairs to the kitchen with the empty dishes, she would stumble; he'd take her arm and again she would look. Her name was Lisa.

She was imagined, changing to a face from a magazine, newspaper or television, then assuming qualities of her own. Andy felt complete when he was with her. They shared the same things, she was someone he could talk to, someone to confide in. She knew about the worm and held him tight, stroked his belly and kissed it better. Rotten old worm, she said.

What do you think of this? he'd ask while in the garden; Not much on tonight, when they sat down to dinner; Let me hold you, when they went to bed.

That was when he could talk to her properly, when they could plan and whisper. During the day they were interrupted; at night, before sleep, they were always alone. There was an unnamed dependency, as though the world were oblivion, that Andy was a shadow whose life and habits, talk and gestures were mirrored and reinterpreted in another world.

Like everyone else in jail, he masturbated; three, four, five times a day at first, to relieve the boredom or simply to be empty, to be cleared of distraction.

She did not take part in this; sometimes, alone, in the garden or looking along the library shelves, he told her why it happened. She smiled and covered his hand with her hand. When he masturbated he thought of women doing what they had done. Cathie perhaps, maybe a girl in one of the hotels, he sometimes thought of Margaret and her indolent ways. Then it stopped; easier to say why it started or continued than to speculate on why it stopped. He was empty and bored.

Great mysteries inhabited his threshold, like the sky before rain or a sparrow battering itself against the wind. None of these things were important. He left them in jail. Lisa and the Open University course came to West End Park Street. She moved into the room beside him, helped him choose and told him all would be well and all manner of things would be well; they would save and one day have a place of their own.

*

He lied. He phoned and told her he was passing. 'Good,' she said. 'Come and have some coffee.'

It was waiting on the table in the living room. 'Hope you take milk and sugar,' she said.

Her daughter was in the bath. Cathie shouted, 'Is it all right, Emmy?' and she said, 'Of course.'

'Stick your head around the door and say hello.'

The girl in the bath was reading a comic. 'I know you,' she said. 'You're the waiter.'

Cathie sat with her legs across the arm of a chair. They talked about her husband, now divorced, in Pakistan supposedly importing carpets; he was more likely to be dealing in dope.

'Ian's a junkie,' she said. 'There's a court order banning him from here. I don't want him to have anything to do with Emily, not that he cares. He's hardly seen her; needless to say, she idolises him.'

They chatted about the area, the houses and their price, the neighbours' eccentricities: God alone knows what they must think of her, but most of them knew her father, so it was all right.

The second time was half past nine of a midweek evening. He phoned from the hotel: 'I've just gone to bed,' she said.

'Sorry. I'd no idea. I'll leave it till another time.'

'No, come on up. I'll put the central heating on.'

January 27. Driving south in the misty sodium light, the roadside, pavements sparkled in the swirling orange air. Hot air blew across one side of the windscreen and wipers slapped across the other. The car was warm and slow. Boots and coats and woolly hats bent against the wind on the pavement. He found a foreign station on the radio. The signal fluctuated beneath electric cables, snatches of fiddle music and a girl singing, like the hotel.

He'd got off early because of a Burns Supper. The meal was

served and quickly cleared. The waiters were around for the early entertainment, waiting to be told to go.

Something had gone wrong. The people did not know what they were doing; it was as though they were performing a ceremony from some other occasion because they did not know, or could not devise, an appropriate ceremony for their celebration. A girl with neatly coiffed and permed hair, a Royal Stewart tartan sash and a white mid-calf-length dress, stood with her hands clasped to her front:

At midnicht hour in mirkest glen
I'd rove and ne'er be eerie, O,
If thro that glen I gaed to thee,
My ain kind dearie, O!

He imagined the foreign girl on the radio. How was she dressed? Would her audience understand what she was saying? Or would they need protection from their past?

They actually talked about the weather: 'Do you think it'll snow? I hope it snows. I love the snow.' The house was warm. She wore jeans, socks and a white woollen sweater.

He kept saying he meant to go and she said there was no need, now she was up and Emily was in bed. Did he like music? She played the Rolling Stones, 'Girl With The Faraway Eyes'. They danced, holding each other around the shoulders.

'When I'm stoned I play that song all the time,' she said.

They had more coffee and told each other stories. He told her about Orlando, life as a waiter, behind the scenes in a big hotel. She told of being little and going to her Daddy's printing works and loving the smell of the ink and metal. She showed him a book her father printed, her grandfather's book, privately circulated, the story of his life in business. 'He does other books as well,' she said and they looked at an awkwardly-shaped collection of photographs of Scotland throughout the year, beautiful and evocative, a landscape without people.

'We stayed there,' she said on the last page.

'I'd better go.'

'Fancy some chocolate?'

'Sure.'

'Wait a minute. It might be snowing.'

They looked out the kitchen window; the back garden resembled a page from the book, the first snow of the year.

'Right,' she said. 'A snowball fight.'

Her jeans were tucked into wellington boots and she tied the top of her sheepskin jacket with a blue woollen scarf. 'I love this scarf,' she said. 'It's my school scarf. I got it in primary when I was seven.'

'What will your neighbours make of this?'

'I don't care. They're all half dead anyway; ancient.' She drew him close and whispered. 'The man next door wears long woollen drawers, you know, the sort of baggy things old boxers fought in.'

'Long johns?'

'His wife hangs them out. Emmy giggles every time she passes him in the street. Don't worry, he won't waken. I can sometimes hear him snoring through the wall. I went to a party in their house. The most boring party I was ever at; as soon as I got there I was dying to leave, nothing to drink but cheap wine and the food was atrocious. He talked to keep me company. Can you imagine two hours with a civil engineer who can talk about nothing but his work, burst lavatory pipes and the damage they do.'

The high cheekbones gave an appearance of her eyes being pulled apart and her hair was soft and brown and straight, cut short and long at the same time, as though the energy had been washed out. None of these features were unattractive. It was the mouth; small, pert and with a heart shape on her upper lip which obscured her lower lip and gave her mouth an imbalanced appearance, as though one single feature had spoiled the others, though there was a beauty about her.

There was more snow than they thought. She threw a snowball and squealed, then put her hand to her mouth as though her shriek would waken the neighbours. He threw snowballs so she would throw them back. He enjoyed watching her throw, enjoyed the way her body stretched, the taut movement of her arms and chest and the lift of her legs. Small-breasted, she moved like a bird on spindly legs.

They ran out of energy and when they stopped were suddenly cold. They ran into the house and she switched on the electric kettle while jumping across the linoleum floor, removing her wellingtons with one hand, her coat with the other. He watched. They made the coffee together, carried the cups into the living room, turned up the gas fire and drank the coffee sitting on the floor, both hands around the mugs, leaning against each other in silence, sometimes giggling.

'I thought we were going to have some chocolate.'

'It was you that made the coffee. You can have chocolate if you like.'

When the coffee was finished she took his mug and laid it by the fire with her mug, then settled back against his body. They sat that way for a very long time, till they were uncomfortable, both feeling there was something to do, but neither knowing how to do it, though the shiver and fear were exciting.

'I'd better go,' he said.

She did not answer. He moved and she sat upright, staring at the carpet. He kissed her twice, reaching round to find her mouth. There was no response. Twice he ran his finger down the side of her face, from cheekbone to chin, using only the middle part of the forefinger of his right hand.

'I'm sorry,' he said. And she kissed him.

They went over the events that followed many times. It was their favourite moment. 'Tell me what happened after the snow?' she'd ask, lying in bed; and always when he got to the bit about running his finger down her face, she'd say, 'I remember that did it. That was very sneaky; sneaky but wonderful. Everything opened when that happened.'

'It wasn't deliberate. You just looked sad.'

'Then what happened?'

'I'm not too sure.'

He remembered things he could not tell her, things it would have embarrassed him to talk about. He remembered her movement beneath him, the fear of coming too soon, then of never coming at all. He remembered the way the bed bounced when she did a Fosbury flop onto the dark blue sheets, how she lifted the downie every once in a while to look.

'What's going on?' she said. 'I can't stop kissing you.'

Lying later facing each other: 'Can you tell from the way I walk?' she asked.

'I don't think so.'

'How about from the way I dance?'

'Why are you asking?'

'Just wondered. Ian told me he knew what I'd be like in bed from the way I danced.'

Some time later, her father asked him to the works' dinner dance; him in a dinner suit, she in a little black dress.

'We'll go soon,' she said, dancing to something like an old-fashioned waltz. 'I want to screw you in the car.'

The tempo suddenly changed. She moved away from him,

dancing on her own, just for him, oblivious to the others on the floor. She danced towards him, smiling: 'I want to suck you off,' she said.

And over her shoulder he saw her father, his face a mystery, watching his daughter's back as she danced towards her lover.

Later that night and every night she got up to piss. The sound of her pissing at three in the morning, the lonely trickle and her sigh, her cold body coming back into bed and her arm stretched around him, was the strongest memory. When he thought about Cathie, he wondered if she still got up to piss in the middle of the night.

*

Something was wrong. Just when his room was settled: when he was beginning to find his way around Glasgow and to see himself like everyone else who neither listens to the sea nor stares at the sky, someone cooped up in an office, or a factory, a street, house or prison, just when he was about to discard the past and had started the process, was thinking about sharing his room with another human being, even for an hour or two, Lisa left. When he expected to find her and she wasn't there, he thought of living someplace else.

Orlando now stayed in Granny's house, which was substantially the same apart from the occasional house guests and Geordie Anderson, the daft man, who had mostly moved in Orlando's room, which used to be Andy's room, who at parties sang the songs he made up for himself standing beneath the bare electric light-bulb, his face black and shining with Jolson make-up in the middle of the room.

'His favourite programme's 'The Black and White Minstrel Show'; he's never forgotten them,' Orlando said. 'Care in the community is Geordie's problem. Nowhere to go, walking around bewildered. There is a lack of resources. The new slums of the city, the houses which cannot be let because of what are officially described as the social problems of the area, will now be given to souls like Geordie who won't know what to do with them. The only other takers are the lassies with weans. You ought to be like them, get on the sick; invalidity benefit, that's the thing. More money; £48 a week I believe. Come here and live on the b'roo for a month and the doctor will put you on the invalidity, quite genuinely because you'll be ill all right. And if you can arrange for a sex change and a wean, you can get a house, a housing grant and a settlement officer as well.'

Next day in the library, Andy looked up the *Evening Times* and *Glasgow Herald*. A company called Dial-a-Home offered a list of rooms and houses to let. 'We do have to charge, unfortunately yes sir. £50,' said the girl who had answered the phone in a Midlands singsong voice.

He spent two days looking at cards in windows: £35 a week was the cheapest room he could find, smaller than the one he had in a house where every other room was let with a Baby Belling cooker on the landings. 'A hundred pounds deposit for the key and a month in advance. £250,' said the Asian landlord.

He went to see the waitress with the semi-shaven head, the girl he had almost asked out. Walking across the park he rehearsed the conversation. He had enough money for a couple of cups of coffee, but figured she would be able to carry the conversation. All he had to do was look for an opportunity.

She was wearing an engagement ring and was growing her hair, standing with the two other waitresses.

He went to another café where the waitress smiled and asked what he wanted. When he was paying the bill, he asked, 'Would you like to go out with me tonight?'

'I'm washing my hair.'

He didn't feel as bad as he thought he would; it was good to hear the sound of his voice in that sort of confrontation.

Back in the room, Mahler on the wireless. Mahler who had worked himself to death and the Fourth Symphony, which the announcer said was descriptive of heavenly life. Andy lay on top of the bed and thought about the Horenstein recording, the one he had on tape. Why then was he listening to this? He felt better at the end.

Next day he ran into a café, having been caught in an ill-tempered squall. The waitress smiled as he shook himself dry. He looked out the window at the string of cars waiting for the lights to change. Rain always brings the cars out early. She was in her late twenties, her dark hair was pulled in to the back of her head by a hinged comb. She sat at a table and read a newspaper, looking up every now and then to see if she was needed. She caught Andy's eye, smiled and carried on reading.

'Do you think it'll stay dry?' she asked as she handed him the bill.

'I hope so. I was looking forward to walking home.'

He turned at the door, walked up to the table and sat opposite her. She put the newspaper down, and smiled.

'Can I help you?'

'I was wondering if you were busy tonight. I wondered if you were doing anything?'

'What were you thinking of?'

'I'd like you to go out with me.'

'Out where?'

'I don't know. Pictures, a pub, anywhere.'

'I don't fancy sitting in a pub, thanks all the same, and I'm working until half past nine or quarter to ten so the pictures are out.'

'I could walk you home if you liked. We could go for a coffee.'

'I get more than enough coffee here and I don't fancy a hike. Does it have to be tonight?'

'Not if you don't want to.'

'Okay then; I'll see you at a quarter to ten. If it's dry we'll go for a walk. If it's wet we'll come in here.'

'Where'll I meet you?'

'Here. And my name's Myra, by the way.'

*

When he was wee, Andy liked to explore a drawer in the dark oak sideboard beside the bed in Grandpa's room.

'I hate it,' said Granny. 'The brass handles make it look like a coffin.'

'That was my mother's sideboard. She got it in a wedding present frae my faither's work.'

'I knew there was something else I didnae like about it.'

The sideboard had a wooden and brass galleon lamp resting on the top. The lamp had no bulb and the red shades, which were also the galleon sails, were torn. The ship was the only ornament. The bottom opened out to a big press where the sheets and blankets were kept, there were two drawers where the good pillowcases and tablecloths which had never been used were stored amongst the mothballs. The drawers were in the top, at the back of the sideboard; four drawers behind the ornamental leaded glass fronts, all were empty except for the topmost drawer of the right-hand section, the bit farthest away from the bed.

It was stuffed with items found in hotel dining rooms and bedrooms, the sort of things guests would miss but would not know where they'd lost them: glass cigarette holders, tie-pins, a red leather wallet, a satin purse, four small boxes, beads from a dress, cuff-links, shirt studs, badges, a watch with no hands, a bracelet, earrings, a scarf-ring, four cigarette lighters and a bundle of sporting cigarette cards tied with a yellow elastic band; Tommy Lawton, Dixie Deans, Denis Compton, Len Hutton and so on: the only tangible items the family had gathered from a lifetime in service.

Jake used to bring home the leftovers, often from the diners' plates. Andy's earliest memories were of waiting for his father, who would bring home Roquefort cheese, roast beef and ham, butter, cake and broken eggs. The family were often without food, then they would eat petit fours; have nothing to drink and Jake would bring home a half-empty bottle of claret. They'd talk in the William Street room and kitchen, behind Anderston Main Street. He remembered his father talking about buildings.

'Look up in Glasgow. Ground level's the same as anywhere else, but raise your eyes to glory.'

Jake took his son to see the now demolished Anderston railway station by J. J. Burnet and the James Salmon Savings Bank. 'Look at the mosaic in that door,' his Daddy said, sighing. He talked about buildings to Andy. To everyone else he talked about work.

'Do you mind the time that drunken bugger, what's his name again?'

'Nicky Ross.'

'That's him. He sent out poached salmon with custard on instead of hollandaise sauce.'

'And nobody noticed.'

'That's right. Eight portions were out before one was sent back.'

'That's not it. No salmon came back. Everybody ate the

salmon and custard, but a man sent back plum duff with hollandaise sauce because he said the custard was too runny.'

All the hotel stories were centred round the kitchen or the dining room, about wee waiters who took small steps like a woman and sang a song with no words in the dining room, working.

'Tommy Flanagan never wore socks.'

'And he dyed his hair with shoe polish.'

'Peter Cameron never wore a shirt, boiled front and cuffs only.'

'And he always served sparkling Moselle for champagne.'

'Everybody does that.'

'Was it Flanagan who had the glass eye.'

'No, that was Flaherty.'

'The Singing Waiter.'

' "When Irish Eyes Are Smiling" was Conar Flaherty's song.'

'I was working with Flaherty in the Grosvenor and an old man that was in with this young lassie, no more than eighteen or nineteen, said his steak was too bloody. Flaherty took out his glass eye and held it over the steak: "Bloody," he said, "It's fucken red raw." '

This was at an end of season party, held at Granny's, when Andy came back with money and Orlando made the punch.

Andy learned the recipe when Granny died: 'Let me tell you a good recipe for a party punch,' Orlando said one night. 'Cheap as well. Three parts Eldorado red and white to one part American Cream Soda. No one knows what they are drinking, it's pink; and since you boil the Eldorado previously, it's also hot. The cream soda gets added to the hot Eldorado. Throw some apples, oranges, grapes, bits of fruit on top and serve as punch. Excellent for any function, the more pretentious, the better; book launches and art exhibitions are a must, the sort of function where no one would expect to be drinking a cheap fortified wine under any guise.'

Orlando's punch, Granny's soup and cans of beer; sandwiches, sausages and potato crisps. This was where Geordie Anderson first appeared. No one knew who brought him, but some had seen him before, with his Jolson make-up.

'God love him,' said Granny. 'He could be wan o yer ain.'

'If you kid on you're daft you'll get a hurl for nothing,' said Orlando.

At some point Geordie would stand to sing, would carry on with songs of his own devising until told to sit down, whereupon he sat down immediately and waited for another opportunity to stand up and sing until told to stop.

'I was a proud woman then, when I wore my collarette,' said Mrs Esplin, otherwise known as Here I am Again or It's Only Me. Her contribution to any party was the album of photographs taken at Orange walks: 'Here I am again in Saltcoats,' or 'Here I am again in Greenock. That's me there, with the white hat and the pink coat.' Doors were usually left open and Mrs Esplin would enter without knocking and shout from the lobby, 'It's only me.'

During a lull in the singing she went round the room displaying the album. Granny once asked her to sing: she la-lahed her way through 'The Sash My Father Wore' and when asked if she knew the words said, 'They're a secret.' Granny persisted. Mrs Esplin la-lahed her way through 'The Cry Was No Surrender'. Baby William stood up and saluted. Baby William was Geordie Anderson's pal.

'Everything is done by the Bible. We march behind the Bible,' Mrs Esplin told Baby William because he had saluted. 'It's a lovely sight coming up Buchanan Street. Of course, I don't walk now. I leave it to the younger ones. I haven't walked for twelve years. I've seen me exhausted and as soon as the band starts up again, away we'd go: *Dah-dah ree dee dee*. One time we went to Stevenson and we were supposed to be there for a quarter past one. Do you know we didn't get in that park until half past four and at a quarter to five we were told to marshal up. Some of the men refused to marshal till they'd had their dinner and we had to carry the banner till they were ready. I was a proud woman that day, carrying the banner. We marched up Cowlairs Road, through the officials and dispersed when The Queen was played. Springburn at that time was full of Catholics and five minutes after we'd dispersed you'd never know there had been a walk. The police used to congratulate us, Number Ten District. It wasn't always that way. They'd throw chanties of stuff over you. But we tamed them.'

'Will you take me to the toilet,' asked Baby William.

I am very fond of grub, grub is very nice,
I like bacon, I like chips and I like bread and rice;
There's lots and lots of stuff to eat, there's soup and meat and stew,
And if you've got a minute I will name them all to you:
There's peas and beans, potatoes,
Sausages and ham
Cornflakes and porridge
Marmalade and jam;
Trifle, tripe and a wee pig's feet,
Chicken, eggs and chops;
Fruit comes from the greengrocer
And the meat from a butcher's shop. Oy.

'Geordie, sit doon.'

'Aye, that's enough Geordie; gie's peace.'

The punch atmosphere poised on the edge of recklessness.

There were a few bletherings which could have developed into argument, a series of breenges which could have become a fight. No one wanted soup or sandwiches and when Geordie stood up to sing again, he was shouted down. Bernadette O'Hara began to talk loudly, staring at Mrs Esplin: 'If there's one thing I hate, it's a bigot. Bigotry's worse in a woman, and the worst type of woman bigot is a black Protestant woman bigot. God knows, they've got nothing to crow about, with the wee bits and pieces they get, but as long as there's somebody beneath you then I suppose you're entitled to feel yourself better off.'

Someone started to sing and they all joined in, though why they should have chosen to sing rather than fight about religion was a happening as random as the gathering. The lights were put out when George Hewitt sang 'Just An Old-Fashioned Lady' and Granny sang her favourite:

The skies are not always blue,
The sun does not always shine for you;
Sunshine or rain,
Pleasure or pain,
What's the use of us sighing.
Dark clouds may come and may go
But brighter days' in store;
Always remember,
The skies are not always blue.

And so it went, around the room. And because everybody had to do a turn, at the end of the evening Baby William stood on his head.

Joe came down to take Andy for a pint, usually once a week. He phoned to say he was coming, parked his car in West End Park Street and they walked to the Halt Bar on the corner of

Woodlands Road. They always sat in the main bar and left when the music started up in the lounge. Joe bought the drinks.

'Eileen wants you to come for lunch this Sunday.'

'Thanks all the same.'

'I'll say you're busy.'

'When was the last time I was busy?'

'Two or three weeks ago.'

'I'd better face it.'

'This Sunday then.'

Eileen opened the door and pushed her left cheek to Andy who kissed it. Her face was greasy.

'Nice to see you at long last,' she said. 'We thought you were dead, didn't we?'

No one answered. Tracy and her husband were on the sofa. They leaned over to one side and pushed themselves up when Andy came in.

'You haven't met my husband,' said Tracy. 'Thomas, this is my Uncle Andrew.'

Thomas had a gold earring and streaked blond hair. His jacket sleeves were turned up and his arms were bare.

'Well, Tracy, you've certainly grown. You're getting more like your mother every day.'

She smiled. 'I was sorry you couldn't be at my wedding, Uncle Andrew.'

'I was elsewhere at the time. What kind of work do you do, Thomas?'

'Thomas is a financial adviser.'

'I thought he was a plumber,' said Joe.

'He used to be a heating engineer, Daddy, but now he offers financial advice.'

'Who to, the government?'

'He has his own selected clients.'

'And where do you get them, Thomas?'

'He gets them from the papers. The company advertises, customers fill in a wee form and the company sends the ones in his area to Thomas.'

'So he's a society man.'

Tracy went to help her mother in the kitchen. Joe and Andy talked about football. Thomas wiped his hands with a handkerchief.

'Come and eat this while it's hot,' Eileen said when all the food was on the table. She then told everyone where to sit.

Andy could think of nothing else to say, nor did he feel a need to talk. He said the meal was lovely. Eileen asked how he was doing, how were the digs and when was he going to find a job. Did he still go to the Job Centre?

'Of course. There seems to be a strange thing happening to the economy of this country. The jobs we are being offered pay less than the unemployment benefit. And there are a variety of new hassles to encourage folk to work. The only recourse is to appeal against the DHSS decision and everyone I know who has appealed has won their case. I am doing nothing but stating the obvious. It is a well-known fact: anyone who works for the DHSS despises their clients. They are neither civil nor do they serve anything other than the anti-working-class legislation this Government brings in whenever it feels like it.'

'I'd prefer not to talk about politics.'

'My wife's a Tory,' said Joe.

'I was talking about the Job Centre.'

'I expect you won't have had much of a chance to see your wife.'

'Please don't feel obliged to answer that,' said Joe. 'There are times when even I find my wife's behaviour unacceptable.'

Eileen left the table. Her daughter rose to follow. 'Stay where you are,' said Joe. 'If you want to comfort your mother, take her to the doctor and tell the man the truth. Tell him she moans about tiredness and headaches but does nothing about it and that's on a good month. Tell him why you got married and left home at the first opportunity. Tell him why I'm on tranquillisers. The only one who isn't on pills is the one who needs them.'

'No signs of a family, Tracy?' said Andy.

After dinner, Joe offered a lift. Andy preferred to walk home, figuring it was time to become something else. Life did not operate like folklore. He could not become a bat or an owl to flap off in the moonlight. He would have to change what made him feel a stranger to himself, that which placed him on the outside, made him distant and alone.

He knew the time would come and he welcomed its arrival, was open and ready for it, but was aware it would have to appear on its own, like his sense of smell. Jail was the catalyst. If he used it properly, he would be strengthened by experience, retaining something of his old self, as the sea retains some of the water which fed it, the way a fog displaces distance or rain erases vision, the way the wind shifts a cloud from the top of a hill.

He passed a traffic island in Queen Margaret Drive. The direction lamp and paving had been shattered so long ago, a tree grew through the disturbed stones, opposite the Botanic Gardens. Further down the road he remembered the cabbage he found growing through the motorway concrete beneath the approach bridge to the Clydeside Expressway at the Whiteinch Roundabout. He passed a box where the phone was ringing, walked up the hill and turned into West End Park Street.

*

The second time they slept together, Cathie said, 'This is real, isn't it?' He said, 'I think so.'

They saw each other once a week, usually on his day off. He phoned every night, sometimes talking for an hour or two. 'You can come every night,' she said.

'If I come over I won't make it into work next day.'

'Yes you will. I've got to put Emily out to school. You can leave with her.'

'When has that happened?'

'There's always a first time. Why don't you want to come over?'

'It's not that I don't want to; I don't trust myself when I do.'

Once a week meant they stayed quite high; they did not settle into a comfortable order, retained their ability to surprise each other longer. They retained their novelty value, which made them believe they had stumbled onto something which had taken them to a higher level. They explored each other's secrets and became a source of excitement.

'What are you doing for Christmas?' she asked. 'They say it might snow.'

'Christmas,' said Granny. 'Christmas; I'll gie ye Christmas. What the hell do I care where you eat your dinner or who cooks it. We'll be having a quiet time. We're getting a turkey and giving it out. We'll keep you some.'

His room was at the back of the hotel, on the top floor where the sounds of the station echoed like a bathtub. The pain came at night. He screamed and no one heard, tried to make it down the corridor to the telephone on the wall at the top of the stairs. He remembered feeling ridiculous, telling himself that pain or no pain he ought to able to walk down the corridor. He stumbled, carried on, stumbled again, fell and crawled to the phone. He either had to dial 999 or call hotel reception on an outside line to get reception to send someone up to him. He didn't have a ten pence piece. He closed his eyes and thought he had fainted, but there was still the pain. He opened his eyes, shut them and fainted. When he wakened in the Royal Infirmary, Granny and Orlando were at his bedside.

Granny said, 'The polis were here. They never bring luck.'

'Summonses, warrants, heartache and grief,' said Orlando.

'I've brought you some fruit,' said Granny. 'They had paper trays with oranges, apples, a couple of grapes and God knows how much for the nice red bow. It'll taste the same from a brown paper bag.'

'Fruit is good for the bowels,' said Orlando.

'The nurse said you need a rest, so do what you're told and none of your gallivanting.'

'Hospitals always remind me of death,' said Orlando.

'I never brought you any flowers because they were too dear. But that's yesterday's paper and I picked this up, somebody left it, I think it tells you what's on at the theatre and the pictures, places like that. And this is a wee thing the man sent round from the church. You don't look well,' she said.

They stayed until seven o'clock, smiling at the nurses. 'This is my grandson,' she told them.

'God help him,' she said, looking at Orlando. 'He's a poor soul and a cratur, but I think he means well. I'll ask him to get you a book to read. He likes having something to do. Did we tell you, Baby William can stand on his hands.'

They came every day, around four in the afternoon and stayed until visiting finished, bringing meat pies, fruit, sandwiches and a flask of soup. At the end of the week, the nurses were giving them tea and biscuits, Orlando was talking to the men in other beds while Granny offered them food.

'She comes from the generation who lived through the war,' said Orlando, 'as I do myself. We are the generation which considers it wasteful not to eat food. We never throw out what can be eaten and we always clear our plate.'

Cathie came two days before he was due to go home. He looked up from yesterday's newspaper and she was standing by the ward door, a bunch of flowers in her hand, wearing his favourite dress, her hair newly done.

'We'll go,' said Granny.

'Good afternoon,' Orlando said, raising his hat as he passed.

When they had gone, Cathie came down the ward, staring at him all the way. 'I've brought you these,' she said and put the flowers on his bed.

'How did you find out I was here?'

'I phoned the hotel. What happened?'

'Appendicitis. I am supposed to be very lucky it didn't become peritonitis. The police and ambulance brought me here, blue lights flashing, the works.'

'When do you get out?'

'Supposed to be tomorrow.'

'Can I look after you? We can have a belated Christmas for our anniversary.'

'I'm an invalid. You can come and see me.'

In hospital and home, resting in Granny's bedroom he imagined the worm and his appendix, that the pain was caused by it trying to escape.

Cathie wrote to say something had come up, she could not manage over, but would explain later. The letters were cheery, but something was wrong. They were too short.

There was a party on the Saturday to celebrate his return to work. 'Back to stay with the riff-raff,' said Granny.

There was usually some Saturday night activity, a party, a card school or drinking after work, so Jake never got home until some time after two in the morning. He always wakened around nine.

'Come on. It's Sunday. We don't want to waste it. Up.'

Andy watched while his father cooked breakfast. He dipped the bread in the egg for french toast and put it in the pan where his father had fried the bacon and sausages; he broke the eggs into a bowl and stirred them for scrambled eggs or omelettes; he watched the toast and boiled the kettle for the tea. He went to the shop for the papers, which were read over breakfast, two-way Family Favourites on the wireless.

'Out you get,' his mother said. 'We've got work to do.'

His mother and Eileen washed the dishes and put on the dinner before their afternoon walk in the park. If it rained, Jake and Andy went to the Art Galleries. They stood in front of the Van Gogh windmill. 'Wonderful,' Jake said. 'Wonderful.' He always pointed out the poppies in front of the fence and beside the shed at the foot of the picture, little splashes of red. He liked the Rembrandts and they queued to see the Dali when it arrived. They always looked at the British painters, at Guthrie, Lavery, Henry and Hornel and from them to Spencer, Sutherland and Lowry. He always told Andy how Churchill destroyed a Sutherland portrait, gifted by a grateful nation.

Andy remembered walking through nearly empty streets, looking at buildings, his father pointing out the shape and design, the architects and their work. He remembered the evening meal, washing dishes, then sitting by the fire, his father, mother and sister, reading until it was time for bed.

*

Myra was waiting.

'Where to?'

'I don't know.'

'This is great. A man that cannae make his mind up's aa I need.'

'We'll walk along Sauchiehall Street.'

She caught the last bus home. They went to the pictures the following night and sometime during the week Myra insisted on taking him for a meal.

'I don't have anything to wear.'

'You sound like me. What are you supposed to wear?'

'I don't know.'

'Neither do I. We're only going for a curry, so I wouldnae bother buying a new suit.'

He had forgotten about curries. Every so often the scent would remind him, but it would mean saving up. He thought of making a curry for himself, but never got round to it.

The first mouthful was too hot and halfway through the meal Andy was very uncomfortable.

'You look as if you're gonnae have a heart attack.'

'I haven't had a curry for a while. It's a bit warm.'

'It's supposed to be warm.'

When he finished he ordered ice-cream.

Myra worked in the café part-time. She temped as a secretary and studied at college. 'I quite like temping. They can send you here, there and everywhere, but £3.50 an hour's not bad and I'm never in the one place long enough to like or dislike it.'

He told her he got out three months ago, after serving two years of a three-year sentence for drug dealing, that the polis raided his home at three in the morning and found vast quantities of stuff in the bedroom.

'My wife said she would stand by me and was as good as her word for about six months. I have spent a fair bit of time considering my luck and I intend to find out what happened. Sorry. I can tell you're losing interest. Heard it all before, I suppose.'

'I'll get the bill.'

They did not speak, walking down Woodlands Road from Charing Cross. Outside the Halt Bar he asked if she wanted a drink.

She nodded. He had a pint and she drank a glass of lemonade. People were singing next door.

Then they walked down West End Park Street and sat in Andy's room drinking coffee. Myra looked around her. 'Was it like this in jail?'

'Suppose so.'

She smiled at the finches. 'Them as well?'

'No, they're new.'

'Listen. It's got nothing to do with the fact that you've been in jail, but I don't think we should see each other again.'

'Okay.'

'No, Andy. Listen, please. What's the use. I don't know what to say. It's me, not you; I'm not up to it. Things are a bit fragile and I don't think I'm ready for a relationship, whatever that is, but you know what I mean. I don't want to get into anything heavy.'

'I won't bother you.'

'Don't be silly. Please, come in to the café. I want to see you, but this scares me. I hope you understand.'

'I don't.'

'Christ Almighty,' she said. 'Time to go.'

She caught a taxi on Woodlands Road. Andy walked back to his room.

*

Grandpa's death was a relief. The funeral service was memorable for its brevity. The minister obviously did not know Andy's grandfather and asked nothing about him. He spoke of a race well run, of forges and furnaces, of metal and the strength to fight the good fight in a changing world whose values are topsy turvy, where we constantly ask ourselves what God has in store for us.

Andy felt a loss, but was unaware of its significance. When the funeral was over he realised he would not see his grandfather again and felt foolish at such an obvious discovery. In the weeks that followed he felt lonelier than usual, regretful he had not known the old man better. Old age was supposed to bring wisdom and dignity, rest and a time for contemplation.

Andy never considered these things during the day; only at night and alone, only when he listened to the city flaring into darkness.

He had no curiosity about his father's death. It was a matter of public record, public property and the intrusion had removed the possibility of private grief. All personal aspects were removed. When he thought of his father's death, he also thought about his mother, Malky and Eileen.

Around the time he met Myra, Malky's cancer was declared inoperable. 'He's riddled with it, poor man,' said Eileen. 'All we can do is wait. Thank God he's in a private nursing home.'

'If he gets sick they'll have to send him to an NHS hospital. Could you cope with the shame?'

Malky had a theatrical ending in the side room of a hospital without wards, small private rooms off Great Western Road. Malky's room had a television, fresh flowers every day and a Tretchikoff reproduction above his bed.

When he was given two weeks to live, Malky called his friends and relations to visit and join him in prayer. He had found Christ.

Eileen was at the hospital for most of the day. Joe picked Andy up at Saracen Cross. They drove down Bilsland Drive in silence. On Maryhill Road, Joe said, 'Some carry on, eh?'

'How are you managing?'

'Getting by. It's hard to take this seriously.'

Andy waited in the corridor. Joe and Eileen came out of the room and closed the door. 'You'll find him a changed man,' said Eileen.

'I hope so,' said Andy.

The curtains were drawn. The window-ledge was lined with get well cards, the top of the bedside cabinet was crowded with fruit and sweets, soft drinks and tissues; there were four separate bunches of flowers and the room smelled of lilac. An armchair was by the bed.

Malky turned when Andy closed the door. 'God bless you,' he said. 'I am going to meet my maker.'

'Looks like it, Malky.'

'I am also going to meet your father.'

'I don't know what kind of reception you'll get there.'

'I am ready.'

'Just as well.'

There was silence, an awkward pause as Andy felt for something to say, but this was as much as he had ever said to Malky. He hoped Malky would not be sick, cough or anything like that.

'Have you thought of giving your life to Christ?' said Malky.

'No really.'

'Then take this tract, read it and come back and see me. I have wasted my life and do not want you to do the same.'

'Did you find the Lord when they found the cancer?'

'I went to a faith healer.'

'She doesnae seem to have done much good.'

'It was a man, who gave me a gift more precious than life, he guided my footsteps towards the Lord.'

'That's good, Malky. So you'll no mind going?'

'I am a witness for my Lord. Blessed assurance, Jesus is mine.'

'I'd best be off then.'

'I wanted to see you because I know and you know and we both know what each other knows and that's okay because that's the way life has to be sometimes.'

'Fair enough, Malky.'

He died four days later.

*

They drove to Rowardennan.

'We have a choice,' he said. 'If you feel energetic we could climb Ben Lomond; otherwise it's the bit of the West Highland Way.'

'Isn't Ben Lomond awfully high? What about Inverwhatsit?'

'Inversnaid's about six or seven miles away. The path's a bit rough, can also be steep, but it's manageable.'

There was an aimless breeze on the forestry road. It blew the smell of pine and bracken, peat, moss and brackish water across their path, or occasionally sent dragonflies spinning. It rustled the silver birch leaves three colours of green; it whistled through the hazels and the tops of the pines but did not diminish the traffic noise from across the water or the occasional rattle of a train. It freshened their faces and hummed in their ears, so they had to speak louder to make themselves heard.

Then came the reversal, when we meet the expected in unexpected surroundings, when the familiar occurs in an unfamiliar place or the usual wears an unusual guise; in the sun and the breeze and the noise they passed a robin on a holly tree.

They were at the end of the forestry trail, where it disappears into the wood and becomes a path to Inversnaid. The small wooden bench to the left was surrounded by cans and paper. 'You'd think they'd leave a plastic bag for the rubbish,' said Cathie, clearing the bench and sitting down. She set out the sandwiches and flask while Andy stared across the water.

'Tell me about it,' he said.

'About what?'

'Cathie, for Christsake. Stop it. I want you to talk to me.'

'Don't you want your sandwiches? I've made up some egg and cress, there's a lovely smoked ham with real German mustard, there's a sort of salady mixture and that's real coffee.'

'Tell me about your operation.'

'What do you want to know? That one's cheese, I didn't tell you about that, did I. I've made up some cheese sandwiches too.'

'Please, Cathie. Sit down. Stop footering and tell me what kind of operation you're going to have, when you are going in and how long you'll be there.'

'I'm only fixing the picnic. I thought you said we were going to have a picnic.'

'We are having the picnic. I am capable of eating a sandwich and listening, so tell me about your operation.'

'Can't talk with my mouth full.'

They sat on the bench and ate in silence. Cathie gathered the remnants of their meal, put it in her haversack and asked if they were going on to Inverwhatsit.

'Do you want to?'

'I don't mind. We'll do whatever you want to do.'

'Then let's go back. By the time we go on to Inversnaid and walk back to Rowardennan it'll be dark.'

They walked back the way they came. Going down the hill towards Rowardennan after an hour's silence, she said: 'I'm going for a woman's operation. It's called a D and C but I don't know what it means except it's also called a scrape.'

'Is that all?'

'What do you mean, all. I've never been in hospital before. That's why it took me so long to come and see you. I'm scared.'

Granny said: 'I know you're seeing a woman. Is it her in the hospital? I can smell her off you. What's up with her?'

'Nothing.'

'Then why haven't you brought her here?'

'No reason.'

'I'll say this about Winston Churchill, God rest him. He was never a whoremaister.'

'When do you want to meet Cathie?'

'Is that her name?'

'Cathie Kavanagh.'

'Bring her on Saturday.'

Orlando prepared the punch on Friday. Granny made soup.

'Boiling bones is an ancient art,' Orlando said as Andy prepared himself for work on the Friday night. 'They believed you could distil the strength of a beast by boiling the bones and feeding yourself on the mixture, a practice which, it must be said, is literally as well as theoretically correct, so when we eat a bowl of barley broth or lentil soup we are ingesting the strength of the sheep or the cow, maybe even a bull, whatever kind of beast had its bones boiled for our benefit. God knows where these packet soup concoctions get their strength, or that stuff to which you add only water. They belong thoroughly to this century and have nothing whatsoever to do with a tradition of any kind, other than the longstanding practice of providing cheap, unnourishing food for the poor.'

Andy made a cup of tea, using leaves rather than bags, while Orlando stirred the punch and soup with the same wooden spoon. Granny was asleep.

'I assume you are aware of the fact that your grandmother's not getting any better. She has lately taken to travelling by bus and introduces herself to the driver and some of the passengers in case she dies during the journey.' Orlando poured some punch into the soup. 'It came as something of a realisation that she could reach her destination quicker by bus than on foot, though, as you will doubtless be aware, this is truer at certain times of the day than others.'

Granny spent Saturday cleaning windows, changing curtains, polishing and dusting, as though it was the New Year. 'I've not got long to go,' she said, 'and I want to see you settled in this world before I leave it.'

Andy met Cathie at seven o'clock. They had a meal and he tried to tell her what to expect. 'Sounds fine,' she said, clutching the box of chocolates she had bought for Granny.

They arrived at the house just after ten. The windows were open; a piper was playing 'Cock o' The North' to accordion, mouth organ and drum accompaniment.

Orlando kissed Cathie's hand when he opened the door. He took her coat, handed it to Andy and, his hand on her elbow, escorted Cathie into the living room where Geordie Anderson was singing:

He says to her, 'You're gey weel built,
You've a rare pair of legs and a wee short kilt . . .'

'That's enough, Geordie. That'll dae ye.'

'I'm very pleased to meet you,' said Granny, rising from the chair. 'And so are all my friends.' She gave the chocolates to Orlando. 'I'm a poor widow woman who's had to work, scrimp and scrape all my days and I'd like to see my grandson settled before I go.'

Granny's wedding photo was framed and hung over the fire, with the Royal Family scattered around the room.

Cathie sat on the stool beside Granny's chair. She sipped a little punch, placed it on the floor beside her and did not drink from the glass again.

'I hope you're going to give us a song,' said Granny.

Cathie smiled. 'I don't think so,' she said.

'Everybody has to sing here.'

'No they don't. They can only sing if they're any good, that includes Elvis impersonators and women with beehive hair-dos who sing hits from the Sixties.'

'Cheek,' said a woman Andy had never seen before. When the noise was shushed she sang 'Why Did You Make Me Care'.

Andy sat opposite Cathie who looked at the floor, as though she might either want to laugh or cry. She was polite, applauded with everyone else, shook her head and said, 'No thanks, it's lovely, but I'm driving,' when Orlando offered her more punch, took a few spoonfuls of soup and bread, looked at him and realised there was nothing else for it. She ate the soup and bread and lit a cigarette immediately.

Mrs Esplin shouted, 'It's only me.'

'God is trying my patience this night,' said Bernadette O'Hara. 'It comes in threes.'

The first was when the strange woman, whom no one knew, had sung her song. Then Baby William asked if she would do up his buttons.

'You've a zip,' she said.

'Gonnae you do it?'

She turned her head the other way, smiled at whoever may be looking and pulled up the zip, suddenly snatching her hands away: 'You're a dirty little pig,' she said.

When everyone was quiet, William sang 'Away In a Manger'.

There was a break while the box player played a selection of Scottish waltzes and while the rest talked, Cathie and Orlando waltzed round the room. Mrs Esplin was at her seat when the dance was finished.

'I saw you looking at my hat,' she said. 'Do you like it?'

'It's very nice,' said Cathie.

'I hate it, but it keeps me warm. It was either that or a green one, and I never wear green.'

'Don't you think it suits you?' asked Cathie. Mrs Esplin showed her the picture album.

When it was her turn, she snatched the album from Cathie and holding it across her chest, opened at pages with four pictures to a page, all of her in full regalia, she sang:

All good Protestants must maintain
That nothing but a Protestant king shall reign;
And if the Pope says, No,
Then we'll have another go
On the banks of the Boyne in the morning.

And simultaneously, Bernadette O'Hara sang:

If I had a yard of an Orangeman's skin,
I'd turn it into drums for my bold Fenian men;

And every Sunday morning as I went off to Mass
I'd bang the drum and then I'd kick the great big Orange arse.

'One singer, one song,' said Granny.

'No party tunes, ladies, please,' said Orlando.

The piper and accordionist played 'Scotland The Brave'.

'Right, dear,' said Granny. 'Your turn.'

Cathie said, 'I'm not very good.'

'Don't let that bother you; think of us as family.'

'I don't know any songs.'

'You must know something?'

'I've never sang in public. I can't keep a tune. I think I'm tone deaf.'

'It doesn't matter; you're amongst friends.'

'She doesn't want to sing,' said Andy. 'She doesn't have to sing if she doesn't want to.'

'I thought it would make her feel at home,' said Granny.

'No you didn't.'

'Perfectly all right, my dear,' Orlando said. 'You don't need to sing if you don't want to. I have only sung once at such a gathering: *Il mio tesoro* from Don Giovanni. Didn't go down too well, I fear. Never again.'

'You at least tried,' said Granny.

Andy looked at Cathie and said, 'Let's go.'

'Just like you to put a damper on people's enjoyment,' Granny said as Geordie Armstrong stood up to sing.

She came out on the Thursday, having been in for two days. Andy saw her at the weekend.

They ate in silence, watched television and argued when he said he was going home. 'Why don't you take what's yours,' she said.

He was late for work next day. That week a pattern developed. When he did not see her he phoned, sometimes standing in a call-box for more than an hour, using two or three Phonecards, or he stayed with her, stroking her hair.

'Where was my wandering boy last night?' asked Granny.

'Young men,' said Orlando, 'are inconsiderate in these matters. I was myself and so I dream of going back to be. There are many stories to substantiate this assertion, but I fancy employers' notes on the subject are generally reliable.'

He saw her every day for the next six weeks. In some ways these weeks had been their happiest: 'Like the beginning,' she said.

Then Emily left home, two days after her sixteenth birthday, which she spent eating pizza with friends. At first she was untraceable, but she contacted her grandparents within a week.

'Looking for money,' said Cathie. 'She always gets round my Dad.'

Emily phoned. She was well, living in a room in Kersland Street, looking for a job and thinking of going to Edinburgh.

'What about school?'

'I'm not going back to school. I've left.'

Next night Andy met Geoff, the man next door, the man who wore the long johns and was widowed a few months ago. Cathie had known him all her life. He came round to offer advice. 'Not much to say, really.' Geoff avoided Andy's eyes. 'All my kids, three of them, left and came back. She'll come back. She's like the rest of them; thinks it's fine till she tries it for herself. In the end she knows what side her bread's buttered on.'

'And what does Cathie do in the meantime?'

'Not much she can do. Emily doesn't want her to have the address.'

She later lifted her nightdress and snuggled her back towards him. He squeezed her nipple.

'Talk to me,' she said. 'Tell me what you want me to do.'

'I want you to lift your skirt for me, right in the middle of the street. When we get out the car I want you to shout, "Andy" and when I turn round your skirt's at your waist.'

'What'll you do?'

'Look at you. Just stand there looking at you.'

'Then what?'

'Take you round to the nearest lane and put you up against the wall.'

'Up a close.'

'And shag you up against the wall, standing there with your skirt up.'

Cathie came. She lay still while Andy continued.

'Don't tell me you're jealous of old Geoff,' she said a couple of nights later, when Geoff had taken her to dinner, then sat in the living room till one in the morning discussing the sanitary arrangements of a recently-built hotel.

'Not at all. If you want Geoff you can have him. It wouldn't be too difficult. I don't go in for beauty contests.'

'He's an old man. He's Daddy's friend. They talk about old men's things together. Besides, he's boring, wears pyjamas and slippers and horrible ties with shirts that are striped differently. Look at him. Apart from anything else, I can't stand him. Don't say it again. It isn't funny. What do you mean about beauty contests?'

'He's sniffing around, Cathie. He's sniffing around for what he can get, pretending to offer a shoulder to lean on in a time of crisis. His wife went through what you're going through, his kids left home. He knows how you are and is ready to take advantage. Lonely people will do anything for company.'

'I've told you, shut up about it. The idea's disgusting.'

Her mouth wakened Andy in the middle of the night. She was under the covers. He rolled over onto his back and opened his legs to let her head slide into the crevice. Her hands were wet. Hands, mouth and tongue slid down to his balls. He raised his legs and she put a testicle whole in her mouth, then bit and held on. Andy fainted.

*

Some prisoners develop a liking for sentimental expressions of love. The day before St Valentine's Day sees hugely stuffed, satin hearts leave jail by post.

A middle-aged man who wore a dark green corduroy jacket, suede shoes and dandruff on the inside of his spectacle lenses took creative writing classes at Dungavel. The class was popular. Those who could write earned some reasonable money writing love poems and letters to order. The poems were suitable for letters or home visits.

*

Orlando was in the habit of beginning a sentence, then pausing. His conversations were either punctuated by long silences or he said something irrelevant, for no reason other than it had occurred to him; it was in his mind.

'Any woman I fancy is afraid of me,' he said, smiling apologetically. 'And any woman who fancies me is having hormone replacement therapy and is therefore in a state of semi-permanent ovulation.'

'Is this you telling me I'd be better off without them?'

'Not at all. I am sympathising.'

Orlando had asked about Cathie. Andy said he had not seen her for some time. He found it difficult to explain what happened.

Two nights later, leaving the restaurant, he met Sandra, a friend of Emily's who lived next door, coming up Hope Street with a couple of girls. She'd been drinking and was going dancing. She talked to Andy while the friends looked bored, shouting her name every now and then to remind her they were there.

'You going out to see Cathie?'

'No.'

'You should.'

'Cathie knows how to get in touch with me if she wants to. That was how it was left.'

The girl with the pink hair and short skirt sighed deeply. 'We'd better go, Sandra. We're gonnae be late.'

'A minute. Do you know she's getting married?'

The sudden rush of fear that seemed like anger made him think he had lost his breath.

'Geoff?'

'Who else.'

'She was seeing him for a while?'

'No she wasn't, not really. He came round a couple of days after you left. My mother said she was in her dressing gown, moping around worse than usual. Next thing I know he's never away from the place. Funny man. Never says much. You don't know what he's thinking.'

'When's the happy day?'

'I don't know.'

'Sandra, I'm freezing.'

'Okay, I'm just coming. You should go up and see her. Please. Give her a ring.'

'Sandra, we're going.' The other girl was walking away.

'Where's Emily? Is she back yet?'

'No. She says she's no coming back. That's the trouble. Cathie lost her daughter, then she lost you. She doesnae want him.'

'Sandra.'

'Emily told her mother she left home because of you. It wasn't true. She was seeing a boy and didn't want her mum to know. I hope I'll see you again,' said Sandra, running off.

They came into the restaurant, Cathie and Geoff, her mother and father. The head waiter showed them to Andy's table. Cathie did not look at him. She wore a diamond solitaire engagement ring. Geoff ordered for everyone. Andy spat in the soup, gravy, ice-cream and felt no better. Geoff paid with a credit card. Andy thought of him in pyjamas, his sunken face and the way he would gather himself, taking time to adjust to the day. How she would hate the blue veins in the legs beneath his pyjamas.

Three months later, coming up from St Enoch's subway station into the light, Andy turned to talk to the people he was with and saw a strange, untidy young woman staring at him.

'Hello,' she said.

He stared.

'Hello,' she said, by now smiling.

Her hair was dyed four shades of orange, her face was spotted and dirty, flushed red and chubby. Her shoulders, arms and upper torso looked thin, her hips were fat and she was dressed in black. Andy recognised none of her features. Her teeth were yellow. Then he maybe recognised her smile, or at least her mouth.

'Emily?'

'Yes.'

'I didn't recognise you because of your hair. How are you?'

'I'm fine. How are you?'

'Very well, thank you.'

'Good.'

And because he had nothing else to say, he smiled and gestured towards Buchanan Street.

'See you.'

And she said, 'Bye.'

*

Andy discovered Radio Three by twirling dials on the greenhouse transistor, bored with the repetition, the resnatronic doggerel that seemed to be the consequence of having a radio in jail. What he later learned was the second movement of the Mozart Clarinet Quintet was playing; he realised he had been looking at the radio, stirring when the sleeky voice announced the players. He switched the radio off.

Next day he listened for an hour in the morning and again in the afternoon, rationing himself in case it was discovered and taken away, rationing himself from ridicule. He saved up, bought a portable transistor and carried it with him, buying blank tapes, keeping a record of what he heard and what he recorded. He preferred Mozart, Scarlatti, Haydn and Beethoven then avoided the nineteenth century until Mahler, Berwald, Sibelius, Nielsen, Prokofiev and Shostakovich. He especially liked composers such as Ferdinand Ries, Johannes Mayr, Giovanni Paisiello, Niccola Porpora, Gabriel Pierné and Ivan Jirko as though their work was a secret, the performances especially for him.

He left jail with over 130 hours of music, including more

than one performance of the late Beethoven quartets and sonatas, the middle to late Mozart piano concertos and the Haydn symphonies. He recorded every available performance of Nielsen's Fifth Symphony. Again the clarinet, with the belligerent side drums and timpani in the first movement, stopped him. He closed his eyes and allowed the earphones to eliminate distraction, as though this music was him, was happening inside his head. The announcer said this was the finest symphony of the twentieth century. Andy wondered if the earphones made it secret.

Charlie Sloan had told him, 'You'll go deaf wi they fucken things on your heid aa day.' Perhaps the other prisoners believed he was deaf. When they spoke, they exaggerated their lip movements and raised their voices.

He did not take the portable tranny and earphones outside. The sound of the city was still fresh and unfamiliar, but it was mostly the sky and the Glasgow light. The Dungavel gardens made him aware of sky, light, air, sun and wind; he was always aware of the rain. Dungavel rain was different, fresher, cleaner, less annoying and incongruous, more to be expected, functional and necessary. Rain did nothing to concrete and stone, glass and metal.

Hoeing is a mindless job. He learned a pleasurable intensity in disturbing a stubborn weed and enjoyed raking the ground after hoeing or turning weeds into the soil. It was sore as gardening was sore, but hoeing was unexpectedly sore; rather than being painful to the shoulders, arms or hands, it was painful in the small of the back, like digging. It also required constant stretching. Hoeing was an early job, given to learner gardeners; hoeing and digging for a year, then planting.

After a day he learned to rest the arm of the hoe on his shoulder as he stretched, his hands tucked behind his head, tensing his legs and groin, raising his feet, bunching the energy into the small of his back. He closed his eyes, snapped them open and saw the sky. Every day he looked at the Dungavel sky. He watched the clouds and air, noticed the way wind shifted, the scent in the air, the way the feel and density of the air changed before rain, after rain, expecting thunder, for a week in the spring and during the first week in October when the geese flew symmetrically and called across the sky.

Coming back to the city, he noticed the light. There were times when the sky was too intense, when the light penetrated the stone and concrete, penetrated the buildings, when inside his room with the curtains drawn he could still feel the light and warmth, the direct radiation of the day, when he opened the curtains to confirm what he already knew. Outside, the buildings sparkled. Small, unrecorded lives took on an aura of light as they walked the city streets, pushing prams, carrying shopping bags and children or simply standing, staring into windows, into space or queueing.

As queues changed the political face of Eastern Europe they increased in Glasgow. The poor queue for everything, for transport, food and shelter. They especially queue for officialdom, dying by inches.

The sky changes and light fades around the bus-stops in the quarter-hour winter sunsets. Glasgow is built on a series of drumlins, which makes surrounding hills constantly visible, snow-topped in the dying light. Andy often stood at a bus-stop just to see the sunsets, walking home in the newly crisp and darkened air. The stars were kept secret by the street lights and buildings, visible from the parks and open spaces, the vacant bits of ground and tops of buildings, the disused factories which showed eternity glittering above the city.

The finches sang when he came in the room. The noise of the

door made them sing. When he came in the room, he sat on the bed, listened to the finches and stared at the wall. Then he lit the fire.

*

Cathie visited the house four or five times more. Twice she came for dinner. They ate tinned soup, stew, peas and boiled potatoes, ice-cream and trifle on both occasions. Cathie said, 'Thank you, Granny. That was lovely.' She sat by the fire with her legs crossed, her hands on her lap.

'I'm glad to see you ate your dinner. Did they tell you never to leave food on your plate?'

'I got a row if I left food.'

Afterwards they played a hand of whist, sometimes solo. Orlando always went on reckless misère ouverts, abundances or even solos. Granny would go a solo with an abundance hand. Cathie learned the game well enough to play.

'I threw away a two of diamonds. That was a signal for you to lead diamonds. I had a hand full of them,' Andy said during the post-mortem that followed every game.

'Explain that again,' said Cathie. 'I don't understand.'

'God love you, hen,' said Granny. 'You have to watch the hands and remember what's been played. Solo's a selfish game, but you need to be sleekit as well. I think that's where you fall down. You're no very sleekit.'

'It means crafty,' Andy told her in the car. 'She doesn't mean it as an insult.'

'I don't think I'll ever understand,' said Cathie.

He started gambling. Not thinking about Cathie had something to do with it. He gambled seriously after she left, knowing it was short term, the way some men go drinking, an expedient thing, something which served a purpose he could not define.

There were games and carry-outs in the staff bedrooms. There was usually a bookie in every hotel and someone would always cover up for a runner. A group from work joined a casino. They ate the free sandwiches, drank in the bar and watched the Chinese players with their lonely dedication. Andy went back and lost his wages, walking home with a fiver in his pocket.

'You're well rid of her,' said Granny. 'Not that I had anything against her, mind; but she was an awful genteel kind of lassie, which made her difficult to talk to. You want somebody a bit more like yourself, somebody whose background's a bit nearer your own.'

'Can you suggest where I might find a woman whose father was murdered, whose mother married the murderer, a girl whose Granny sells cardboard boxes to dossers.'

'That's enough,' Orlando said, quietly.

'What's it got to do with you?'

Orlando stared at him: 'I won't have your grandmother spoken to in this way.'

'And what are you going to do about it?'

'I've just done something. I've told you to stop it.'

'And what if I don't?'

'You already have.'

'What is it with you: have you got to be right all the time? Is it not enough that you are constantly hanging around here, uninvited as far as I can see, that you are continually wittering on about this or that piece of crap, but now you are leaping to defend someone who is not being attacked and butting your nose into a private matter which is none of your concern, is the concern of this family and this family alone.'

'If you weren't attacking, what were you doing?'

'Keep out of it, Orlando. It's got nothing to do with you.'

'I beg to differ.'

'You do whatever the fuck you like.'

'Please don't use that language in front of your grandmother. It is very disrespectful.'

'So that's it. Very clever; ever consider politics as a career? Ignore what I say and attack the way I say it, or pick one part of the argument and ignore the rest.'

'I don't especially want to fight with you.'

'Fight? Is it a fight now? I'll tell you something, you are here on sufferance and don't you forget it. You contribute nothing to this household. You don't even live here. God knows where you live, though even he might be forgiven for assuming it was here, because you spend enough time here.'

'I'm sorry. I'll go.'

When Orlando stood up, Andy for the first time noticed how tall he was, five feet ten or six feet high, wiry looking, lean and angular. There was a slight hesitancy, just enough for Orlando to take a breathful into his lungs while he looked at the solemn pink and marbled roses symmetrically strewn across the wallpaper, long enough to inhale and turn at the same time, avoiding the chair; the sort of hesitancy you might miss if you did not know the person rising.

'Goodnight,' he said. No one answered. Orlando was at the door when Andy spoke, his face overlooking the square of brick-built middens, the railings with the gaps, the wired-glass-panelled back doors and the flickering light in the closes.

'Walking out now? That's really great.'

'If you have something to discuss with me, then please do it when you are in a reasonable frame of mind. Whatever has upset you, I know it wasn't me. I happen to be the nearest target least likely or able to defend itself.'

No one heard the noise of the door scraping the carpet or the click as the ballbearing locked into its socket, neither did they hear the front door close.

'Is that you pleased?' said Granny.

Andy did not answer. In the silence, he wished he smoked so's he could do something with his hands. He sat on a kitchen chair, his elbows on his knees, hands clasped, doing what the soul does in times of humiliation, he was trying to think of something different, wondering why he had never smoked, had never liked smoking, though he did not mind being in a smoky room.

'Don't you ever talk to him like that again, or anyone else I bring here for that matter. You have no idea what he does or does not do. You have left this home before and as far as I am concerned you can do so again. I have tolerated your guests, I may not have liked them and at times I even showed I did not like them, but at least I tolerated them.'

'I've only brought one here recently.'

'If you treat him like I treated her I'll have no complaints.'

'I thought you didn't want me to humiliate him.'

'I am only glad your grandfather is not here to hear you speak to me like that. God knows what he would have done.'

'He'd have gone to his bed.'

'If you're half the man he was, you'll do. Now I'll need to get Orlando something nice for his dinner; and God knows where he's gone. See the trouble you cause.'

Andy had felt like this once before, in the school playground within a year of his father's death and the family's scattering. This was the new school; coming up for Christmas, he was still the last pupil on the school roll.

There was a small girl, something Campbell, maybe Alice. She appeared friendless, played hand-clapping games in a group, never with another girl forming a pair; she wore National Health spectacles coated in pink plastic, one of two frocks and a cardigan buttoned to her neck with embroidered flowers down either side of her chest. She wore plastic shoes and never wore socks. Her hair was straight, tied with a ribbon at the top of her head. She was a skinny girl whose legs bulged inwards at the knee. She neither skipped nor played peever.

Morning playtime in the week before the Christmas break in the days when kids got a third of a pint of milk each day. The Campbell girl was never seen eating other than at mealtimes. She got free dinners. She was in the girls' playground by the railings which separated the girls from the boys. She was eating a bar of chocolate. Two girls took the chocolate. Andy told them to give it back to her. 'What for?' asked the Campbell girl, looking at her shoes while the other girls ate her chocolate. 'I gave it to them.'

'I'll need to get him a chicken,' said Granny. 'God love him, he likes a chicken, always said it was an important creature and when you think about it he was quite right for we get eggs from a chicken as well as meat. We can boil or roast it and use the bones for soup.'

Andy took off his shirt and washed himself at the sink. It was the easiest way of avoiding his grandmother's presence; she left the room when he took his clothes off. He boiled a kettle, shaved and was drying his hair when the doorbell rang.

'I would like a word with your grandmother.' Orlando was no more than slightly embarrassed. He looked at Andy the way he might look at a bus conductor, or a taxi driver who said he had no change.

'She isn't in.'

'Could you tell her I called?'

'Come in and wait.'

'I would rather call back later.'

'Orlando; please, come in and wait. I was going to have some tea before going to work.'

He sat in the sitting room like a guest, in the same kitchen chair Andy used. Andy brought in the tea with some plain digestive and ginger snap biscuits on a plate. He served the tea and said, 'I'm sorry.'

'Perfectly all right. Had to be said. That sort of thing clears the air. I know where I stand now.'

'The thing is, I'm not sure I meant it.'

'Don't feel you have to entertain me. Get on with your ablutions.'

Andy was combing his hair, his empty teacup on the mantelpiece beside the mirror, when the doorbell rang. Orlando shouted, 'I'll get it.'

He knocked on the bedroom door. 'I think you ought to come through here.'

Granny was pale, sitting in her chair by the fire in her coat and black beanie hat. Two substantial men in raincoats, obviously policemen, were standing by the table. Granny had fainted at the supermarket, buying a loaf. They gave her a seat and she fainted again. The second time she fainted her hat came off and a frozen chicken she had been hiding rolled across the floor. The chill caused the faint. There would probably be no charges. They hoped she'd soon be well.

Two nights later Andy and Joe went to the casino. They had a fair night's betting, Joe won some and Andy reckoned he was up a little, which meant he had lost a tenner.

They were in the bar downstairs. 'I'm setting up a wee tank,' said Joe. 'Just a fund of my own, so that I'm never short. This sort of thing is perfect.'

'It's a great idea so long as you don't take anything out.'

'Putting it in'll be the problem, but I'm not in any hurry.'

There was a noisy group of girls at the table opposite. When Andy looked over one of them smiled. He and Joe joined them and stayed till after three in the morning. The smiling girl's name was Margaret and she was waiting outside the Odeon the following Monday at seven o'clock. Andy was glad; he could barely remember what she looked like.

During the interval she told him, 'I don't gamble, by the way. That was a works night out.'

'You told me.'

'That's right, so I did.'

Three weeks later he took her to meet Granny. This time there was no prior warning. 'I'm not sure,' Margaret had said. 'I don't know that I'm into meeting families just at this minute.' She had recently split from what she called a long-term relationship.

Granny seemed unconcerned. 'I'll make some tea,' she said and met Andy coming out of the kitchen.

'My God, son,' she said, 'You and your lame duck women.'

*

Andy wondered why he did it, especially when he was always obvious. There were times when he was talking with a woman in the Post Office, the library or even in the Social Security Office, and happened to look, even glance, allow his eyes to flicker towards another woman, any woman, who was passing. The change in conversation, both in tone and content, was immediate and palpable, effected in the time it took the eye to blink.

Was it this or something else that made him afraid to talk to women? He had never done it, was comfortable with people he already knew and disliked meeting strangers of either gender, though he thought women made him appear more awkward. The idea of talking to a strange woman was especially uneasy.

Once, in the Kelvingrove Art Galleries, he thought he had stumbled on something. He had been out of jail maybe five or six weeks and was renewing acquaintances with things he used to know. He was ready to begin absorbing, finding out if things were what he thought they were, if the reality and the dreaming were the same, if the imagination which had sustained him had been a tool of invention or discovery, if memory was unreliable as time.

The art galleries smelled the same. He walked through the Armoury and up the stairs. The Armoury was the same. He turned right at the top, into what used to be the French Room. It was like a junk shop, laid out on the principle of the antique shop: Look around and you're sure to see something you like. The rooms had been reorganised into headings which presupposed a certain knowledge before an approach could be made. Perfect examples of consumerism. An education was offered in the old rooms, free to anyone who walked through the doors, like a library. Now everything was reduced to an object which only made sense in relation to other objects, a display which said, Stay off unless you know what you are looking at.

He asked the woman beside him, 'Are they changing the display?'

She smiled. His confusion kept him going, 'They must be moving the stuff around.'

'I think it's meant to be like this.'

'Why?'

'I don't know.'

They strolled along the corridor together. She was American, over on holiday with her boyfriend who hated art, but might have liked this. Andy told her what used to be there, what was in the old rooms. 'I know what to expect,' she said, 'I've been to galleries before.'

Walking home he realised he had experienced his first casual conversation with a woman in more than two years; in the anger and confusion he hadn't even noticed.

Andy went to a casino near Charing Cross after Malky's funeral. This was where he had met his wife. Joe was with him on both occasions.

A tea was arranged for Malky's mourners. They were shown into the side room of a small hotel near the cemetery. Three tables ran the length of the room. They were covered in white plastic cloths with three groupings of plastic flowers and tea settings for twenty to each table. Within ten minutes the room was smoky. There were no ashtrays. The mourners used saucers. The waitresses asked the mourners to pass the scones and jam, to serve themselves with tea. There was no coffee.

'Fancy a pint?' said Joe.

Andy's mother was crying. She was with a woman Andy had never seen.

'Who's that?'

'Maureen. Malky's sister.'

A man was talking to Andy's mother. Eileen was smoking and staring at a picture of lovers at a stile. Tracy was singing to herself, 'Scooby dooby doo, Where are you?' Thomas held her hand.

'I'm going for a pint with Andy. I'll see you later.'

'How are we supposed to get home?' Tracy stopped singing.

'I thought you'd ordered taxis.'

'We haven't ordered them, but it looks as though we're going to have to.'

'You told me you were getting them anyway.'

'I suppose it'll be all hours before you're back.'

'Excuse me,' said Andy.

Maureen looked up and smiled.

'We haven't met. My name's Andy Paterson, Rose's son and Eileen's brother, Tracy's uncle.'

'Pleased to meet you.'

'I've always wondered. Was Wee Malky really with you the night my father died?'

Her bottom lip quivered. She scanned his face for a sign, her own face pale, her eyes like glass, sheep's eyes.

'You understand, it's important to me. The truth can't hurt anyone now. Put yourself in my position. I need to know.'

Her eyes never left his face. She pushed the chair backwards, said, 'Excuse me,' and left the room.

Andy looked at his mother, wiping her nose with a tissue, looking at the tablecloth. The wee man held her left hand in both his hands. 'If there's anything I can do, ask me. All you have to do is ask. Anything.' He was wearing a wig. 'Maybe when all this is settled and things are back to normal, I'll call round one night.'

Joe tugged Andy's arm. 'Let's go.'

'Delighted,' said Andy. As he left he saw his mother, sister and niece all reach for a scone from the same plate.

'Who's the wee guy?'

'A bookie, one of Malky's pals.'

'What's he doing?'

'Fuck sake, Andy. Sober up. What does it look as if he's doing.'

'He must think he's in with a chance.'

'Put it this way, as long as he thinks he's in with a chance, he's got no chance, but as long as he thinks he has a chance, your maw will be kept in the manner to which she has become accustomed. She's about as interested in him as the Aga Khan is in having a bet at Shawfield.'

'I thought Malky left her plenty.'

'As far as I know she got a good wee whack, but women get lonely, son, especially widow women, and when that happens all bets are off. Now, shall we go and get pished.'

The taxi driver had a tattoo shining through his balding hair. 'I know what yous're looking at; good, intit? I got it done when I was young and daft; fourteen, so I got my head shaved and a tattoo of a spider's web done. You want to have seen the state my heid was in; bealing, yella pus and scabs. I don't know what was worse my heid or my maw when she saw my heid. Guess what they called us?'

'Spider?'

'Scabbyheid. I wanted to be called Spider because everybody else was called Tam or Billy, some fucken daft name like that. I grew my hair when they called us Scabbyheid. I forgot about the tattoo till I started going bald. You want tae've heard the wife. Still, it's good for this job. Gets you talking with folk.'

'Smoke?' asked Joe. The driver took a cigarette and lit it without stopping talking. 'Bad time of night, this. Not that there's what you would call a good time for traffic, but this is a bad time – no thanks, I've lit my own – this time is fucken desperate. Look at it. Dead slow and stop. See that M8, fucken useless, so it is. They should've built it or left it alane. The state of the traffic in this city's deplorable.'

The taxi driver pulled his window down and threw the remains of his cigarette onto the road. Andy watched it bounce into a single burst of sparking red when it hit the roadway. 'If you ask me – ' the driver stopped to raise his middle finger up and down in the direction of a young girl in an old car: 'Did you see that cunt there, that's what should be banned, private cars. They should take daft bitches like that off the road. See when they do that, take their surveys or whatever the fuck they do, they never ask the folk that use the roads, they never ask the taxi drivers or the bus drivers. They sit in their daft wee offices and count the cars. "I think we'll make St Vincent Street one way chaps. That'll really fuck them up." They want to ban these fuckers that cannae drive. It's the same as the drink. If you ask me, everybody should have a drinking licence. If you're caught drinking and driving, if you wallop some guy when you're bevvied, anything like that, you get the licence taken off you. This it chief? Great stuff.'

Out of jail, walking around to remember, Andy added up the car registration numbers. If three in a row came to thirteen, something unlucky would happen, unless he got another three of the same number, or a sequence, which could include the number thirteen. Sequences could be down as well as upward.

Then he began to add telephone numbers, the numbers on digital clocks and watch-faces, the price list on a menu, supermarket window or along the shelves. Prials and sequences were easy to find on menus. Most telephone numbers came to somewhere between thirty and fifty, so under thirty or over fifty became lucky. A car registration prial or sequence which came to single figures or to more than twenty was very unusual. Most were between thirteen and nineteen. Low and high sequences became extra lucky.

*

The casino was glass and light; bouncers in dinner suits, croupiers who smiled when you won, sandwiches with watercress sprinkled across the top, and coffee.

After an hour they knew it wasn't working. 'A bit early,' Joe told the checkout girl, as though he had to explain to someone. 'We'll come back later.' They went to the Griffin, which they both called the King's Arms. An hour later, this wasn't working either.

'What's the point of drinking if it neither changes your mood nor gives you the simple pleasure of a numbed set of frontal lobes.'

'We could have a little low life,' said Joe.

'The British sherry.'

'Can you stand the thought of a fat woman in a spangly dress, her hair piled up like a cake, singing "I Don't Know Why I Love You Like I Do"?'

'What is it then?'

'A carry-out and a seat in the park?'

'Might as well.'

Woodlands was deserted, except for an occasional taxi avoiding the lights at Charing Cross. The street lamps gave the buildings, the misted air and pavements an imaginary colour, like a black and white film on a colour television, lots of blues and greys. The park was open. Through the gates and the air seemed cleaner. The city was both below and around them. The scattered, sluggish western sweep and illuminated buildings gave the same cosy air of unfamiliarity as the first fall of snow. The noise felt like silence and was quiet enough to pass for stillness.

'Fucken freezing.'

'What do you expect?'

'A bit of civility and a drink out the bottle.'

The whisky went down like a rip saw and lay like a boiler, sour and anxious, warming, though their hands and faces were cold. They drank in silence for more than an hour, Joe smoking, nudging each other with a fresh can of beer or when it was the other's turn for a slug out the bottle.

'Something about this,' said Andy.

'What do you mean?'

'I don't know. Just, there's something about it. All these people concerned with themselves, all that quiet desperation, all that obsession. If you sit here long enough it'll come up to meet you.'

'Do you ever wonder what's going on?'

'All the time.'

'I don't mean that; and I don't mean who made us all either. Just when you see something spread out like this, d'you no think some sort of pattern emerges.'

'Not at all. The opposite. When I see people together I find it hard to believe in God. Groups of people together are bad. When I see crowds like that, a mass of humanity, at a football match or even in the street, I find it hard to believe in anything, in God, in man's supremacy or even the theory of evolution. I find it dead easy to believe in God when there's no one around, when I look at the sky or the hills, the sea, moonlight on the water, snow, a starry night, that sort of thing makes it hard to deny the existence of something other than what we know.'

Joe lit a cigarette and gave it to Andy. Andy said, 'I don't smoke.' Joe laughed. 'And what about the Wee Malky? Where's he?'

'Wee Malky's snuffed it.'

'But what about his soul? Or did the likes of Wee Malky no have a soul, him having broken every one of the Ten Commandments.'

'Especially the ones about murder and coveting your neighbour's wife.'

'So what about Wee Malky's soul, son? Has he gone to meet his maker?'

'Wee Malky's soul is about as interesting as anybody's soul.'

'What does that mean?'

'It means that Wee Malky'll need to find out for himself if he has a soul or no, and if he has then it's his business and nobody else's. Did it never occur to you that no bastard knows they've got a soul until somebody tells them and they always find out in times of trouble. Anybody, anybody at all; ask them; ask any bastard who found their soul, found the Lord or anything like that and they'll tell you it happened when times were tough, because when things is fine naebody needs it.'

'What keeps them going?'

'Judgement. Fear. And the two of them thegither. Plus, of course, the fear that it might be right.'

'And is that what's happening to Wee Malky?'

'I suppose Wee Malky'll have the same judgement as the rest of us.'

'And, as a murderer, we can safely assume he will not be bound for glory?'

'Gey few of us'll be making that trip.'

'You see, Andy, what I'm trying to find out is how you feel about that little bastard. How do you feel now he's gone?'

'Dying hasn't made him any better.'

'I suppose that means you don't like him?'

'I've never liked him.'

'Because he murdered your father?'

'It's a good enough reason.'

'Is it him you don't like or your mother who married him?'

'What is this, Joe? What are you getting at?'

'Nothing. I just want to know how you feel.'

'What difference does it make, how I feel? What has that got to do with it? Who asked my opinion; who asked me for advice; who took my feelings into account? Malky? Or my mother? Surely to Christ you'd expect a mother to think about her children, to wonder if they'll get picked on at school, to worry about them getting a kicking from the other weans, or maybe they'll get spat on, maybe they get their hair pulled, maybe nobody talks to them or plays with them because their Mammy's a cow. Surely to Christ you'd think; you've got a kid, Joe, don't ask me questions, fucken tell me, tell me, surely to Christ you'd think a mother would take her children's futures, never mind their feelings, into account. She thought about what her daughter would feel and look at the fucken mess that turned out to be, so maybe I got the best deal after all. Sorry, Joe. I didnae mean nothing, you and Eileen.'

'Nae bother.'

'I didnae mean to hurt you. I got carried away.'

'You never told me anything I didnae know. Can I tell you something?'

'Sure.'

'Promise you'll forget it's about your sister?'

'I don't have a sister.'

'Think of it as my wife rather than your sister? Promise?'

'Sure.'

'Say it.'

'Say what?'

'Say, I promise.'

'I promise.'

Joe lit a cigarette, took a slug of whisky and rested his elbows on his knees. A dog barked on Kelvin Way and a car sounded its horn and from somewhere came the chimes of an ice-cream van playing Greensleeves.

'I married her because she was pregnant.'

'I know.'

'I know you know. Shut up.'

'Sorry.'

'She told me if I didnae marry her she'd kill herself wi shame. She said she couldnae stand it, having a baby and no man, what with Malky and her mother. She told me more or less what you told me. Guys at school, wee guys, fourteen, fifteen, that sort of age, would ask her for a ride, would talk to her different than they'd talk to other lassies. They'd show other lassies some respect, or they were scared; know what I mean, they wouldnae talk as if they were slags, but they'd talk to Eileen as if she was a slag because of Rose, because of her mother. So I married her. The thing is, Andy, she never stopped me, know what I mean. The boys in the playground were right. She never stopped me. Listen, the first time I tried the hand, she let me in there, straight away, nae bother and I was her first boyfriend. She never said anything either, never mentioned it. Second time, same again and so on. It was as if she was expecting it and she let it happen, up a close near where she lived. We used to call it our single end. Christsake, can you imagine her doing that now? I can hardly believe it myself. The funny thing is, I thought she was doing what she must have believed was expected of her, but I don't think that now. I believe she got pregnant deliberately. I believe she let me ride her to get herself pregnant, knowing I would marry her and that would save her getting hurt, that would save her feelings. She would never have to face her background. She'd never need to look at her past.'

'And you're stuck?'

‘That’s it. That’s the thing. That’s what I want to tell you. She’s still at it. She still does it, still blackmails me, still tells me she’ll kill herself if I leave.’

‘And you believe her?’

‘You don’t know her, Andy. She’s daft enough for anything.’

‘Is the drink done?’

‘Aye.’

Joe stood up and threw the bottle downhill: it clattered into some bushes. Andy gathered the cans in their bag and dumped them on a waste bin, already overflowing. Joe was standing still.

‘Shh.’

‘What is it?’

‘Listen.’

Very faintly, above the traffic, the sound of geese flying south. The two men faced each other and smiled. Andy touched Joe’s arm, Joe turned and they hugged each other, dancing around in the cold for warmth. Andy jumped up on the bench and shaded his eyes, Joe looked upwards in the other direction, but they could not see the geese because of reflected city lights.

*

Andy was called Plato because he used to be a waiter. Everybody had a nickname; some were more obvious than others. Andy didn’t mind his name, others got very upset. To show you were upset was to guarantee the nickname stayed.

By and large, prisoners do not allow themselves to get upset. They walk away from trouble and argument, even the mildest political argument, because they do not want to get angry; if they become angry they get into trouble. It was common for someone to come into the greenhouse and stare out the window because the gymnasium was being used. They’d tell Andy, I’m on my own today. I've been on the phone to the wife. She's winding me up again.

There is no privacy. Everyone has to establish a way of dealing with being locked up. Simple physical constriction is worst. The small gymnasium is very well used; they sweat until pectorals, deltoids and trapezii bulge with mass and sharp definition. Aggression is rarely reported. Dungavel is a good guys' jail; break the rules and you finish your sentence in a place like Barlinnie, which is not so nice.

Some times are worse than others. Publicly, New Year is worst of all; small griefs and personal anniversaries are also bad publicly, though far worse privately.

Andy had been brought up celebrating New Year, rather than Christmas. School finished for two weeks on Christmas Eve and though there was a small exchange of gifts and cards, the real celebration was New Year.

Granny spent Hogmanay cleaning, polishing and scrubbing. The windows, floors and woodwork were washed, cupboards were cleaned, bedclothes and curtains were changed; the house was tidied, the doorstep scrubbed and the brasses polished. Orlando made punch, Granny made soup and the guests arrived with an assortment of drinks, food and a lump of coal. The wireless went on at half past eleven. Granny, Grandpa and Andy listened to Jimmy Shand until five to twelve, when Grandpa would get some black bun, seed or madeira cake, a bottle of whisky and a lump of coal, put on his tie and jacket and wait outside the door until the bells. There was never any difficulty knowing midnight: boats on the river sounded their horns, people cheered, the band on the wireless played a jig and Granny cried. Grandpa always knocked the door. 'I wonder who it is,' said Granny, wiping her eyes with the corner of her apron.

Orlando later opened the door and entered with great

ceremony. 'I am the spirit of the future,' he said. He kissed Granny's cheek and shook Andy's hand. They had a drink and waited for the guests to arrive.

The best New Year was when Maisie O'Brien, everyone said she looked like Rita Hayworth, and three other women from Grant Street who used to be Granny's neighbours, arrived with four German sailors, schnapps, vodka, brittle white cheese and black cigarettes everyone liked. Maisie wore red shoes, though they weren't the shoes she wanted to wear. She saw a nice pair in the Dolcis window. These ones were too red, too rory. Another woman told everybody's fortune. She told Andy he was going to get a nice surprise, and winked. He blushed and everyone laughed, including Granny. They rolled up the carpet and danced an Eightsome Reel, Strip the Willow, Dashing White Sergeant, Petronella and the Gay Gordons. Then they drank punch; Geordie began a song while the dancers were resting, his face black and shining:

I don't like the Germans.
The Germans started wars.

'Geordie.'

Mrs Esplin told her husband to stand up and sing like a man. He sang 'Granny's Hieland Hame' and sat down.

'Me next,' said Mrs Esplin.

The lily, O; The Lily O;
The pink, the white, the daffodilly, O;
Beneath the sky, no flower can vie
With the loyal, royal Orange lily, O.

'That's it,' said a woman called Wee Agnes. 'Any more party tunes and I'll clear the place. I've had to put up with that all my life and I'm not doing it now.'

'She got to sing her song, how can I no sing mine,' said Bernadette O'Hara.'

Wee Agnes stood up: 'Carry on,' she said.

Bernadette looked at her husband who was lighting a cigarette: 'I've told you before to stop smoking,' she said. 'It's bad for you.'

'I thought you were going to sing a song.'

'You sing it.'

'Indeed I will not.'

Bernadette closed her eyes and sang 'Forty Shades of Green'. Wee Agnes sat down.

The Germans sang a jolly song together and everyone applauded politely. A girl put a poker and a pair of tongs on the floor, lifted her skirt and danced. Mrs Esplin and Bernadette O'Hara took their husbands home and Baby William turned a somersault.

'These're nice fellas, they Germans,' Granny told Maisie at half past three. 'You'd better make sure they get back to their boat.'

'Their boat's at Greenock. They're staying with us. Think it's great. They save up for it. Come twice a year. That big yin there's supposed tae've said he was gonnae marry wee Agnes, but they keep their money in their shoes and haven't changed their socks for three days.'

Andy remembered that New Year because of the Germans and the girls. He got drunk for the first time and fell asleep with Agnes under the table while everyone sang. He wakened being put to bed, unable to do anything other than smile, as two Grant Street women took off his shoes, trousers and pullover. 'It's aaright, son. We've done this before,' one of them said as she kissed his forehead. He went to sleep thinking about the woman who winked and the dancer's legs.

He often slept thinking about the dancer's legs. Something cosy sent him sleeping, especially in jail; and the unspecific area of remembered lust was as cosy and comforting as being tucked in or sleeping with Lisa.

New Year was a time of strain. Unstated tensions hung around. One time, around his first New Year, Andy was in the dining room. A fight broke out at the table opposite. He was taken as a witness and asked what happened.

'Don't know.'

'You were there. You saw it. All we want to know is who was involved and how it started.'

When a grudge fight started other fights broke out simultaneously so the grudgers could have the maximum time together.

'I never saw nothing, sir.'

'You know what's going to happen, don't you?'

'I'd rather take it off you than take it off them.'

He was sent to Barlinnie where he spent ten days in The Digger, solitary confinement. Then he was sent back. The Worm was very active then.

It was the middle of January and snowing. He looked out the Maria window at the receding road; sheep and turnips and spidery black trees. The landscape was various shades of grey, like a pigeon's wing or a road stained with petrol. There were only certain things he could think about and one of the things he could not think about was why he was there.

*

The night of Malky's funeral, they left the park and went back to the casino. The tables were busy. They had a few bets and drank more whisky.

'Caliper's?'

'I'm no going in there to drink.'

'She'll give us a carry-out.'

Caliper Mary had a very nice shebeen not far from Charing Cross. On the pavement outside the casino, Joe counted his money: six fives, four tens and three twenties. He divided the money into two bundles and winked at Andy.

They waited for a taxi outside what used to be the Locarno. 'Did I ever tell you my parents met in there?'

'A few times,' said Joe. 'Here's one.' The taxi stopped, asked where they were going then said he had to go to the garage in the opposite direction.

'Not far enough, ya bastard,' shouted Joe.

'I don't think we're right wing enough for him,' said Andy.

Jake was in the army, a national serviceman, home on leave. He met Rose in the Locarno.

Four months later, in a hotel bedroom at Portobello, she told him, 'I don't want to marry a soldier.'

'I'm getting out,' he said.

'How?'

'I'll tell you when I've done it. I promise, it'll work.'

'It'd better. I could face my Mammy and Daddy better if I told them we were getting married.'

'I know. Don't worry, I'll be out in time to wet the wean's heid.'

Jake got out the army by being a good soldier. Not for him the mild insanity, the sexual perversion or the sudden physical ailments brought on by smoking 100 cigarettes in a single night, eating glass or drinking bleach.

Jake told everyone he loved the army and wanted to become a regular soldier when national service was over. On the parade ground, instead of marching as the others marched, left arm forward with the right foot, right arm with the left and so on, Jake swung both arms forward at the same time, back at the same time, forward, back and so it goes. The sergeant shouted.

'I know,' said Jake. 'I've never been able to do it, but I'll practise.'

He spent hours marching up and down, swinging his arms from front to back. When others were in the pub or cinema, were reading, playing cards or chatting, had gone to night classes or were asleep, for hours every evening, Jake marched across the parade ground or along the roads and lanes around the barracks, arms forward, arms back.

He spoke to officers, doctors and even asked to see the psychiatrist. 'Does this mean I can't be a soldier?' he wanted to know. 'More than anything, I want to be a soldier.'

Everyone, including the commanding officer, was sorry. 'You would have made a fine soldier,' he said, shaking Jake's hand as he left.

Back home his da, Winston Churchill, was reading the paper in his chair by the fire when Jake walked in. Granny was shopping.

'It's you.'

'It worked.'

'Of course it fucken worked. I learned it during the war and if it worked then it'd work for you. They tell me you're getting married.'

'Who told you?'

'That lassie was up here with her Ma and Da, a right couple o warmers, nothing tae drink and plenty tae say for themselves. She's either about tae drop a wean or she's hiding a big drum under her coat. Is it yours?'

'I think so.'

'What do you mean, you think so.'

'Aye. Aye, it's mine, if that's what you mean.'

'What I mean has nothing to do with it. If it's your wean you'd better marry her. If it's somebody else's wean, tell her tae fuck off.'

Jake signed his marriage certificate four weeks after his demob papers. His first child, called after the patron saint of Scotland, was born ten days later.

*

Sometimes he couldn't sleep.

For the first few weeks he slept twelve hours a night, sometimes dovering for twenty minutes or half an hour in the early evening, wakening in time for the evening concert.

Then for no reason the pattern changed. He slept for four hours or five, wakened for a few hours and slept again, relaying throughout the day and night. This was broken by fighting sleep, by sitting up till eleven o'clock, going to bed with a book and chocolate or camomile tea and rising with his alarm at eight. He could understand the temptation of staying awake at night and sleeping through the day, of finding no good reason for rising.

He was called to the dole office at eleven o'clock. The lad with the shell suit and trainers in the next seat kept yawning. 'I was supposed to've been here at ten,' he said. 'Slept in.' Claimants were called in the morning for that very reason.

'Are you still looking for work?' the girl asked. She had lipstick on her teeth and a ribbon in her hair. 'And are you prepared to travel to find work?'

It was best to provide the answers they needed; otherwise benefit was automatically stopped. Then a reclaim procedure would have to be instigated; the claimant would need to appeal and appeals could take four or five weeks.

'Are you prepared to take whatever work is offered?'

'Yes.'

'Thank you, Mr Paterson.'

The lad in the shell suit was smoking a roll-up. 'I'm waiting for wee Mickey,' he said. 'Fancy a score?'

'No, thanks.'

'Nae bother, big man. Thought you'd fancy it, know what I mean.'

'Another time. What happened up there?'

'Benefit stopped. Another fucken hassle. That's how I've got to sell the stuff, know what I mean. Win some, lose some.'

At first he thought it was the room temperature; if he was disturbed in the first few minutes of sleep he was awake for at least a couple of hours. He used to read till he ran out of books; he listened to the World Service till neighbours complained.

So he started walking, rising rather than staring at the ceiling with the bed too warm, remembering snatches of conversation, missed opportunities, the dancer's legs and a past that always ended in jail. At first he imagined he was crazy. The illusory disapproval made him do it. He walked round the block, got back to bed and slept. The third time a policeman stopped him.

'Where are you off to?'

'Nowhere.'

'What do you mean nowhere?'

'I'm out for a walk.'

'At this time in the morning; around here?'

'I live here.'

'Where?'

So it went on, ending when the policeman said, 'Right, then.

On your way, but watch it. Okay. Just watch it.' His breath smelled of whisky and peppermint.

Andy loved the night and was slightly scared. He was like his Granny, loved what could never happen in daylight, loved the possibilities, which also scared him. Night was frantic and a little nervous, night was alone. The city changed. There was an easier, carefree attitude, another play in the same setting, different lights and shadows, different players. What was easily ignored by day was obvious at night, easily seen and hard to avoid.

He was walking by the river, once a source of commerce, manufacture and storage, now a relic, a river like any river, passing through any city, a place of no significance. The docks were ruined or turned to sites for brick-built tenements, three storeys high, a joint venture. The district council sold the land, a developer built the houses.

Sometimes, to wonder what went on, to visualise lives behind the curtains, because he tried to imagine what sleepers would think if they knew he was passing, he wandered through a residential area, usually in the west end. He did not expect houses by the river and wandered around the small estate.

An environmental health van was parked at the end of a small street. A man in overalls and a donkey jacket watched him walk down the road.

'Help you?'

'Just passing. Out for a walk.'

'You live here?'

'No.'

'Fucken lucky. See they hooses, riddled wi rats. This was the docks, right? And what've docks got plenty of? Rats. Big as dugs, so they are, fucken rats yon size.'

He had been rolling a cigarette. He lit it and shook his head. 'See if they folk sleeping nice and cosy knew what was going on, they'd shite themselves. They took away the docks and the sheds, so the rats had nae place tae stay. But rats don't go away and the company that bought this place, the fucken developers spent a fortune on a private firm that was supposed tae get rid of them. But the rats is still here. You'll never shift them. Rats'll survive a holocaust. Look at it. The rats think their coupon's up. They build centrally heated houses with a chute for flinging your rubbish down into a big midgie. Perfect conditions for breeding rats, food, warmth and shelter all in the one place. So what do the rats do; they're sitting down there with wee napkins roon their necks at the bottom of the chute, waiting for the mugs to send the grub down. They're the best-fed rats in the world. They don't need to go looking for grub. The punters send it doon to them, doon the chute. The rats are the only thing on the increase here, rats and beggars, there's fucken thousands of them. And guess what: we're here because a woman saw a rat in broad daylight. Jesus Johnny, it must've been one of their relations coming doon tae Glesca for a feed, or else it was a rat that was lost, cause I can assure you any rats around here know they're on a good thing. There's two main packs to every building. Unless the yuppies never sent the vol-au-vents doon the chute in time and this was a wee warning party coming out to check them.'

He laughed: 'Fancy a hoose here? Seventy-five thow for a three apartment facing the river and aa the rats you can catch.'

Was it then or later, around that time or nearly, he read about the new city, the emerging place. Consumerism's victory over manufacture promoted a tourism and conference centre, with no extra facilities to support the influx. Millions were coming to the city, using the same sewers, the same water, gas and electricity as served the population prior to the goldrush.

A couple of weeks later and further upstream, a man was

trembling by Glasgow Green, a blanket and a carrier bag beside him. 'Polis've flung us aff the Green,' he said. 'Nae place tae sleep.'

In the jail they'd talked of a good skipper on the Paisley Road West or maybe out Duke Street. 'Come on. I'll get you a cup of tea, auld yin,' Andy said. They walked up the Saltmarket towards Glasgow Cross.

The man was talking. Andy could not make out what was being said. The man kept talking. His wife was dead. He was glad she didn't have to see him like this, with the family scattered.

'There's a bit to go for the tea, auld yin.'

The man said something Andy didn't understand. He went to move off and the man grabbed his arm. Andy almost vomited as he caught the smell, bending his ear towards the voice. 'I'm not an old man,' he said. 'I'm fifty-three.'

They were on Argyle Street. A young man, maybe in his twenties, with spiky hair, three earrings on the lobe of his left ear, a raincoat tied to his neck and a dog on a bit of string, was standing in a doorway. 'Where yous off to?' he asked.

His hands and fingers were covered with the do-it-yourself tattoos Andy recognised from jail, boredom or both, like schoolbag graffiti. 'There's a skipper doon here,' he said.

His name was Davie. He had a sign: HOMELESS. NO DOLE. HUNGRY. PLEASE GIVE SPARE CHANGE PLEASE. THANKYOU. Four hours a night at the Central Station and he splits the take with the lookout. Begging's illegal on railway property, though it's worth the risk; the station's a good pitch, especially if you have a dog. People feel sorry for the dog, he said. He gets about twelve quid and finishes by nine. No point after that.

'The businessmen and yuppies give you fuck all,' he said, going down Stockwell Street towards the river. 'And the casuals give you a kicking. I got a doing off them last week. The trouble's getting worse, on both sides. Sometimes when somebody stops you in the street to tap you, they're sizing you up for a mugging.'

They work the grid, Central Station, Argyle Street, Clyde Walkway, St Enoch Square. 'I'm fed up eating they Dunkin Donuts and McDonalds shite. Carry-oot food's all you can take. By the way, have you any grub on you, auld yin?'

The other man shook his head.

'Fine. Just checking. There's rats where we're going. They'll no touch you as long as you've nae grub on you. You get bitten bringing grub in. They run over your body looking for it. There's aye too many for the dug to get.'

The skipper was a hut beneath the bridge. 'Better than the Queens Park, though that wee lane up there's no bad. This hut's moving soon. Every night I expect it'll be gone. The corporation workmen left it.'

'See you,' said Andy.

Davie said, 'Please yourself.' The older man went into the hut without speaking.

Next time he couldn't sleep, Andy went to Charing Cross and stood opposite the casino. He didn't see anyone he knew.

He had finished his tea and was reading a book about hillwalking. The man in the next-door room who worked funny shifts and sometimes sang to himself while shaving, little songs in Gaelic, knocked on the door and looked at the wall.

'There's a woman to see you,' he said.

Myra smiled self-consciously. She wanted him to think she'd come straight from work, or maybe she was passing, but he knew she had taken some trouble with her appearance. 'Can I come in?' she asked.

Ten minutes later she sipped a mug of tea. 'Hasn't changed much,' she said. 'You've still got the birds.'

'It's nice to see you.'

'Are you still listening to that music on the wireless?'

Nerves made her talk. She used her left hand as a saucer for the mug and looked at the tea every once in a while, thinking of something to say. She obviously wanted to appear as natural as possible, as though they had seen each other recently or were renewing a casual acquaintance.

She sat on the chair with her knees together and filled the room with her scent. Andy knew the chatter was preamble; he was content to wait, happy she was talking because he did not know what to say. Her fingernails were filed to an oval shape and painted with an opalescent varnish which caught the light like a piece of jewellery. She finished the tea and put the mug on the carpet beside the chair.

'So, what's been happening?'

'Nothing much.'

'Still not found a job?'

'Not yet.'

Maybe she wouldn't tell him. Maybe she would go away feeling foolish and never come back. He would have to say something. He would have to tell her.

'You never come into the café.'

'I didn't think you'd want to see me.'

'I thought you'd've come in.'

'I will then. I'll come in tomorrow.'

'Have you put your name down on the housing list?'

'I didn't think it was worth it. I don't know what to do. One minute I think I'll go, then I don't know where I'll go to or what I'll do when I get there.'

'You must have a lot to straighten out. I was thinking, it must be hard trying to get your life together after all that time.'

He looked away and hoped she didn't notice. He felt angry: there was a sudden flash, a tightening like fear in his stomach and a numbness around the mouth when he narrowed his lips. Later, he would not know why he had felt angry, nor why it had happened so suddenly.

'What's the matter?'

'Nothing.'

'You looked angry. Did I say something?'

'No. I'm okay.'

'Listen, I'd better go. Maybe, if you like, I could come with you when you're putting your name down, if you want to that is?'

'No, of course, that's great. And thanks for coming round. I'm really glad to see you.'

'Good. I'm glad I came now. So, you'll come into the café?'

He nodded.

She stood up and gentle as a pickpocket kissed him goodbye.

Possil had hardly changed. One or two shops had different owners, but it was still the same straight semi-treeless street. The Lido Café was there with the same sign, black lettering on a green background; Andy wondered if they made their own ice-cream, but was too cold to try.

The Blind Asylum had been demolished; it always looked a rickety structure, twentieth-century and temporary, unlike the red sandstone Rockvilla Church and the wee hall on the other side of the street. Sometimes, just before sleep, he would remember the frozen sermons, the wooden pews with long, padded crimson cushions and the other boys restless in their heavy uniforms.

After a while he never went back, long after Watson left. This was an unpredictable cause of misfortune, easily explained in the hours before sleep when it returned like a debt collector. He always excused himself, said he was adolescent, had lost his father, mother and sister, in the emotional confusion he clutched at comfort, warmth or maybe someone showing an interest. It was all over quickly. Billy Watson was in a hurry, the toilet was small and the caretaker might find them. He wondered how he got there, why he went; was he asked or did he go into the toilet and find Billy Watson waiting? There was the pain, the impossibility of it all, even while it was happening, there was fear. It was the terror he remembered most, the anxiety of his cheek rubbing against plaster, the smell of dampness and the sound of the cistern. Watson never spoke. He wiped himself and closed the door; Andy heard the snap of the lock and let out a yell. 'You've hurt your face,' the caretaker said when he found him. 'What happened? Did you fall?' Andy nodded.

Next week Watson was back for more. He walked Andy along to Saracen Cross and took him into a close, the close beside the Balmore Bar; again Andy's face was to the wall, again the pain and the stickiness, again the useless feeling. He never went back.

'Is that you done wi the Scouts?' said Granny.

Now there was a new church, a new hall and a new name, built of brick like most new buildings. The lime leaks after a rain and it does not catch the light. There are no shadows on brick buildings.

Orlando warmed his hands on the fire. Geordie Anderson was living in Andy's room and writing poetry. This was the first time Andy had seen him without make-up.

'You'll need to let me hear some of your poetry,' said Andy.

'There's some good stuff,' said Orlando. 'He took to verse when the parties stopped. Somebody wrote them down for him and now he goes to a wee writing group. He's written poems in praise of the Mosshouse and Keppochhill Road, one about Saracen Street and one about Life. There doesn't seem to be a shortage of subject matter. He wrote one I liked called Grace: *Thank you God and make us good / As we sit down to eat our food*, something like that at the beginning. Food is still an important subject for Geordie.'

Geordie carried in the tray with three mugs of tea. Andy had brought a wee Dundee Cake and a packet of digestive biscuits which Orlando liked to dip in his tea. They were bought in Saracen Street.

Two girls were standing near a bus-stop beside the shop, giggling and pushing each other. They were pale girls, maybe fourteen, no more than fifteen, in their panstick make-up and high-heeled shoes. Andy was looking down the road towards the Mosshouse, watching the light as it crossed the street and lit the lamp posts, flattered the tenements and sparked in the hair the girls had backcombed together, laughing at each other's reflection in the mirror. He realised he was staring. One of the girls was nodding towards him, a single downward jerk of her head, mouthing a word whose meaning he could not understand.

'Business.'

They looked at him. The girl on the left put a hand on her hip and opened her legs. The other's smile changed to a slightly menacing stare, brimming with confident bravado; she had obviously mistaken his confusion for innocence or fear. From a close, a young man, whose hair was matted and whose back was stooped, moved between them, his back to Andy, who went into the shop. When he came out with the cake and biscuits all three were gone.

He told Orlando. 'Ten pounds each,' he said, 'or the two for fifteen. Am I alone in thinking there was a time when drugs were not an issue, when whatever threat or problem they represented was easily containable because we live on an island. Look at it now, our only growth industry. How did this happen? How did they cease to become containable? What was the springboard to their undoubted success, apart from cutting the customs staff, and where does all the money go if it doesn't go into the economy?'

The house was the same, smelling of cats. Granny's wedding photograph was on the mantelpiece in its leather frame, Granny and Grandpa, stern-faced and shy. Andy expected her to come in with the shopping. He expected to hear her complain.

'The changes are all very well,' Orlando said. Geordie poured more tea. 'They are the same as any other of this city's so-called changes. Did you hear about the woman who gave birth to a heid? No arms, legs or body, just a heid. She visited the heid in hospital every week and on its twenty-first birthday said "I've brought a nice surprise for your birthday. Will I open it?" The heid said "Yes please" and watched the parcel being unravelled, first the ribbon, then the tape and finally the wrapping. "Oh, Mammy," it said, when the parcel was opened, "Oh Mammy. No another bunnet." '

Orlando went into the lavatory. He was older, stooped and walked with an old man's limp. Geordie handed him another piece of cake and a sheet of paper:

In the field near St Theresa's chapel
There's a balloon as big as a corporation building,
A balloon with stars.

I get in the balloon and float
Above the city,
Rising into the warm darkness
With stars all around me.
I could be anywhere,
America, Perth or Russia,
On the other side of the world.
When I come back to reality
I do not know if I've seen it
Or dreamed it.
You would need to be there,
You'd need to see it for yourself
To know.

He waited three hours. By the time his number was called he had finished the novel he brought and exhausted conversational possibilities with the people on either side, he had become accustomed to the tension, noise and smells. The noise was the perpetual grind of voices, crying children and complaint.

'Paterson?'

'That's right. Andrew Paterson.'

'What is it?'

'I live in a bedsit with shared facilities and get housing benefit. I am thinking of changing my house, or rather, of applying for a house and – '

She leaned her left forearm on the counter and raised herself up by pushing her right hand down on the chair. She said nothing, opened the door and walked away. Five minutes later, she was back.

'Here.' She handed him three forms printed in different colours; plum, orange, puce. 'Fill these in and send them back in this envelope.'

*

A vertical stripe of light arrives in blocks, angled between the buildings. Density changes with the seasons. It glimmers on the rooftops, turns slates to amber or radiates in the opalescent mist. It reflects on the buildings and makes the buildings reflect upon themselves.

The night architecture of streets, motorways, theatres, cinemas, advertising, the floodlit buildings in the centre of the city, even the car headlights, create the illusion which hides the light, can even hide the green diamond of Venus and the eternal snows. West of Scotland light glows in the embers of day, turns rain to sparks of silver, spins around the telephone wires and moves amongst the leaves of the trees like a birdwing through air or small shards of electric glass.

The morning light is mysterious, new and solitary. On a dry day the city is pastel, on a wet day oil. When you breath in the morning light you inhale the walls and the pavements, the junk on the pavements and the writing on the walls. When you exhale, you exhale gold and rouge tinted gauze to wrap the city round your little finger, to bandage your cuts and bruises, heal your wounds.

The river runs black and stony, hard as fuck; mist rises from this river and clouds the city like a memory. It blends all the greens to one green, all the blues to grey. In the half light the brightly coloured children's clothes can make you believe anything is possible. The air can make you drunk and fankle the cherry trees. Memories pass downriver like barges.

In this light the orange, red, fawn and grey buildings are churches and churches cathedrals. The carvings, adornments, protrusions, wood and glass reflect the early sun and shadow.

Birdsong in the traffic; flowers beneath stone.

*

The wedding was at three o'clock on a sunny afternoon. It was the minister's second wedding that day; he was due a third at half past four and the brown envelope went into his hip pocket.

Andy wore a grey suit; Margaret's suit was ivory. She wanted a quiet wedding; most of the guests were Andy's friends and family. There was no reception. Granny, Orlando, Margaret, Andy and Margaret's parents went for a meal after the service. The couple went to Dublin for a three-day honeymoon.

'We cannae ask Geordie Anderson and Baby William; nor Bernadette O'Hara and Mrs Esplin.' Granny was going over the guest list.

'They gave presents.'

'We could have a wee party for them here. Her people are very stuck up. They're not asking many.'

'The reason their guest list is tiny is obviously because they do not know many people,' said Orlando. 'Not that it has anything to do with me, but why not ask as many as possible to the wedding, have a small reception in a hotel or restaurant for the family, the happy couple can go off on honeymoon while we come back here and mingle.'

Andy's mother and sister did not come, though they had been invited. Geordie Anderson and Baby William played Chinese chequers during the ceremony. Bernadette O'Hara, her husband and their three children blessed themselves continually. 'Don't you give me a showing up in front of they black Protestants,' she told her eldest daughter, who was sniffling with the cold. Mrs Esplin wore a powder-blue suit and hat. Her husband and son wore black.

Andy thought he had met most of Margaret's relations before the wedding. Small men in checked suits pressed envelopes into his hand and wished him well. They nodded, as though he was now an initiate.

The two parties grouped in opposite sides of the driveway outside the church. The photographer stood on a chair he had brought with him; because there was no reception, the wedding guests watched as he plowtered around with his equipment, asking Andy and Margaret to stare at each other with her bouquet between them or hold hands and look over their shoulders. One girl complained because he had not asked Margaret to kneel on the grass with an assortment of bouquets in a circle around her. 'Oor Ellen's got that picture,' she said. 'Beautiful, so it is.'

Andy had cut himself shaving. There were spreckles of blood on his collar and he had grazed the end of his stubble with a new blade. When his grandfather shaved, Andy was cleared out of the room. When he asked what to do, his grandfather had told him he did not need to shave. He asked a barber who suggested an electric razor.

'They're too dear,' said Granny.

'You don't get a decent shave with them,' said Grandpa. 'Soap and watter, that's what you use. Soap and watter and a new blade.'

Grandpa wrapped his razor in a white canvas case which rolled into itself. There was a metal tube for soap, a slot for the brush and a container for the blades. He untied the tapes, unrolled the canvas, placed the implements along the draining board with a cracked and handleless cup, then he cleared the room.

One afternoon Andy asked Granny if he could see the equipment, so that he would know what to get. 'He's awfy particular about these things,' she said. 'I've never touched them before.'

The outline of the implements showed through the canvas. Andy untied the linen strands and opened the case. There was a small metal mirror his grandfather never used; the metal razor had a short wooden handle and no maker's trademark. 'That's the one he made himself,' said Granny. The shaving soap was a stubbly cone and the brush bristles bent to one side. The bone handle base was patterned with hairline fractures, like enamel. Andy folded the canvas sides across the implements, rolled the case and gave it to Granny. 'We'll get one tomorrow,' she said.

They went to the co-operative in Springburn Road. The Cowlairs Co-operative Society Men's Department was through the back. Granny went down the steps and looked around. 'I want a razor for this boy,' she asked a man in a suit.

'Is it just the razor you require?'

'No. He needs to know how to use it.'

'Wait here,' he said.

'Honest to God,' said Granny. 'What kind of man takes a job like that.'

She bought a metal three-part razor, a packet of Blue Gillette blades, an Imperial Leather shaving stick wrapped in silver foil and a brush whose bristles came out every time it was used.

'What's the cup for?' asked Andy.

'Hot water. Boiling really.' He was shown how to fit the blade to the razor, how to soak his skin, lather the brush then apply it to his face. He was told he must always shave with a clear head, to remember bristles grew in patches and in different directions; ignorance of this fact was the usual cause of cuts. 'If you should cut yourself, you must patch it immediately with a corner of newspaper, which you wet with your tongue. Place the newspaper over the wound. The blood will ensure it will stick to your face. There is also a caustic stick, which you apply directly to the wound. It will staunch the flow of blood.' He left with the caustic stick in his pocket.

The stag night was organised for his evening off. Hotel staff were invited to the wedding since it was after lunch. He had taken a week's holiday, which meant he had to work the night before he was married. He had intended going back to Granny's, but the staff arranged another party.

Two prostitutes were employed for the second evening. They entertained Andy for an hour and a half, joined the party and told the men to fuck off. The duty manager dispersed the revellers at 4 a.m.

Next morning Andy had a hangover. 'Hell mend you,' said Granny, presenting a greasy plate of sausage, bacon, egg and fried bread. 'It's not too late to change your mind,' she said.

When Granny died he remembered the razor and the wedding-day breakfast. He remembered Orlando made a pot of coffee, which Andy drank with two aspirins a cup. He remembered he cut himself shaving: 'It's your throat that should be cut,' said Granny. He remembered the way she posed for the wedding picture in her fur coat and felt hat, how she went round the hotel folk to invite them up for the party and sent Orlando to the reception.

When Granny died she could not stop dying. Andy did not know what to do; he closed his eyes and Granny was dead, sat down to eat and his Granny was dead; around the grounds, in the greenhouse and garden, all day and every day especially at night in Dungavel jail, Granny died and kept on dying.

He remembered things he did not know he had noticed. The nail on her right forefinger was bent. It happened when she was wee; watching a door open and shut, she wondered what would happen if she stuck her finger in the jamb. Her hair was downy, fine and soft as a child's hair, baby hair she called it. Granny often laughed for no apparent reason. When asked why, she repeated the tag line of her favourite joke: 'Is that wee sailor away?'

The governor told him. He expected confirmation in the form of a letter and a copy of the death certificate to appear. 'There should be no problem about you going to the funeral,' the governor said.

'I don't want to go. I couldn't face it. I'd rather remember the way she was.'

The day before the funeral he was sent to the psychiatrist, who had a red, largely expressionless face and stared continually, except when he wrote on a single sheet of paper, folded twice, with termite writing. When Andy looked up, the psychiatrist looked away.

'Don't you think it's natural to grieve?'

'I don't think I need to go to a funeral to grieve.'

He was prescribed a course of anti-depressants.

Granny was buried on a Thursday. The following Saturday Orlando arrived, angular and blousy. He had a Safeway carrier bag with three apples, three bananas and a couple of oranges. From his raincoat pocket he gave Andy a bar of Cadbury's Dairy Milk chocolate. 'That's for yourself,' he said.

It was the way Orlando pushed the small bar of chocolate across the table while looking the other way: Andy knew Orlando considered sweets, especially chocolate, a useless frivolity and therefore the ultimate treat. It was like a hug which is meant as a comfort but reminds you of the loss.

'She'd never have come here,' he said. 'Though it's a nice enough place.'

Andy stared at the marbled Formica pattern, like the base of his grandfather's shaving brush. He could not look at Orlando. If he wept they would discontinue the visit. He knew he was being watched.

'I've never had to see any of my family in the jail, she said, and I'm not starting now. I've seen my son lying cold and stiff in the mortuary. I've been forced to hear details of his life and marriage scattered to the public as if he was a stranger, as if he never had a childhood, that what he did when he left my house was none of my business; because of that I've lost a granddaughter, the thing every woman wants, a granddaughter to talk to, to tell things to, I've lost all that, though I had my boy, but I'm not going to see him in jail, even though he is my grandson, my boy, God love him. That's what she said.'

'I know.'

'And that's why she never came to see you.'

Andy nodded.

'She talked about you all the time. Sometimes it was as though you were there. I suppose it was when she stopped going out, she had no interest other than her own history, the history of her past. Are you all right?'

'I'm fine. Just keep talking. I'll be okay. When did she stop going out?'

'Hard to say, maybe a month or two back; no, more than that. I don't know when it was; a while. When we did go out together, she got to know everybody, got to know the dossers and why they were there. She knew the alcoholics from the schizophrenics and the temporary homeless from the permanent or even semi-permanent strays. She knew their names and their stories. If she saw a shirt or a jumper, some wee item of clothing, it wasn't enough to say it would do somebody, she knew who it was for and if she didn't know someone it would fit, she didn't take it. All in the dark too; that's what amazed me. She never saw them in daylight. This was all done in the dark.'

'She used to take my shirts and pullovers, once or twice a pair of trousers went for a guy named Dougie.'

'She liked Dougie; he slept in the Botanic Gardens. Worked at the BBC one time. God knows what as. She was always doing that, picking up things, nothing much, bits and pieces for this one or that one, a hat or a coat, scarves and gloves, useful things. It's a nice enough place here.'

They stared past each other, over the other's shoulder. Orlando looked greyish; he sighed.

'She hadn't been going out for a year or more. She was confined to bed for the last six months, after she caught a chill. The trouble is there are too many of them now; she thought she had to see them all, had to deal with every one, see every dosser in the city of Glasgow, give them soup and a box to sleep in. She stopped selling, or rather, she sold to some and gave to others. I don't know how she did it, but she knew if they had money. Must have been a kind of gift, maybe a kind of second sight.'

'Was she in bed for six months?'

'More or less. It all began when she said she hadn't thought of Annie for a while and supposed she must be dead.'

'Who's Annie?'

'Her sister; the one she never knew. She lost the will, that's what it was, she lost the will to live. Her last conversation was about her family. It lasted for a while. On and off it lasted weeks. I had a good wee family, she said. The feeling I got was that she could accept the death of her son because death is final, but she could not accept you going. That was as if you were dead but still alive; missing in action, drowned at sea, a death without a funeral, a running sore. When her son died she took on the lost, the helpless, the folk who needed looking after became her children. There were too many of them; thousands, with more arriving every night, young people too, that was what upset her, the age of them, kids really, children, fifteen and sixteen years old, young adult bodies, children's emotions. They needed a cuddle. They were too near the truth, too near you and your age. They could have been you.'

'I'm older than that.'

'Not to her. You were her boy. You don't want to know any more, do you?'

'Was it a big funeral?'

'Hundreds. God help the folk going in after us. The place smelled like an old pair of socks. The team were lovely. They asked if they could carry her coffin. The flowers were great. I don't believe there's a flower left in a Glasgow park. And you wanted to have heard them singing the hymns: "Guide Me Oh Thou Great Jehovah" was very fervent. The minister said a nice thing: her work is here, her work is around us, he said. Nice that. How did you adjust to being here?' Orlando asked. He shrugged and wiped his eyes. 'Especially if you didn't do it, I mean. Sorry. Don't answer. Best if I go. I know how you adjusted. Hellish, isn't it. Waiting for the day, waiting to get at it, waiting to get out and find the bastards and pay them back. Keeping it down all the time, keeping everything down. And now there's this. We'll talk again, when you're out. Come and see me. I'll be there. Promise me you'll come.'

Andy nodded. 'Thanks, Orlando.' He closed his eyes. He screwed them shut and opened in time to see Orlando's back as he left the room, maybe after turning with a cheery wave.

That night Andy went to the dormitory. Since word got out that Granny had died, the prisoners had not left him alone. He did not know it had started. He thought he could hold it in, thought it would be okay, thought he knew the limit he had not yet reached, thought he would get to cry in the night.

Orlando's back, the raincoat and the carrier bag, the bunnet: something fell, dropped inside him. He knew because of the bruises, but could not remember getting them. This was necessary. He could not stop himself. There were no flashing lights, the sky did not crack wide with fire, animals did not leave their lairs, beasts did not stalk the forests, there was neither water, flood, nor tide. The sea had nothing to do with it. No dam burst anywhere.

He howled and was immediately aware of other wailing. Furniture was smashed and beds were thrown across the room. It did not last long. He did not know the damage. Other prisoners cleared them out. No one was discovered though the room was wrecked. Andy was bundled into the lavatory, where he cried alone for an hour while the riot went on.

After the honeymoon, when he was living with Margaret's parents in their four-in-a-block Carntyne two-bedroomed house, Andy wondered why he was married.

He would later tell the prison psychiatrist: 'I don't know how it happened. She wanted it more than me, at least I think that's how it was. She kept on about it, saying how nice it would be if we were married. I went along with it because I couldn't really think of anything else. I could have said no, but I didn't have a reason for saying no any more than I had a reason for saying yes. I agreed because my life was pretty lousy. Looking back it seems unbearable, but that's not to be trusted either. I was on the rebound. So was she. But she'd been on her own long before me.'

He was working at the Mal, serving lunch and dinner six days a week, with two or three hours off in the afternoon, like a barman. He spent his afternoons in town, went to the pictures or to the bookies, walked around and looked at the shops. He stayed in the hotel when it was raining, playing cards and talking with the staff, cellarmen and porters.

Margaret typed receipts and invoices, share certificates, deeds of sale and the occasional letter for a firm of stockbrokers in West George Street. She started work at nine and finished at five-thirty, five days a week. They sometimes met for ten minutes or a quarter of an hour when she finished work. He would wait outside her office and together they walked to the restaurant. This was their only time alone. Often she would find him waiting. She always smiled. They walked in silence, without touching, back to the hotel, where their first words would be something like, 'See you later.'

They had a whole day together every Sunday, usually with Margaret's parents, though they occasionally visited Granny. Andy looked forward to Possil, going every three or four weeks. Orlando made a steak pie.

'Your house is lovely,' Margaret told Granny. 'Did you get it done up or did you do it yourself?'

'I'd like a terrazzo doorstep,' said Granny.

Margaret spoke when spoken to; she smiled in the right places and stared at the television or into her lap during a lull in the conversation.

'Have your parents always lived in Carntyne?'

'I think so.'

'And there's only you?'

'Just me.'

'You said your father works on the railway, is that right?'

'He used to.'

'What did he do?'

'I think he was a signalman.'

'And your mother?'

'She worked on the railways too. She was a tracer in the Hyde Park Loco drawing office.'

'They built the engines, didn't they?'

'I don't know.'

'They were a private company, not part of the British Rail conglomerate, though they suffered as much as anyone did with the Beeching closures and the great move south.'

They played cards. Granny switched the television off, whispering the word 'Rubbish' to herself. Orlando covered the table with a heavily embroidered dark green cotton cloth and turned on the radio. They played Newmarket until three or four money cards were turned, a few games of Sevens, perhaps some Blackjack or Rummy and always finished with a hand of Solo.

Andy and Margaret had a cup of tea, a slice of cake, chocolate biscuits and left before ten o'clock, walking down Saracen Street, along Craighall Road, across the canal at Port Dundas and down towards Cathedral Street where they caught a late bus to Carntyne.

After a week or two, Joe asked: 'What the hell are you doing going out with her?'

'Don't know. I suppose it has something to do with getting back seeing women.'

There were women at the hotel, but that confused him. He had gone to a couple of parties after finishing with Cathie, but found the atmosphere was either strained or melancholic. He had slept with an Irish girl called Patsy. 'What's your name again?' she asked in the morning.

He had heard of animals who return to the corpse of their partners, or to places where their partners died, to sniff the air. He wandered around the public places they'd been, cafés, bars, cinemas and so on; the restaurant did not matter, lots of people came in there. He did not know why he did it, could not understand the need which forced him past her house in a hired car. Geoff's car was in the driveway, a red Sierra with a Count Me In Edinburgh sticker on the rear window.

He took Margaret to the cinema. This was their first date. They saw the film of Horace McCoy's novel *They Shoot Horses Don't They?* Margaret found it very depressing. They walked to the bus station, waiting with the other couples for the last bus to Carntyne, which went out the Edinburgh Road.

'Do you fancy going out again next week sometime?'

'If you like,' she said. He asked because she was upset. Had they seen a happy film, they might have parted.

They saw each other five times in four weeks, going out on Andy's night off, usually a Sunday, which meant they walked round the art galleries, saw an old film, had an early night home.

The breakthrough came when Margaret's father went into hospital for a gallstones operation. 'Ever had gallstones?' he asked Andy. 'No, I don't suppose you will have had them; you're too young. It affects your water. They give you stuff to melt them, except mine never melted and now they have to operate. I've never had the knife and don't fancy it much. I mean, these guys are only human. It's no like a butcher cutting up a slice of steak, is it.'

They were in the Horse Shoe Bar in Drury Street, a Victorian gin palace designed to make drinking respectable and attractive.

'I am what you might call a family man and I'd like you to go up and see that things are all right while I'm away.'

'You're only going in for three days.'

'Maybe four, they're no too sure. Still that's a long time when you're used to having someone around the place. Just go up and see that everything's all right with Margaret and her Mum. If you'd do that for me, I'd be much obliged.'

'They're not going to want me running around the place. They've got visiting hours to run their life now.'

'That's a wee part of the day. We've worked it out, to be at the Royal for two you have to leave our place at the back of one, that's to ensure the buses are okay.'

'An hour to get down Alexandra Parade?'

'We're punctual people. We like to be on time. It's bad manners to keep folk waiting. God; would you look at the state of him. Don't speak to him.'

'How's it going, Squeezy?'

'Desperate.'

'I've no money.'

'I never asked you for fuck all. Who's this cunt here?'

'Peter Mulholland. Lives in Carntyne.'

'And what's he doing drinking with you? Is he a poof?'

'I know his daughter.'

'Jesus Christ, say no more, know what I mean. Must be serious if you're drinking with the old man. Did you stick her in the club?'

'Fuck off, Squeezy.'

'I was a deprived child. That's no way to talk to someone who's never known a mother's love. I might turn violent and use an inarticulate rage to express my emotions.'

Two men and a woman were at a table behind him. The woman had a high, irritating laugh. Squeezy moved towards them. Margaret's father touched his tie and looked across the bar.

'Squeezy comes round the hotel from time to time, like every night. He cleans the bar and does some work for the night porters. They let him sleep on a sofa and throw him out at six in the morning. I know him because he sometimes sits in watching the cards and, needless to say, he's always around if a drink's going.'

Margaret's father was buttoning his coat. 'I'd best be getting back to work,' said Andy.

Squeezy moved between them. 'Daft cunt's trying to impress her. Told me to get what I wanted cause she felt sorry for me. The other one's a panhandler, except he's no fucken use at it. See you later, Andy son. Is Daddy taking you up the road for a wee family conference?'

Mr Mulholland moved towards the door and Andy followed. In the lane, a man was leaning across the bonnet of a car, trying to be sick. Mr Mulholland moved around him: 'I'm going this way,' he said, walking towards West Nile Street, leaving Andy by the door.

This was an odd feeling, like the start of something; a beginning rather than an end. He did not contact Margaret, but phoned the hospital. 'Mr Mulholland was admitted this morning. Quite comfortable,' the nurse said.

Andy phoned Margaret during his break. 'Mum saw him tonight,' she said. 'He's settling in.'

'Do you need anything?'

'I don't think so.'

'He asked me to keep in touch while he was in hospital, to see you were okay.'

'He never said anything about that to me.'

In the morning, Margaret's mother answered the phone. 'It's the company we miss,' she said. 'We keep ourselves to ourselves. It took us a long time to get used to Margaret growing up. We expected changes, but found them hard when they came. I'll never forget the first time she went on holiday without us. She was away with the Guides for a weekend. We sat here and didn't know what to think.'

'Would you like me to come round?'

'That would be lovely.'

Margaret's father was in hospital for ten days after the operation. 'He's caught a wee infection,' the sister said, 'but he's coming along nicely.'

Margaret slept with her mother. Andy slept in Margaret's room. He grew used to being around the house, to being looked after. His shirts were washed and ironed, his trousers pressed and shoes polished. 'Waiters have to be smart,' said Mrs Mulholland, who bought him a pair of black socks. She made his breakfast every morning and supper was waiting when he came home at night.

'What's happened to you?' asked one of the waiters in the changing room, sometimes called the dressing room, the place where they changed their civvy clothes for their working clothes, morning coats and trousers, white waistcoat, front and tie, where they washed and shaved, smartened themselves up and prepared for the show.

'What's going on?'

'Nothing.'

Granny tried to let events take their course. 'Did you have a nice time when you were away wherever you were?' she asked.

She gave him presents, secretly slipped him things she picked up in the streets, string, wire and scraps of carpeting for his bedroom, as well as the usual assortments of wood and metal she continually brought home. It was difficult to find a pathway through the house; but now Andy was disturbed at having to step over boxes or avoid an assortment of clumps: tea chests filled with clothes, random golf clubs and bags, umbrellas, a car engine, old cases, handleless holdalls, prams, disused radios and television sets, bundles of newspapers, the smell of cats and the firewood Orlando sold around the doors at a price he fixed according to the type of wood: 'I have some nice rosewood sticks,' he'd say. 'A wee bit dear because it's rosewood, but well worth it.'

A week after Mr Mulholland's return, Margaret told Andy her mother was asking for him. 'She was asking when you were coming round for your tea again. She misses you.' By the end of the following month the matter had been decided.

'I hope you know what you're letting yourself in for,' said Granny. 'She looks as if she's getting what she wants, but I'm not too sure about you.'

'A step into the unknown,' said Orlando, who softened his crusts and biscuits by dipping them into his tea.

'I hope you don't bring disgrace to this house,' said Granny.

'What do you mean?'

'I think your grandmother is referring to the possibility of marriage being forced upon you by the conventions of society, at the point of a shotgun as it were.'

'Not at all,' said Andy. 'I want to get married.'

'Then hell mend you,' said Granny.

Margaret said, 'We'll manage fine. You'll see.'

They had been married for eight hours when she undressed in a room at the Excelsior Hotel, a room overlooking the airport, filled with the noise of planes. They caught the Dublin flight just after nine the following morning. They had lain on opposite edges of the bed, their backs to the centre, aware the other was awake, afraid of turning for fear of wakening the other. At first they lay in the dark awake, he thought because of the noise, the heat of the room and the fact that she did not like flying.

'You're cold,' he said.

'Just a wee bit shivery.'

They looked at each other and when he moved forward to kiss her she pulled back the bed covers and complained about the cold. 'Funny that the bed's cold,' he said. 'The room's warm enough.'

She kissed his hair and moved her head to the crook of his arm. He put his hand beneath her nightdress.

'They're not very big,' she said. He thought the cold had stiffened her nipples.

They shuffled to find a comfortable way of lying together, ending with Margaret on her back and Andy on his left side, his head on her shoulder. 'I never know what to do with the extra arm,' he said.

She played with his hair, stroked his face and kissed the top of his head. He lay with his hand on her left breast, brushing her nipple with the palm of his hand. 'They're different sizes,' she said.

Their bodies were relatively familiar, though they had never before been able to continue, fearing interruption. Andy was aware there was a moment when he could move, when he could raise himself on his elbow and kiss Margaret's mouth. He stretched downwards, lifted her nightdress, touched the tip of her pubic hair and moved his hand back to her breast. He felt pinned, unable to move properly, dependent on Margaret to move towards his touch. He wriggled round and kissed her cheek, moving his mouth downwards towards her right breast and his hand towards her leg. Margaret's breathing did not change; there was neither a change in intensity, nor a direct invitation. She seemed happy to have him lie in her arms like a child, for him to caress her softly. He was afraid of falling asleep. This change in pace, this mellowed approach distracted him.

Margaret had a way of interrupting his thoughts, as if she

knew what he was thinking or was aware of how he felt. 'I like to be loved,' she said. Her eyes were closed. 'I like to be made love to. I don't want to go at it. That's no use for me. Kiss my earlobes.'

The following afternoon, with a Dublin street map, they were by the pond in St Stephen's Green, looking down Grafton Street, when she said, 'Excelsior.' Every afternoon they went back to the hotel. The girls on reception smiled and looked at him when they handed her the key. Then they looked the other way.

Andy and Margaret moved into Carntyne. The arrangement had been suggested by Margaret's mother: 'There's no good the room going to waste. It'll give you a wee start till you find your feet,' she said.

Mr Mulholland did not comment. He had lost his job as a messenger, delivering letters and documents between solicitors' offices. When Margaret and Andy came back from honeymoon, her father had a job as a night watchman, guarding a building site near Pollokshaws.

'It's not like him, but I don't think Daddy likes you,' Margaret said.

'What makes you think that?'

'I don't know, just the way he is, I suppose. There's something about him. I can usually tell when he isn't happy. Maybe it's because of me; I mean, fathers dislike their daughter's husbands, don't they? Not that it matters much; Mum likes you. She thinks you're great.'

Andy and his father-in-law were never alone together. Everyone was in bed when Andy got home, he usually had the house to himself in the morning when Margaret's mother went shopping. Her father slept till midday, by which time Andy was at work.

It might have been five or six weeks later. Andy got up, walked to the bathroom and heard the sound of a man pissing in the bowl, water rumbling into water.

He was in the kitchen waiting for the kettle to boil when Margaret's father came in, put half a teaspoon of instant coffee into a mug to the sound of the flushing toilet. He looked at Andy: 'Job's finished,' he said. 'They've cleared the site. Nothing to protect.'

'Ever thought of being a hotel porter?'

'Ever thought about getting a house for your wife to live in?'

*

The letter was from the Social Security. He had an interview at 10.15 a.m. the following morning.

They had installed a video player and a number of television monitors. He watched two films, *Conan The Barbarian* and *Robocop*; adventure movies where good triumphs over evil, helped by superhuman powers.

'We're running a bit late,' the woman said. 'Staff shortages, I'm afraid.'

'I thought there were three million unemployed.'

'I believe you're not long out of jail?'

'About three months or so, maybe four months.'

'That's right, the date's here. And you haven't found work?'

'Not yet.'

'This is just a routine check-up we make to see if there's any scheme or training programme we can offer that might interest you.'

'I was up here last week. I got called in last week about this. The girl I saw asked if I was working and that was it.'

'Have you considered a training scheme?'

'No.'

'Why not?'

'I haven't been offered anything.'

'But you would be prepared to consider a scheme we offered?'

'Of course.'

'Did you do a Training For Freedom scheme when you were in prison?'

'I was a gardener.'

'That's right. You would get out and about a bit then?'

'They have a fairly big garden in Dungavel, so I spent a lot of my time there. I was also involved in community schemes, doing old-age pensioners' gardens, public schemes and stuff like that. There were a lot of working parties outside the jail.'

'That's right. It says here you were out a lot. And would you like to go back to gardening, or do you fancy something else?'

'I don't mind. I liked being a gardener.'

'Seems a waste not to use a skill you've got, doesn't it. Very well, Mr Paterson. We'll be in touch. And could you fill these forms in please.'

She gave him three forms printed in different colours; plum, orange and puce. She gave him a stamped addressed envelope.

'I've done this.'

'I beg your pardon.'

'I've filled these forms in.'

'No you haven't.'

'I think I would remember filling three forms in.'

'Are you sure it wasn't three other forms.'

'I am quite sure. It was these forms.'

'And did you post them to us, here at this office?'

'Yes.'

'Are you sure the envelope was addressed to this office.'

'Uh-huh.'

'Hold on.'

She was gone for half an hour. 'Sorry to have kept you. I thought it best to check. We have no record of these or any other forms being issued to you and have not received the completed forms. I would be obliged if you could complete these replacement forms and I think it would be best if you could hand them in personally this time so as everyone will know they got here safely.'

She wrote *Second Issue* on the top left-hand corner of each form and handed them to Andy with a smile.

He walked back through the Botanic Gardens, watched the ducks on the Kelvin and the grey squirrels on the fence who took food from your hand. He watched the gardeners lay a new flower-bed and walked around the Kibble Palace, a glass cathedral, brought up the Clyde by boat. He intended buying a newspaper and sitting on a bench by a marble statue, reading in the Kibble Palace light. The statues were allegoric Victorian public art, a handsome, modestly naked man with a monkey on his knee, a young, small-breasted girl squatting by a pool, and another called *The Thorn in the Flesh*. A child was crying because she could not catch a goldfish from the pond by the door. Andy smiled and the yells increased.

Hillhead Library has a concrete facing, vertical strips of aggregate panels and glass. The electric light is always burning inside the building, making it difficult to read. Window seats are always taken.

He borrowed an Ed McBain, *The Good Soldier Schweik* and *The Munros*, a hillwalking guidebook. He took recordings of the Shostakovich Fourth Symphony because it had been banned, the Melos Ensemble playing the Prokofiev and Shostakovich quintets and the Mozart Divertimento Trio, K563, which he later played continuously, fresh and mysterious every time. He took a tape by Tom Waits, who was popular in jail. He met Myra on Byres Road.

Orlando maintained you would meet everyone on Byres Road if you stood there long enough. It is difficult to see why it's popular, an ordinary street with grand tenemental canyons, gardened streets and ornamental ironwork rippling away on either side. The grandeur is mostly on the façade; tenement flats are let as rooms and houses subdivided. They met by the newer buildings, the library and the supermarket.

Myra seemed embarrassed. She was wearing jeans, trainers, a sweatshirt and jerkin. Her hair loose around her face.

'Have you been to the supermarket?'

'No, I'm just going. Are you off to the Botanics?'

'No, I've just been. Fancy a coffee?' He remembered he had no money.

'No, I'd better get this shopping done. I'm going to a meeting this afternoon.'

'What kind of meeting?'

'Nothing much, just a few friends. Listen, we have to talk.'

'What about?'

'I don't know. You said you'd come into the café and you never came. Did you put your name down on the housing list?'

'Not yet.'

'I shouldn't have come to see you that time. It was none of my business. I always interfere in other people's lives. My motives are usually good, but folk don't like it. Using words in a context that removes their meaning is another defect. Words like actually and absolutely are the current favourites.' She smiled.

'I meant to come round, Myra. I'm sorry. I don't know why

I didn't. I've been having a bad time lately. I mean to do things and they never get done, or I get round to doing them when it's too late.'

'Put your books in here. We'll go for a walk; if you can stand the Botanics again.'

'Why not, it's quiet round the back.'

The gardeners had planted a bed of begonias. Andy and Myra walked round the hothouse. She trailed her hand in water amongst the fish and lilies, bounced the pom-pom flowers on her finger and stroked a bird of paradise plant, she whistled at the birds who flew around the hothouse and laughed at the orchids. 'They're wonderful,' she said. 'They look like artificial flowers.'

She took his arm going up the hill. 'Tell me about it,' she said.

'Nothing to tell. Lousy day. I've been to the Social, which is always a bummer.'

'It isn't just today, is it?'

'It's pointless. Everything. You're beat before you start. All these things I wanted to do and I've done fuck all. Dreams of grandeur, really. Pathetic. Too many books and films. The man of justice gets revenge.'

'What happened today?'

'Nothing new. They've lost my forms.'

'Housing benefit forms?'

'Of course.'

'You didn't tell me.'

'I got them before you came round.'

'You're a sly and sneaky, weaselly old bastard who doesn't need much looking after.'

'Don't kid yourself. Getting forms is one thing; filling them in's another. Especially if you know they're doomed to an arbitrary mediocre reception. What time's your meeting?'

'Half two.'

'You'd better go then.'

'It's okay. I was only going to see someone. I can get there for four, or give her a ring later.'

'Fairly casual meeting?'

'That's right.'

They sat on a bench by the playground. Myra took the library books from the bag. 'Do you go hillwalking?'

'Not yet. I'd like to. I like reading about it. The trouble is the books make it seem easy. A two- or three-line route description of something that is dangerous and can take up to four or five hours. Another dream. Dreams of high places and dreams of flying. Nothing new, is there.'

'I might come with you.'

'I'm only thinking about going. I haven't gone yet.'

'What's stopping you?'

'Money.'

'Are you too proud to accept second-hand gear?'

'No.'

'Then what size of shoes do you take?'

'Nine and a half.'

'Davie's old boots should fit you. You're supposed to buy walking boots new because they need to adjust to your feet, but Davie my brother's just bought a new pair of boots, not that there was much wrong with the old pair that I could see; I think the new ones are more expensive, so the old pair's up for sale. I'll ask him what he wants if you like.'

'I don't know what I can afford.'

'Which is fine because I don't know how much they'll cost.'

A child's ball bounced beside her. She squatted down to hand it to the girl. Andy noticed a price tag on the instep of her right shoe.

When she came back she took his hand and they sat watching the pigeons strut across the grass, the children, and the fieldfares guzzling rowan berries, the seagulls raising their yellow beaks towards the sea and a blue tit perched upside down on a cluster of nuts.

*

Homeless folk came round the hotel. They washed their socks and underwear in the toilet sinks and dried them in the hand driers, used the soap and towels and got to know the night porters. They sometimes worked for the porters, shining the shoes, cleaning or scrubbing the kitchen. They were given scraps of food and allowed to sleep for a couple of hours. Girls were given preferential treatment, especially young girls.

The porters thought young girls were easier to help, were likely to be grateful and encouraged them to come back the following night. Two or three men would turn up at the back door some time after eleven, to be told they couldn't get in; the hotel was busy which meant the night porters would be serving drink all night. They were sometimes told there was a bomb scare or a security clamp-down. It meant the same thing; a girl had turned up at half past ten. The homeless men lay on the hot grating in front of the station, listening to their memories and the three notes BR use to signal train announcements.

The number of homeless youngsters increased while Andy was in jail. He had read about the increases and seen a couple of television programmes which flirted with the problem. It amused him to think his grandmother had anticipated a social trend. Granny was a Tory. 'We need the man with the money,' she said.

'I was homeless myself when I met your grandmother.'

Orlando put two teaspoons of tea into the warmed pot. He did not use teabags.

Most of the rubbish had gone. The lobby was clear and carpeted. The living room and kitchen had too much furniture and it was still recognisable as his Granny's house; her colour schemes dominated the surroundings, her furniture was evident and the house still smelled the way it did when she was there, a trace of cats. Geordie Anderson was singing in the bathroom.

'I'd knocked around a bit. This and that. Here and there. Searching, as I thought. Always looking for something.' Orlando was toasting muffins on the open fire; butter, tea and bramble jam on Granny's chair beside the fire.

Books replaced Granny's trash, her newspapers, vegetables and wonky machines. Every time, another change. Orlando bought a cassette player and, for the first time, there was music in the house: 'I don't care what it is, so long as it's music,' he told Andy. Orlando did not like opera, except for Mozart, neither did he like country and western, nor any kind of popular music, especially what was in the charts, easy listening and light classics. He was especially fond of Gilbert and Sullivan though, almost all ballet music and pibroch, the big music. 'Gilbert's contribution to the English language has been greatly undervalued,' Orlando said. 'I first heard it by accident, being forced to listen when I was a school janitor. Every year the school put on a Gilbert and Sullivan opera. I not only had to attend every performance, but every rehearsal as well. And I like pibroch because it is impossible not to be overawed by the dignity and subtlety of the *ceol mhor*.'

Orlando had sold insurance and motor cars, brushes round the doors, second-hand clothes in a market and second-hand pots in the open air. He had been a seaman and a labourer, a clerk for two days and a barman for one night. He had worked on a farm, down a mine and in a forest. He could plaster a wall, drive a lorry and bake bread. He knew about electricity and twice a week when he visited the Possilpark Library he took home books on science and wildlife, travel, a little biography and Scottish history.

'I do not understand your devotion to fiction,' he told Andy, 'in terms other than escapism. The Possilpark reading room has splendidly inspirational murals on self-educative subjects: Science, Astronomy, Geography, Poetry, Commerce and Art. These murals were painted by students at the Glasgow School of Art when it was under the directorship of the wonderful Francis Newberry. Three murals are by men and three by women, a revolutionary division of labour for Edwardian Scotland, not to mention Edwardian Britain. Possilpark Library reading room is now almost bare. There are leaflets on community care and how to protect your home, but self-improvement screams from the walls. It is similar to Langside Library, was built at the same time and designed by the same architect, though Langside Library, quite properly, has a mural of the Battle of Langside on its walls.'

Orlando did not see many people, though he told Andy he had plenty company: 'All the company I want,' he said.

Some brought newspapers, groceries and a little conversation, though he always had a ready talk when Andy came, as though it was something he had been thinking for some time, something he had been waiting to say.

'How did we begin?' he asked, one night, making the tea.

This was Myra's first visit to Bardowie Street. Orlando asked Andy how his course was doing.

'What course is this?' asked Myra.

'I'm doing an Open University course on Sociology. I started in the jail, but haven't really taken it up again. Everybody in jail's doing OU courses. It passes the time.'

'You'll need to let me see the stuff. I'd like to read your essays.'

'Why?'

'Don't know; just would.'

'What was the way it started?' Orlando and Geordie carried in the trays of tea, cake and biscuits. 'According to Christian belief we were given the planet, made by God to inhabit his creation, which has meant we can do with it what we like. Primitive man has no time for this nonsense. Aborigines have one of the most complex cosmologies of any society; American Indians too. They believe they are descended from God, rather than made by him, and quite right too. The Aborigines have no separate God; they believe their ancestors made them and the universe, that the landmarks and the landscapes, every bush and boulder, have stories behind their creation from the dreamtime; so their mythology is the land, they sang the world into existence. These peoples are tied to the land, there is a give and take between man and the planet.'

Geordie sat staring out the window. He stood up, opened the window and the noise of a pneumatic drill accompanied Orlando.

'Christian history is not the history of the people, or the land or the creation. It is the history of the oppression of the people. The peoples' history begins with water and fire and food and shelter, with hunting and tribal formations, with myths of how the earth began; how the mother became fertile and created us all. Think of the world as an idea, dismiss the reality. Imagine you'd never seen it. Think of the world as an idea and it all makes sense. That's either too simple or too sophisticated, I can't decide or remember which.

'Glasgow was never made. The place developed. What you are doing is in keeping with the place. People educate themselves here. There is a history of autodidacticism, from Anderson's College, where women were encouraged to study alongside men, to John Maclean's workers' colleges. Education was always seen as a good thing, worthy for its own sake, the way forward. When a co-operative society was founded the first thing they did was start a library. Paisley weavers were notoriously well-educated. Education was seen as a beautiful thing in itself rather than a means of self-improvement, a ticket to the middle classes, or a means of understanding socialist philosophy. All changed I'm afraid, all changed and not necessarily for the better. I fear I'm a dinosaur, certainly a threatened species if not a dying breed. And before I finish, let me lay my curse upon the teachers who tried to remove what they and David Hume called Scotticisms from our language: did you know that the phrase "the now" is used by J.M. Barrie?'

They refused an offer to stay for tea. Last time Andy was given a cheese sandwich, two boiled potatoes and a pickled onion.

'Where did you find him?' asked Myra. 'He's gorgeous.'

'He found me.'

*

They looked at houses in Ibrox, Langside, Anniesland and a place the estate agent called Thornwood, which Andy called Partick or maybe Whiteinch. They bought a two-room and kitchen, one storey up in Allison Street, off the Vicky Road, far away from Granny, Orlando and Margaret's parents.

The Sunday before they moved he went walking in Alexandra

Park with Margaret. The sough of the motorway was all around them. They stood on a rise and watched the traffic.

'We could have that hall a deep red, more a rust colour than anything else, which would mean we would only have to paint the walls, though I'd like a wallpaper for the sitting room and the bedroom, maybe the bathroom; no, we could paint that. I'd like a shower for the bathroom. I've always imagined getting up in the morning and having a shower.'

'How are we going to pay for all this?'

'It doesn't need to be dear. We can do a lot of the work ourselves.'

'We'll need to do all of it.'

'Can you lay carpets and paint? Can you tile a bathroom?'

'Never tried.'

'Surely some of your friends could help you.'

'What about your dad?'

'He's busy.'

'Hasn't he found anything else?'

She shook her head. Her dad had been working as a barman for three weeks.

They didn't have much to move in with. Margaret's mother bought a bed, Granny gave them a table and a chest of drawers. The rest came from hire purchase, Habitat and Marks & Spencer. Margaret worked out what they could afford. 'A nice home is important,' she said.

They walked around some other stores. She looked at the fluffed and feathery sofas, the Afghan rugs in Fraser's. She squeezed his arm in front of the window of the bedroom shop in Princes Square. They looked at Liberty and Laura Ashley.

'How much of this stuff can we afford?' asked Andy.

'I don't know; not very much, I should think.'

'It looks damned dear to me. Maybe we'd better work out what we want and price it, then look at what we can afford.'

'I've done that. I know what we can afford. We're only in here to look.'

On the way to Habitat, Andy detoured up Renfield Street to Thomson's coffee shop. In summer the coffee smell crossed the street. He bought a pound of Colombian beans: 'For the mornings,' he said.

'We already have some coffee,' said Margaret. They had instant coffee; the Thomson's coffee became a secret after that, he ran up the road from work during his break.

They bought carpets from a shop with a sale in Victoria Road. The curtains came from Remnant Kings. Margaret bought something for the house every month when the Habitat account was paid. Their first big argument was when she found the coffee.

'Are these beans new?'

'More or less. I bought them about a week ago.'

'And where did you get the money?'

'Tips.'

'We have coffee. I don't know why you need to buy more.'

'That's instant coffee. It's no bloody good. Instant coffee is too weak, it's just a milky drink. This stuff is the business, loaded with caffeine and very nice, strong.'

'It's disgusting. I can't drink it. If you gave the money to me it could go to the house.'

'All my money goes to the house. I spend nothing on myself. I don't smoke and I don't drink, Margaret.'

'You do so drink. You drink every week. I have also been willing to sacrifice things young married people do, things like a night at the pictures together, once in a wee while, or going out for a meal; I have been willing to sacrifice these things so's we could have a nice house to come home to.'

'You're not the only one to make sacrifices. What about me? What have I sacrificed?'

'I don't know.'

'You do know, you bloody well do know.'

'All my wages goes into this house, either for food or furniture. All my wages, every penny I earn, everything. I don't have any money to buy fancy coffee even if I wanted it, because my money's all accounted for.'

'So's mine. This is tips, woman. Tips. Money I make over and above my wages.'

'I don't care what it is or where it comes from any more than I care for the amount. It's the principle of the thing that bothers me.'

She put a pillow between them when they went to bed and did not speak for a week.

'God alone knows what you can do,' said Joe. 'Myself, I said fuck it a long time ago. I have a wee tank for myself.'

'I don't need money. It's easier just to give her what she wants.'

'In that case, let her think she's getting what she wants. Give her a different amount every week and keep a fiver of your tips for yourself.'

'What for?'

'Firstly, there is the principle of the thing. More practically, for a wee bevvy and a night at the casino, anything you like so long as it's yours.'

Within a year, he and Margaret had certain subjects they could not discuss. They blamed each other and got on best in a neutral territory. When he said what she construed was critical, either of her opinions or behaviour, there was an argument during which the main issue was lost and older issues re-emerged. They usually argued over his criticisms rather than their substance. Whenever they argued, she put the pillow down the bed and did not speak.

'Don't you think this is silly?' he asked in the dark.

'What?'

'You know what; not speaking, the pillow down the bed.'

'I am trying to sleep. It's one o'clock in the morning and I have my work to go to.'

'Sorry.'

'You're only sorry because you're looking for something.'

Sex never gave what it promised and became a secret, manipulative affair. The initiative came from Andy. He was not aware of having stopped trying. He thought it was overrated, attractive because it was unobtainable, as soon as it became obtainable it lost its attraction. He thought Margaret did not like sex. Jail showed him what was obvious, she did not like sex with him.

Adultery came because of the promise. Only when he saw how much it hurt his wife did he consider it adultery. Prior to that it was not important.

Andy reckoned he was jailed for shagging a polisman's wife.

'I didn't know it was an offence,' he said.

'We've decided to oppose your bail,' said the Polisman. 'Sorry about that.'

The Polis found out when he was on the night shift. His wife was getting up as he was getting into bed. He saw a damp patch on the bed where his wife had been lying. He phoned in sick and watched the house. Andy came back with the wife and the Polisman followed him home.

No one told Andy this had happened. He assumed it had happened because he was having an affair with his arresting officer's wife and was not dealing in drugs.

He'd met Sheila in the casino. 'Your luck's in,' she said.

In jail he thought about revenge. It was important neither the Polisman nor Sheila the wife knew he was out of jail, important Margaret did not know and important one did not know what the other knew. He suspected the Polisman would know he was out.

It took a while, weeks before he could phone the station. His heart was pounding when he asked for CID. He put the phone down, followed the grid around the block, returned to the phone box, called the station again, asked for CID and again replaced the receiver.

He tried three days later. A voice said, 'He retired about a year ago. Anything we can do to help?'

'Not really, thanks all the same. I'm a family friend, I haven't seen him for some time and thought I'd give him a call.'

'If you're a friend you'll have his home number. I suggest you try him there.'

'Thanks very much,' said Andy The line was dead.

*

It must have been around four o'clock when she said she would have to go. 'This is all very well,' she said, 'but I must be responsible.'

'Can I see you later?'

'Much as I would like to I think we ought to slow things down. Come around for dinner on Friday.'

'What time?'

'I don't know. Seven o'clock?'

The houses to the north of Huntly Gardens are in a three-storeyed terrace, rising in pairs to the top of the hill, with bay windows, cast-iron railings and the remains of lamp standards at the far end, furthest away from Byres Road. Myra lived in what was once the servant's quarters in the basement, two rooms at the back of the house, the bathroom and lavatory shared with the girl in the two rooms opposite.

'Flowers are a real con,' she told him. 'I love them. Now for the Calvinist bit: you shouldn't have bothered because you can't afford them.'

'How do you know what I can't afford?'

'I am supposing you went without food to give me this lifeless sucker blow. I am also hoping this is so because I think I've cooked too much food; if so, you can let me indulge in the deepest need of a Catholic woman, you can let me make you fat.'

She put the flowers between them at the centre of the table. 'No wine,' she said. 'I didn't get any.'

'Do you want me to get some?'

'I don't think we could find a wine that was pretentious enough for this meal. Anyway, I don't drink. We have some overpriced, herbally approved fizzy water and French stuff which ought to be called derrière water, because only an arsehole would pay a pound a bottle. Ice?'

'What's this stuff about Calvinism and Catholicism?'

'In this country even the Catholics are Calvinists: Jews and Muslims, Hindus, anything, all wee Calvinists, running around telling other people what to do for their own good. Anyway, I'm both.'

'How come?'

'My mother was brought up in the Wee Free, made to suffer

for her mother's shame, which was her. My mother was illegitimate, a wee bastard. By the way, there is no starter because I forgot to buy the prawns. The pork chops have been cooked in red wine; these are creamed potatoes, mange-tout peas and little french beans, tastefully done in butter and garlic. The salad is supposed to be for after, but I don't mind when you have it. Dig in.'

'How does the Catholic thing come in?'

'I was brought up a Catholic.'

'I presume your mother was brought up in the Wee Frees.'

'Absolutely. There's that word again.'

'Then how come her daughter was brought up a Catholic?'

'My mother married a Catholic.'

'The chops are lovely.'

'They're not bad, are they. Squeeze some lemon juice on them; brings out the flavour, or maybe you already know that. The book says it enriches the natural juices. I think it changes the flavour.'

'With your mother's Calvinism and your Catholicism you seem to have got the worst of both worlds.'

'I don't know; it has certainly given me an outlook on religion, not to mention the ways of the world. In a society like this, where lassies get pregnant to get money off the social and a hard-to-let house as well, such things don't really matter; but in my granny's day, being unmarried and pregnant was not the done thing, especially in the Highlands. It must have been awful. She wanted to keep the baby, to stay home and face them all. Her parents wanted to send her away, but she stayed and had the child, which effectively branded her for life. She didn't manage: I hate this story, I really hate it; and I hate them, all of them that did it to her and are still doing it and still saying they're right because God tells them what to do, that their interpretation of the Bible is better than anyone else's so they can't possibly be wrong. For all their certainties, they display a severe lack of Christian charity. No wonder we don't like ourselves, no wonder so many people leave and those who stay are discontents.'

'No more than anywhere else.'

'How do you know?'

'I don't, any more than you know we have more self-righteous, small-minded malcontents than anywhere else. Look at America, South Africa for God's sake.'

'Oh, shut up. I've got to tell you, whether you like it or not. My granny committed suicide. She was working in a hotel in London in the Thirties, having left the baby with her sister. There was nothing wrong with her physically or mentally. Her best friend was an Irish girl who said my granny told her she was missing the baby. My mother was brought up in shame, a multiple shame; she was ashamed of herself, her body, her feelings, her background, everything. Not only was she a bastard, but she knew it and was reminded of it every day: she knew it because the children in the playground told her, every day they wouldn't play with her because their parents told them not to; she was also reminded by her aunt who told her to do things, everything was for your shame, bring in the washing, for your shame girl, peel the potatoes, fetch the coal, do the ironing for your shame, the shame of being born and of having caused her mother's death. Stands to reason, if her mother had not had her she wouldn't have died. Her fault. Simple. Needless to say, my mother left at the first opportunity and never went back, not even for her grandparents' funerals or aunt's funeral, but that only proved they were right. She was ungrateful on top of everything else.'

'Did they know?'

'Know what?'

'Know why she never went back. Did she ever tell them?'

'She did and they called her a sinner. That was only to be expected because the devil was in her from before her birth. She had no chance. We're all born in sin, which you might think means they've got you anyway, but she had no chance of redemption except through constant repentance. She had to be continually sorry for being alive, make amends for something she'd never done. Her aunt brought her up and every day said she had sacrificed herself because it was her duty, so she was pleased enough with herself at the end. Her grandparents seemed glad to be rid of her, especially the grandfather who said she was a Jezebel born of a Jezebel. I think he meant she was pretty. Eat up.'

'No thanks. I'm fine.'

'Lost your appetite?'

'I've had enough.'

'Have some more salad.'

'It was the jail, Myra. Every day someone told me what to do, where I should be; everything reminded me of why I should be there. I was reminded of my shame for something I didn't do. How come you became a Pape?'

'I told you, my mother married a Catholic. It's hardly surprising, quite predictable really: think of it, what would offend them most, assuming they ever found out. She hadn't been in touch with any of them for some time.'

'And did they ever find out?'

'Of course. That sort of thing always gets back. I don't know how, but people from the community know all about us. They have long memories that stretch even further than Glasgow.'

'I think I'll have some salad.'

'There's a pudding; don't look at me like that, it isn't anything fancy. I thought to myself, what would this man like for pudding? You look like a crumble and custard man to me, so I made an apple and bramble crumble.'

'Where did you get the brambles?'

'The apples were harder. There were no decent apples around. I like these wee hard buggers of which Glaswegians are so fond. I picked the brambles last year and froze them. Pathetic, isn't it. Typical Catholic, the first time I use them is on someone else.'

'You get the pudding and I'll finish the salad.'

'The custard isn't made. You can talk to me while I'm making it.'

'I'll make the coffee while you make the custard.'

Andy cleared the table, put the dishes in the sink and asked where the cups, coffee and coffee-maker were kept. Myra was singing.

She put the coffee things on the counter and they worked away in silence when she finished her song, smiling when they collided near the sink.

'The crumble was wonderful.'

'It was okay.'

'I chose the word carefully. I can't remember the last time I had crumble.'

'I don't expect you'll always be so easily pleased. I'm sorry there's no more.'

'Tell me about your dad. Where does he fit into the story?'

'My mother was working in a shop when she met him. He was at university. She always said she never liked him till she met his family. There's a whole squad of them, nine in all. They're still down there.'

'Down where?'

'The Renton. My granny and grandad are Irish, from a farm outside Omagh in the County Tyrone. We go back nearly every year, there's dozens of relations there. We're a typical Irish Catholic family: lawyers, doctors, teachers, a nun and a priest. There was a great to-do about my dad marrying a black Protestant, but that was soon sorted out. My mum told me she had a word with my dad's mum and that was that. She was never a very good Catholic. But she still goes to church most Sundays and has herself a wee confession every once in a while. My dad never bothers. He's a teacher in Clydebank; he's actually a headmaster now, due to retire soon.'

'And what about you?'

'What about me?'

'Married?'

'Not any more. I got married because that's what you do. You become seventeen, you have been seeing this guy since you were fourteen and everyone expects you to get married, so we got engaged and then we got married. Me and my granny, same mistake. I didn't know what I was doing. He told me that if I didn't do it with him he'd get someone else. I fancied him, or thought I did and that was that, on the floor of a house in Paisley after a party. I thought, Is that it? I remember wondering if that was what all the fuss was about. Then I got scared, and I was quite right to get scared. I was pregnant. The big temptation was to pretend it wasn't happening, that nothing was going on, that I wasn't very pregnant, only six weeks. Then I told him. He said, We're engaged, so we might as well get married. So we got married. In a registry office. My dad insisted. He also told me, get this, my dad, who is to all exterior reasonings a good Catholic, my dad told me I didn't need to get married if I didn't want to. I lost the baby: seven months pregnant and I lost the baby after my husband kicked me in the stomach. He told me it wouldn't happen again and I believed him. It did happen again, every time Rangers got beat. Your turn. Begin at the beginning and tell me all about it.'

There was a temptation to miss bits, to skip over things like Cathie and Margaret, the casino and the jail, the reason for going to jail. He told her everything. Later, the idea scared him.

'I wish I'd met your granny,' Myra said.

They were lying on the floor beside the fire. The room was lit by a lamp in the corner. They had cleared the table, washed the dishes and tidied the room. It was some time after two in the morning.

'She'd have loved you.'

'Yeah. I think we'd have got on fine, her and I.'

'I'd better go. Can I see you tomorrow?'

'I'm busy tomorrow night. But phone me on Sunday. We'll do something. What do you fancy? Art galleries?'

'No. The rooms have been rearranged. It looks like a saleroom.'

'In that case, we'll go and see our Davie. You can get the boots sorted out at the same time.'

'Fine. When will I come round?'

'I'll come round to you, about half twelve.'

Andy stood and stretched himself. He took his jacket from the back of a chair.

'Did anyone ever tell you you have a nice arse?'

'A guy in the jail told me.'

'How did you get out of that?'

'I tried to ignore it. I kept myself to myself and it worked.'

'I'm bloody tactless sometimes.'

They were at the door. 'I am extremely aware of the fact that I haven't kissed you yet,' said Andy.

'It hasn't actually passed me either. I don't think I'm ready for this, Andy. I don't know what I'm ready for.'

'I thought I'd mention it, that's all. Just in case you wondered.'

'We'll talk about it on Sunday.'

Ten minutes later, walking down Great Western Road, he smelled her perfume from the front of his sweater. She did not push him away as he had expected. She put her arms round his waist, her hands into his back pockets and rested her head against his chest. 'I can hear your heart beat,' she said.

He kissed the top of her head. She unlocked herself and shoved him towards the door.

'That's enough,' she said. 'I probably won't sleep tonight. You and your arse.'

Crossing Kelvinbridge he thought of snowdrops. They are almost immortal. He forgot about them every year until they appeared. Seen in clumps on the edge of a clearing or in the woods they mark the site of a former house. No one told them the house had gone, so the snowdrops appear year after year, right on time at the start of the spring.

*

She asked him to run her home, invited him in at three in the morning and that was that.

Margaret was used to him coming in late. 'This isn't good for us,' she said. 'We're living separate lives already.'

'What can we do about it?'

'You can start coming home after your work.'

'I wouldn't necessarily see more of you.'

'That's not the point. I would know where you were. I do worry about you sometimes, as well as wondering where you are and what you're doing out of the house at two or three o'clock in the morning.'

The prison psychiatrist said self-delusion, and Andy agreed.

There are security cameras everywhere. A pit boss struts the floor in his red clip-on bow tie, pocket handkerchief and cummerbund. Cards are dealt in the same way, the chips collected in the same way and the pay-outs made in the same way. The house makes money by keeping the game going and croupiers are trained to keep punters playing. Punters carry on playing when they are losing, hoping to win in defiance of common sense, reason or the basic gambling knowledge, known to all. This means the house must win in the end.

Andy told Joe it had nothing to do with money. 'My heart is pounding,' he said in the toilet, his back to the sink. 'Just standing there, waiting and I can feel my pulse go.'

'That's the first sign,' said Joe.

Gamblers believe the outcome depends on the players, that they can defy chance with a personal supply of good luck. They increase their bets when losing, because a winning streak must come soon, they decrease their bets when winning because winning streaks cannot last.

Andy went to the casino about twice a week. He had a tank of around £100, playing blackjack or roulette. He played a couple of hands of blackjack simultaneously, betting on both to increase the chances of winning on the second hand by buying off the bad cards with the first hand.

'Which means you lose twice as fast,' said Joe.

Andy's only control was to stay away. Withdrawal was slow. He convinced himself he was doing the right thing, saving to buy a better home for his wife and family to be. Within a week he thought how much more quickly he could get the house if he won the money. He told himself he was going back to look, to enjoy the atmosphere and the crack, to keep Joe company. He was back to have a look when he met Sheila.

Playing roulette, he left his chips on a number which had recently won, believing it would win again. When he lost he placed his chips on the number that lost previously believing it could not lose again. He looked for luck in the near misses.

'You'd be better off pissing your money up against the marble slab,' said Joe.

The police came at seven o'clock on a Sunday morning. Margaret wakened him. 'There's someone at the door,' she said.

Later he wondered about a spyhole. He had first heard of them when Granny said, 'I've met some daft buggers in my time, but this one beats them all. He asked if I wanted a hole in my door.' If he had looked through the spyhole and seen the policemen would he have opened the door?

The dogs found dope in a sock beneath the bed. The Polisman asked Margaret if Andy had unexpected large sums of money. At the trial he said they were acting on information received.

Andy's lawyer lit a cigarette and looked at the wall: 'Obviously, I believe you are innocent or I wouldn't be here. But the evidence is convincing. I must tell you one more time that if I were you I would change my plea.'

'You're not me. Why the fuck should I plead guilty to something I didn't do?'

'Because they're going to find you guilty. Plead guilty now and you'll get a lighter sentence. If this goes the whole way you'll get about ten years.'

He changed his plea and was sentenced to three years' imprisonment.

'I don't know what to think,' said Margaret. 'It's my Mum and Dad, especially Mum, I feel sorry for. She's really hurt by this.'

'Everybody in jail's innocent,' said Charlie Sloan. 'You've no chance of proving anything here. If you take my advice you'll see your way through it, that's all; getting by is the name of the game; getting by.'

Charlie was afraid of the dark and used to fall asleep at dawn.

Margaret came every two or three weeks. 'I'll give you a while to get settled,' she said when he was transferred to Dungavel.

Like all mail, the letter had been opened. The warder stood beside him. Her handwriting was smaller than he remembered, as though she was trying to cram the message into a single sheet of the blue Basildon Bond writing paper with matching envelopes. Yet the writing also seemed thicker; that could be the black ink; she had probably used one of the Bic pens she got from the office.

He wrote asking her to visit and got no reply. He phoned.

'I didn't know you could get calls from the jail,' she said.

'Yeah. We can use the phone. When are you coming to see me?'

'I don't think I should.'

'We need to talk.'

'I've nothing to say.'

'You can't just go.'

'Don't get upset,' she said. 'What else am I supposed to do. Life must go on.'

There were the blue denim prisoners, striped shirts, white T-shirts, scrubbed red faces, hair nicely combed, queueing up for the gymnasium, wanking in the dorms at night. Andy was in the garden talking to Eddie Coyne who told him he thought of nothing when he wanked, even though he wanked every night: 'You'd think I'd think of something, sure you would,' he said. Eddie Coyne had the next bed.

Of course, he spoke to Lisa before sleep, imagining what they would do next day, where they would go and so on. One night he thought of the dancer's legs and after that he thought about nothing.

'You're auld afore your time,' said Eddie. 'I can imagine that auld bastard there thinkin like that cause he's past it.'

'Some folk are made different,' said Charlie.

'Cannae imagine anybody no wantin their nookie. Sport of the kings, man.'

'Naebody said we didnae like it,' said Charlie. 'Andy only said it's worth bothering about when it's there, that right?'

This was during an English class. The teacher told them Wordsworth said poetry was emotion recollected in tranquillity. 'Same as a wank,' said Eddie. 'Sir, how is it a man can weigh eleven stones and have a shite which weighs a couple of pound and if he weighs himself after the shite he still weighs eleven stones?'

The teacher looked out the window. When the laughter stopped the only noise was the wire slapping against the flagpole.

'I went to see Margaret,' Joe told him six months after the divorce came through. 'She's still in Allison Street living with a guy called Frankie. Ever heard of him?'

Andy shook his head.

'He was her boyfriend before she met you. Granny says you're well out of it and there's a home for you in Possilpark.'

The doctor said it was a virus.

'There seems to be some sort of epidemic going on just now and there isn't much we can do about it except the usual things, suggest you keep warm and take hot drinks. I'll give you this to clear your chest. They're small yellow pills and you should take one three times a day. Come back and see me if it doesn't clear up.'

He collected the prescription and walked home, wondering if a virus was a thinking mechanism; difficult to imagine them as anything else. Parasites do not kill their hosts and the virus's ability to replicate itself and strengthen as it does so would surely be the death of mankind. No more water but the fire next time. Can plague be seen as a fire, expecially now with the end in sight when the AIDS virus has attacked and demolished the immune system? The only hope was history. Medieval society invented cures for diseases and ailments we now know nothing about, and we must hope to do the same.

'Where's your prescription?' Myra asked. She phoned on the Saturday morning, to see if he got home all right. He coughed and was told to go to the doctor.

'What are you doing today?' She opened the curtains, raised the window slightly, put on the gas fire and turned off the radio.

'Staying here and being sick.'

'Fancy coming to see my brother?'

'Where?'

'Stirling.'

'How will we get there?'

She dangled a set of car keys.

'I didn't know you had a car.'

'I hardly ever use it.'

She had a dark blue VW Beetle, cramped, noisy and suddenly fashionable. 'Don't worry about the stuff in the back,' she said. 'That's for Davie, Lorna and the kids.'

There were two boys and a girl, David, Liam and wee Lorna, having soup for lunch round a circular table.

'Would you take some soup?' asked Davie.

Myra sat next to wee Lorna, smiled and raised her shoulders in a single movement, then cut the child's bread into little squares and laid them round the edge of her plate. The boys stared at Andy.

After lunch Myra and Lorna drank tea in the kitchen, with wee Lorna on Myra's knee, while Andy and Davie played football with the boys, who wanted to be in Andy's team.

There were clothes for the kids and books for Davie in the back of the car. 'I go round the jumble sales picking up bits and pieces, that's all,' Myra said as Lorna held the jumpers and trousers up in front of the boys. Myra took Andy's hand and squeezed it: 'You okay?'

'Fine.'

'Have you read them?' asked Davie.

'Put on the kettle,' shouted Lorna.

'Get your new clothes on,' said Myra, 'and we'll go for a walk.'

They drove Davie's car past the university, parked in a lay-by, crossed the road and walked up the hill by the side of a wood towards a reservoir. 'We'll need to let you have a look at these boots,' said Davie. 'I suppose you're staying for your tea.'

'The men are cooking,' said Lorna, who was feeding wee Lorna, boiled egg and butter switched in a cup. Myra was reading to the boys.

'What can you make?' said Davie.

'A mess,' shouted Myra.

'Lasagne.'

'Carry on,' said Davie. 'I'll do the salad.'

Someone put on a Van Morrison tape. 'Your man's making lasagne,' shouted Davie.

'How long will it take?'

'Too long. We'll do eggs for the boys and get them down, then we can eat. Is that all right, Andy?'

'Fine.'

'How's the virus?' Myra's arm was round his waist.

'The pills are wonderful. I feel fine.'

She kissed his neck and when he turned, again on the mouth. 'Leave that man alane so's I can get my weans' eggs on.' She squealed when Davie tremmled her waist.

Davie and Lorna were feeding the boys, Andy was reading the paper with the lasagne in the oven when Myra came into the kitchen. 'Come and help me put wee Lorna down,' she said.

The child was washed, her hair combed, sitting up in bed in what used to be her brother's pyjamas. The bed was in her parents' bedroom. The bedside light was on and when they opened the door, she pulled the covers over her head.

'Where's Lorna?'

'I thought you said she was in here?'

'I thought she was in here, but she can't be here now. She must be in another room.'

She was giggling.

'Maybe we should go and see if she's in another room.'

'Here I am.' She threw the covers out the bed.

Myra stroked her hair, singing, while Lorna sucked her fingers.

When she closed the bedroom door, Myra leaned her head against it, her arms around his neck: 'This is getting serious, Andy Paterson.'

'Is it all right for me to take my weans upstairs?' said Davie. 'The poor wee buggers didnae know what they'd find.'

'Don't you listen to him,' said Lorna. 'Right boys, say night-night to everybody.'

'The salad's done,' said Davie. 'There's beer in the fridge. All you need to do is serve the supper.'

It was a slow meal. They changed the tape, firstly *The Four Seasons*, then *Miles Davis in Concert*, though they talked all the time. Andy, Lorna and Davie drank four cans of export between them, Myra drank water and made the coffee at the end of the meal. Davie wiped his plate with bread and Lorna asked if anyone wanted yogurt.

'Keep them for the kids,' said Myra.

'What's the biggest difference you've noticed since being out of jail?' asked Davie.

'The price of stuff.'

'That's the bloody Tories for you, put up the price of everything and blame the working man. I hope you're not a Tory.'

'I'm not.'

'Lorna's a Tory.'

'I am not.'

'Sorry, Lorna was a Tory.'

'I voted Tory once because my father told me.'

'I nearly did that,' said Andy.

'You never did,' said Myra.

'I did. Granny was a Tory.'

'Surely not. I thought you said she hated Churchill.'

'It didn't stop her voting Tory. She had been brought up believing those born to rule should be allowed to do so.'

'It's that generation again; radicals and forelock tuggers. What about old whatshisname?'

'Orlando is above politics. He says politicians trivialise things.'

'You ought to meet this one, Davie. You'd love him.'

'He sounds fine.'

'Who do you vote for now, Lorna?' asked Andy.

'Last time I voted Liberal.'

'I vote SNP,' said Myra.

'This isn't a marriage,' said Davie. 'It's more of an electoral pact; we do it for the kids' sake really.'

'Have you paid your Poll Tax?' asked Lorna.

'Haven't had a demand yet,' said Andy.

'Will you pay it?'

'It's difficult. I don't want to pay it.'

'I haven't paid mine,' said Davie.

'I have,' said Lorna.

'The issue is confused because there isn't a collective leadership.'

'That's the bloody Labour Party for you, all talk. I haven't paid and I'm not going to pay,' said Myra.

'That's all very well,' said Andy, 'but by not paying out of political protest you are surely confusing the issue, especially the genuine cases of hardship which the Poll Tax causes. Those who can afford to pay should pay and those who cannot afford to pay ought not to pay; that way the issues would be clearer.'

'Not at all,' said Myra. 'That way you're dumping the issue onto the poor, making them fight your battle for you, or at least to stand in the firing line. It is my struggle as much as anyone else's; I believe the tax to be morally wrong, therefore I will not pay it.'

'I didn't mean to suggest we leave the poor to do the fighting. I was trying to find a way through the maze of so-called leadership where the SNP are saying don't pay, the Labour Party are saying pay up but don't like it, the Tories are saying pay now and we'll fix it later and the Liberals don't know what the hell they're saying.'

'They'll have a pact with anyone so long as they can change the system.'

'And why do they want electoral reform? Because they'd get more seats under proportional representation.'

'Turn that tape over, will you, love?'

Myra poured more coffee into Andy's mug. She placed her left hand on the inside of his right leg, just above the knee.

'I was just thinking,' said Lorna. 'If Andy and Myra want to stay we could make up a bed with the cushions from the chairs and sofa.'

'We'll go back to Glasgow,' said Myra.

'You're not going yet,' said Davie. 'This man has a pair of boots to get.'

'God, the boots.'

'Are you sure you won't stay?' said Lorna. 'It's no trouble. The kids'll be asking where you are in the morning.'

Myra smiled. Andy followed Davie to the cupboard beneath the stairs to try on the boots.

It was after one o'clock when they left. 'If you break down don't come back here. You were offered a bed and didnae take it,' said Davie.

Lorna and Davie stood by the door. Andy and Myra watched them disappear and sighed when the car turned the corner. She put her hand on Andy's leg. They did not speak till they were on the motorway.

'I've had a great day.'

'Me too. How's the virus?'

'Seems fine.'

Passing Cumbernauld Andy said, 'That's the best day I've had since coming out of jail. In fact, I can't really remember a better day.'

'We should have them down to Glasgow.'

'Pull into that lay-by, Myra.'

'What for?'

'I want to kiss you.'

When his hand covered her breast, she pulled away, switched on the engine and jolted the car back onto the road.

'What was that about?'

'I'm sorry. We need to talk. Honestly, we really do need to talk.'

'Then talk.'

'Not just now. I can't. I'm too tired and too randy, too upset.'

'That's pretty much how I feel.'

Myra did not reply. She came off the motorway at Charing Cross, drove down Woodlands Road and stopped outside his close. She switched off the engine, turned and took his hand.

'I'm sorry.'

'What for?'

'I don't know, I just am.'

'What do we need to talk about?'

'Me.'

'What about you?'

'Did you notice I was drinking water tonight?'

'Uh-hu.'

'Why do you think I was drinking water?'

'Because you were driving.'

'No.'

'Then I give in. Tell me. It's nearly two o'clock.'

'Because I'm alcoholic.'

He didn't say anything.

'Haven't you anything to say?'

'A lot of the guys in jail were alkies. They went to meetings and talked about doing their sentences a day at a time.'

'That's the meetings I go to. I'm more than three years sober and I've never had a proper relationship. You're the first and I'm scared. It was why I ran away the first time and why I'm going now.'

'When are you going to sort this out?'

'I don't know.'

'And what's the problem?'

'I don't know that either. I need to talk to some people. I'm going to a meeting tomorrow, maybe two. I'll phone you.'

'When?'

'I don't know.'

'Then phone me tomorrow.'

'What time?'

'When you've made up your mind what you're going to do, or when you know what you're doing for the rest of the day, say around lunchtime.'

'Okay. This is serious, Andy.'

'So you keep saying, but it isn't any more serious for you than it is for me.'

She smiled and kissed his hands. 'Off you go, you're looking tired. And take your pills.'

'Stop nagging.'

He opened the door.

'Andy.'

'What is it?'

'I want you to promise me something.'

'What?' He closed the door.

'I want you to promise you'll never lie to me. No matter what, I want to know the truth.'

'Okay.'

'Say it.'

'Say what?'

'Say, I promise never to lie to you.'

'I promise never to lie to you.'

'Fine.'

He got out and looked back in the car with the door opened. She smiled and said, 'Goodnight.' Then as he was about to close the door she said: 'I think I love you.'

No one is born in the West End of Glasgow. Everyone moves there. It is a suburb of incomers.

There are times in summer when Byres Road appears festive, as though the flower sellers, buskers, fly posters and beggars, sandwich boards and preachers were there for an occasion.

Byres Road suits the early winter evenings when the light changes and rain disfigures buildings, when the sky is both pewter and lead, frozen solid, though few on Byres Road seem to look at the sky, especially on a night like this.

The district, street and city are a concentration of oppositions, where the buildings are visual reminders of history, where vibrations of privacy and participation mingle. This used to be a port and is no more. This was the world centre of manufacture. The manufacturing heroes lived with poverty and its consequences, violence, low esteeem, escapism. They are not considered as important as the men who employed them. This is a city where tokenism sits beside perpetuality, where one false premise is locked with another, where everyone is right, where myth is reality and history struggles to retain a past which is the same as other pasts: masters and workers and masters and workers and masters and workers.

Glasgow absorbs everything and retains itself. Having incorporated the loss of manufacture it is now sponging the tourists, tarting itself like Edinburgh. By moving across the city, or even a mile in another direction, the city changes. One is capable of the same rejuvenation by moving a mile across London, Paris, Rome or New York, by moving any city mile, made up of villages and small communities. In Glasgow the exchanges are more extreme, from darkness to light, from affluence to poverty, noise to silence, from public to private and so on.

Glasgow has always absorbed the stranger, Native Glaswegians started elsewhere, mostly Ireland or the Highlands of Scotland. Here the native accepts the city he has never seen. He knows it is there because someone told him. The commuter experiences the journey and little else. This city and all cities belong to those who search for something. For them it is the city of magnificent distances, the final destination.

Commuters do not last. They live in the worst of all possible worlds, staying in places with no vitality, experiencing the runt of the city, seeing none of the secret city natives love and searchers see. They have never smelled the George Square hyacinths on the corner of Albion Street at two in the morning; they have never seen the rabbits on the Clydeside Expressway or the packs of Pollokshaws foxes, kestrels in the city centre; they have never read a paper in the park while the band played, never seen the city empty at Easter, never seen a seagull raise its beak in the middle of Springburn, never been wakened by the traffic or a taxi or a shout, never watched the river change or done any of the sentimental and classic trivialities which are the sound of the city's breath. Commuters are the cursed of the earth, constantly forced to retrace their steps.

The city is the most complicated of human devisings; it has harnessed nature. We brush our teeth with water from Loch Katrine and walk above a system of pipes and cables so complicated and essential that when the Parliamentary Road was cancelled, when the grid was abandoned in favour of randomly placed vertical streets, the old road was preserved to give access to the services. A city knows what it needs to maintain itself. We should have destroyed ourselves with hunger or traffic long ago, either that or the plague should have got us. This city is as compressed as a poem, changeless and changing, different to what it was twenty-five or even ten years ago. There are new buildings and old façades with new interiors. The population shifts. The railway station is a shopping mall, the motorway a traffic jam, the high-rise concrete flats and office blocks an embarrassment. We have the worst health record in the world. The newspapers are complacent and patronising, the taxi drivers rude, the police unavailable, the hospitals mismanaged and overworked. We are as discontented as ever we were. We complain about Christmas and love the New Year. We like children and old people, our football teams are the greatest and no one anywhere can drink like us. We are wide and double wide. We laugh in the street and keep going. It is too late now; we'll never change.

This city is redundant as a watchmaker and lost as Atlantis, has been destroyed and regenerated so many times, taken the wrong direction or no direction, survived and persisted, replicating itself in the image of itself with the same name.

The West End is full of students; young aspiring poets and actors, painters, dancers, singers, writers, comedians, linguists, scientists, doctors, crazies and dreamers. It has more than any other part of the city, though every part has some. They live in their rooms and they look out the window. They own what they see.

Andy wakened as though he had slept for three or four hours, or slept with bad dreaming, yet it was almost midday. He could not remember the dreams but knew they were there.

He ground the coffee beans, made the coffee, went back to

bed and stared at the ceiling, aware of what he wanted. Lying in bed would have been too easy. It had happened before, a wasted day.

He thought it was Saturday, but knew it was Sunday. It felt like Sunday; a slow state of dreamy recovery, inactivity and as near to silence as Glasgow gets.

He dare not think about Myra.

When he felt like this in jail, he liked to work. It took his mind off what was happening. He called work what everyone in the jail called work, the things they did for themselves, that which had nothing to do with the regime. Andy's work was the Open University course and at times like this he researched his essays.

There was no point in getting a newspaper. He wouldn't read it any more than he would have read a novel. He wanted to walk, but Myra might phone. He tidied his room, dusted the shelves, wiped the table tops and vacuumed the carpet, cleaned out the bird cage and listened to the radio. The phone rang twice before it was Myra. He answered all calls.

'How's you?'

'Fine.'

'Did you sleep?'

'Not too well. Quite badly in fact.'

'I hardly slept at all. I feel shattered.'

'What's happening, Myra?'

'I'm going to a meeting at one o'clock. Then I'm going out for my tea and going to another meeting tonight. Do you mind?'

'I don't know. What happens?'

'There's a good meeting tomorrow night near you. Woodlands Road; do you know the wee Methodist church on the corner, opposite what used to be the Three In One pub?'

'Would they let me in?'

'Sure. Anybody can go. Will I come round and get you?'

'What time?'

'Seven. The meeting starts at eight and usually finishes before ten. So we can talk after that.'

'Fine.'

'I'd better go.'

'Did you mean what you said last night?'

'When?'

'You know when.'

'Yeah. What about you?'

'I think so, but I've been wrong before.'

'See you tomorrow.'

'Bye.'

'Bye.'

'I miss you.'

'Yeah.'

He did not know when the worm went. He thought it arrived when he went to jail, but knew it was there before that. The headaches arrived with the jail and had to do with the heating system; jail was always warm. The worm came and went. Sometimes it was there, sometimes not. Sometimes it was strong and he could feel it turn inside him, could feel it crying for food and attention. Most of the time it wasn't there.

He remembered the house in William Street. They and the cats lived in three rooms. He lay at night, listening to the trams on Anderston Main Street. Sometimes a blue spark lit the yellow room. The curtains were thin; the light from the street lamps threw shadows on the ceiling.

His bed was next to the wall. He knew the steps and shuffles, who stopped for breath on the landing, who sang, who whistled up the stair for the door to open. He knew his father's step.

Jake told stories about the city, small incidents related as if they were living in a mythical town, Glasgow was as real as Valparaiso or the Cape of Good Hope.

'I worked in the Beresford Hotel at the top of Elmbank Street with a German head waiter called Charlie Kaufman. That place was built for the Empire Exhibition at Bellahouston Park. The exhibition opened on the same day as Hitler met Mussolini; it celebrated an empire that would be destroyed by war, pathetic really. Ten minutes' walk from where we lived in Grant Street is work by the finest architects. John Keppie, the man who gave Mackintosh a start, has a building near there. Mackintosh, of course, designed the art school up on Garnethill. There is a Thomson warehouse on Sauchiehall Street and a church on St Vincent Street, as well as churches by John Honeyman and Burnet, terraces by Charles Wilson and John Baird and a wee sliver of a building by James Salmon. Look them up and see what else they did, especially Salmon. Look at The Hatrack. Ten floors in a single-house plot.'

This was when Jake came in with the food, when cheese and crackers were in the middle of the table, when Jake and Rose drank Mouton Cadet or Château Rothschild from earthenware cups that clicked when they touched, like stones. This was when Eileen was sleeping and he was just about big enough to be allowed up late to talk with his Dad, who sometimes came home smelling of drink.

The information now seemed useless. His father had left him with a clutch of trivia, easily obtainable elsewhere, of interest because of his father's obsession.

Everything was pared to the last night, the dark blue suit, white shirt, silver cuff-links and polka-dot tie, the black shoes with the shiny toecaps. Did Mozart know that K595 would be his last concerto and is it really the rhythm of Mahler's heart we hear in the Ninth Symphony? Did Van Gogh know these crows were his last and why was Goethe calling for light?

Saturday afternoon, after a walk along Sauchiehall Street to get Andy a pair of shoes; Jake bought him an ice-cream and wet his handkerchief with saliva to clean Andy's mouth. 'We'll need to take a walk, you and I,' he said, putting the handkerchief back in his pocket. 'Some Sunday afternoon when no one's about we'll go off on the wander and look at buildings. I never got a chance, but you will. If you don't want to be an architect, fine; but at least you'll get the chance.'

Andy looked at buildings in search of his father. The city was where his daddy got lost. Remembering the trivia kept his father alive.

He remembered the rush around the kitchen, his father in his trousers and braces, putting the studs in his collar while Rose ironed his shirt. 'I won't be late,' he said before he closed the door. He was back five minutes later.

'Where the hell are my keys?'

'Wherever you left them.'

'Rose. I need my keys.'

'Then find them.'

'Andy.'

'His name's Andrew.'

'Help me get my keys.'

Jake found the keys in his pocket. He gave a lopsided smile, put his forefinger to his mouth and said shush. 'Not a word,' he said.

Andy knew before anyone else. He heard strange footsteps on the stairs.

'This is it.'

'Are you going to tell her?'

'I suppose so. The best thing you can do is make a cup of tea and keep quiet.'

He heard the police voices and the constant, repeated questions, counterpointed by his mother's sobs. 'Go away back to bed,' she said when he opened the kitchen door, the two men in their trench coats, cats in the lobby.

No one told him; they assumed he knew. No one sat him down to say the worst. For a while he thought it could not be true, for a while he thought they'd made a mistake. He planned the walks they'd do together, Park Circus, Great Western Road and for the first time alone he went to the art galleries, looking for an answer in the paintings, a sign that his mystery could be solved in their greater mysteries. He absorbed the works and the worm came.

He asked the seagulls in the park. Cats told him his daddy would soon be back and the dogs ran away to fetch him. He saw his father in the paintings of burghers and peasants as well as in every man with a good blue suit. He saw his daddy with his finger to his lips and every night heard his tread on the stair.

He went to school on the day of the funeral. Teachers looked at him and his sister whenever they passed. Previously they had been ignored, now the teachers seemed as if they wanted to say something, but were unsure about what to say. Once the first sentence was out they'd be okay, but they could not think of the first sentence, caught between being teachers and people, staring with a mixture of curiosity and pity. He disliked his celebrity status. Eileen went to sleep with her mother. Now he was in the room by the wall, listening alone.

He knew for sure when he read the papers. His mother told him to stop moping, to pull himself together: 'Stand up straight and act like a man.' He wanted to smell the soap from his daddy's face, to kiss the roughness of his beard.

He was told of the trial when he knew he was going to stay with Granny, when he knew he was going to another school. Kids in the playground told him. They never quite said anything, never more than innuendo till the trial was over and the engagement announced.

'Your maw's a bun,' said a boy with short hair and impetigo.

'A fucken ride,' said his pal.

'Imagine letting the guy that murdered your da ride her. Cannae have any self respect's what my da said.'

He knew it could never happen again. 'Your son was like an animal,' said the impetigoed boy's father, whose shirt did not button around the belly. 'He was screaming and spitting. He kicked my boy in the privates and clawed him like an animal. Your son should be put down.'

'I'm sorry,' said Andy's mother.

'Sorry's not good enough. What are you going to do about it?'

The worm disappeared while he was fighting, or maybe he just forgot it was there, for it came back, worse this time, demanding food and more attention.

While it was away it was gathering its strength, resting like the Calgacus army. This was the same, the same injustice. First his dad and now the jail.

He spent the afternoon with a newspaper in the Kibble Palace. This was Sunday.

It rained. The sky was red and grey. The lights lay on the wet black streets and for a moment or two the smell of dust and rain was there, like a memory.

In the Palace, the grey light was tinged with blue. A woman sat on the bench beside him, crossed her legs and smiled. 'Do you mind if I smoke?' she asked, inhaling.

Andy shook his head.

'Thanks. It's a filthy habit, sure it is. I've been smoking since I was thirteen. Embassy Regal was my first cigarette. We saved up the coupons and sold them. You could get gifts and things, but we just sold them. I got twenty Embassy Regal from a man in a shop when I was twelve. He gave them to me and I gave them to my mother. She asked me where I got them and I told her I found them, but I never found them, I got given them by Mister Edmund Wallasey, shopkeeper of Dumbarton Road. He asked me what I wanted and I said cigarettes, though I didn't smoke. I didn't want anything. Dirty old devil. Edmund Wallasey. That's the bastard son's name in King Lear. Edmund, the bastard son of Gloucester, a whoremaister. He has two sisters on the go. Dirty devil. Wallasey took me into his back shop and footered with himself. He told me to unbutton my blouse and he gave me cigarettes.'

She moved her leg back and forward, bouncing from the knee. Her right shoe dangled from her toes. The tip of the heel was metal screwed into white plastic. The black plastic covering was frayed around the heel and the shoe was split at the foot. Her right hand rested on her knee and the cigarette smoke rose in a single line, diminishing into air. Andy went the other way and she did not look.

The air was cleaner. Sunday evening on Byres Road: people on their way to the pub, returning rented videos, buying bread and milk, finishing afternoon walks, going home.

He passed the house, knowing she wouldn't be there. He saw the car and paused for a while, then hurried away in case she came out, scared of getting caught; as if he was doing something wrong, as if he shouldn't be there.

He followed the grid, like butter on a kitten's paws, back onto Byres Road, over Gilmorehill with the University on the right, down Gibson Street onto Woodlands Road. He had too much energy to go indoors and with nothing else to do carried on walking past West End Park Street, down towards the Charing Cross.

He waited by the traffic lights on the corner of St George's Road, with Grant Street down to the left. A heavy tremolo rose from the shallows of the motorway, no more than a primeval hum, like breath passing over bamboo. The volley increased as vehicles entered or left the tunnel. The hum was constant, like wind in the telegraph wire or the slap of wire against a flagpole. Turning the corner of the Charing Cross and Albany Mansions, into Sauchiehall Street, he saw Fenian McGuire.

The story goes that Fenian went into Glasgow's most expensive tailor and said, 'Make us a suit that disnae fit like this one, wi a Crombie to match, two white shirts and a Celtic tie.' He was rounder in the belly and his hair was thinner. Fenian was a gambler and a lawyer, outside the casino trying to hail a taxi, looking down to Charing Cross and the one-way system.

'Look who it is.'

'How's it going, Fenian.'

'Mustn't grumble. How long have you been out?'

'Maybe a week or two.'

'I imagine it's more than that. You working?'

'Not yet. How's the Polis?'

'If you mean who I think you mean, my client left the force. Started up on his own in a wee security firm, you know the sort of thing.'

'Debt collection?'

'Cracked it in one. Rounding up the Poll Tax defaulters. Maybe you've no heard of the Poll Tax but?'

'I've heard it mentioned. How come you're vacating the premises this early?'

'I have to go a place to see a man about a dug. Here's a taxi.'

A girl ran across the road, got in the driver's side and the cab moved off. She gave Fenian the V-sign as the cab passed. Fenian offered Andy a cigar. 'That's the kind of city you've come home to,' he said.

Andy sat in the Social Security Office for two hours, long enough to do the *Glasgow Herald* crossword and read *The Odyssey* up to Book V, 'Calypso'.

'Paterson.'

He told her he was thinking of going on holiday.

'When?'

'I don't know yet. In a day or two.'

'And where are you going?'

'I don't know.'

'Can you say how long you will be away?'

'Not long.'

'Come back and see us when you have further details.'

Walking back through the Botanic Gardens he smiled at the ground elder amongst the bushes. He didn't know, could not say what he would have done if Fenian had asked him to go into the casino. He could not understand why the possibility scared him. He had no desire to gamble, not even cards. Of course, there were card games in jail, but not seriously, nothing more than a game of cribbage or solo, that sort of game.

He phoned Fenian from one of the boxes at the foot of Great George Street. A secretary voice told him to wait.

'Hello.' Fenian had a way of answering the telephone which made him sound like someone else.

'It's Andy Paterson.'

'When I told you to get in touch I thought you might give it a day or two.'

'Sorry. I was a bit confused after last night. I thought I'd better phone up and check.'

'Check on what?'

'That you want to see me.'

'What's your plans?'

'I'm busy tonight.'

'Glad to hear it. I meant for the next day or two.'

'I might be going away. I'd like to get out of the city. I've a lot on my mind.'

'Sensible man. Call me when you get back. Are you strapped for cash?'

'I don't think so.'

Because the weather was unsettled as himself, grey like tarnished silver, he spent the afternoon in the Mitchell Library.

A hinged comb gathered Myra's hair at the back, giving her face and neck a sculpted look, not unlike the first time he saw her. Andy smiled, imagining the time it had taken to look so casual.

'What's funny?'

'Nothing. You look great.'

'Can I leave my car here? I thought we might walk down.'

They arrived just before eight. Four people in the church foyer welcomed visitors. It seemed as though everyone shook Andy's hand as he moved through the crowd from the door to the serving hatch. The men kissed Myra's cheek. There was a smoking section nearest the door. They got a polystyrene cup of instant coffee and sat in the non-smoking section.

The meeting began promptly at eight o'clock and was over by half past nine. The first speaker spoke about drinking, the second about recovery. Andy was surprised by the way they discussed personal horror, how simply and directly they spoke and how much he indentified with their experience. Everyone shook hands with their neighbours at the end of the meeting, had tea, sandwiches and cake and gathered into informal groups.

'What did you think?' Myra took his hand as they left the meeting.

He smiled. 'I can see why you like it.'

'I've grown to like it. In the beginning I went because I had to go.'

She hung her coat behind the door. He made coffee. She smiled when he came in.

'Watch you don't spill it,' she said. Andy turned on the gas fire and covered the bird cage. He put out the central light and lit the small reading lamp by the side of the bed. Myra put her coffee down on the carpet. 'I'll try not to spill it,' he said.

'Sorry. Tell me; tell me when I do it, will you. Please tell me. I don't want to be like that, I don't want to be that kind of woman. Did I tell you? My mother thinks men are poor souls who need looking after.'

'You said. That was a very mild example.'

'I know, but I don't like it. That's one of the troubles with AA; you can lose your sense of perspective. It's possible to hide in it, avoiding all contact with civilians in the outside world. You only meet other alcoholics and you use the standards you have for them in dealing with other people. Recovering alcoholics set themselves very high standards, but are usually quite tolerant of others.'

'Are you all right there?'

'Yes. Why?'

'You look as if you're going to start on something which could be quite difficult. I wondered if you were okay, if you wanted to sit near me?'

They moved down to the floor, beside each other, facing the

fire. She drew her skirt around her legs and rested her face and hands on her knees, speaking in whispers. 'Things like that make me love you. It scares me sometimes. I don't know why you're doing it, whether it's concern or if you're as unsure of yourself as me. I don't want to know, though, and I don't want you to stop doing it.'

'Did you know you've still got the price tag on your shoe?'

She smiled and started picking it loose, removing ticks of paper, leaving a patch of adhesive.

'You were saying?'

'I wasn't. I don't know where to start. There was a while when I thought it was like an artificial leg factory.'

'What was?'

'AA. You go there if you only have the one leg and have an artificial leg fitted, so you can seem normal and get on with your life. Then you spend your time talking with other people who have artificial legs and there are two topics of discussion: you either feel sorry for yourselves and tell each other how horrible it is to have an artificial leg, or you tell each other how well you're managing, that you've found the secret and feel sorry for the poor souls with two good legs.'

'Do you still feel that?'

'I changed my mind. I really do not want to drink again and booze is only a symptom of what was wrong with me. I know that. AA gives my life a purpose. It makes me feel useful. When I sobered up I was scared. I was unsure of myself, constantly seeking the approval of others; there's still a tendency to be like that, to give people more importance than they deserve, to please them. I know, I know; there is also the business of taking over. That's it, pal. That's the way we are, from one extreme to another, no half measures, no middle ground.'

'When I came out of jail, I thought everybody had been in

jail. It's only now that I'm beginning to believe it's permanent, that I'm out for good and I'm not going back. It's only now I'm thinking about what I want to do.'

'Exactly, and we need to talk about that. Because I was unsure of my opinions, I thought everyone else was unsure of their opinions. It took a while, almost three years, to realise this might not be so. For months after I stopped drinking the simplest things became a source of wonder. It sounds silly. I had no idea how much I'd lost: the taste of a buttered roll, the smell of grass, flowers, that sort of thing. Sounds corny, doesn't it. Pathetic really. I think it was just the fact of being alive, as though there was a misted window which had been wiped and I could see again clearly. It is difficult to explain to someone who has never known it; recovering alcoholics immediately know what I'm talking about.'

'Maybe I understand more than you think. As I've said, I'm not long out of jail.'

'I know, darling. I'm sorry. I'll never forget the first time I heard Monteverdi on the radio. It paralysed me. I was forced, compelled to do nothing but listen. Then I went to a jazz concert and cried because it was so wonderful. I did the same in the art galleries.'

'The old galleries?'

'I haven't been for a while.'

'They've changed the rooms.'

'You said. It's odd, isn't it. How much a part of everybody's collective experience that place is. I spent my first year going to theatre, to opera and to AA meetings. It was wonderful. I'll never forget the first time I read a book sober. Silly things people take for granted were new to me. They were exciting and I was embarrassed to say, I was frightened in case folk thought I was foolish. I believed only an alcoholic could understand. I'm sure you'll understand. That's why,' she stopped speaking, staring at the floor. 'That's why I didn't want to sleep with you until we'd talked,' she said, 'so you could know what it means to me. This is my first time, Andy.'

She looked into the empty coffee mug, cupped in her hands like a mouse; then she jerked her head up and stared at him, demanding a response.

'I think it's that way for me too. I mean, I want to get it right, but I'm scared I'll fuck it up the way I've always fucked it up or had it fucked up for me. I don't trust myself to be good at this. I'll expect it to go wrong and I might even try to make it go wrong.'

The clatter of voices came in from the street, noisy voices coming from the pub. They obviously thought they were speaking normally, walking in groups of four, five or six down West End Park Street. A car passed and the group outside the window, three or four voices, male and female, young voices, confident, slightly slurred voices, shouted, 'Lights.' They repeated the word two or three times, rising louder and running after the car: 'Lights.' 'Lights.' 'Lights.' Down towards West Princes Street they raised a cheer.

'People sometimes think we do it for religious reasons, because we want to be good people or better people.' Myra put the mug on the floor. 'We don't do it to be closer to God. We do it because we have no alternative. If we don't do it, we drink. I'm not going back to that, not for you, not for anything. I stopped for the same reason I started, I wanted to feel better. And that's why I don't want lies in my life. It was all deceit. I'm trying to cultivate an alternative way of living. A day's as much as I can cope with, that's what I'm saying. I feel the same way as you do and I'm promising nothing except to try, to really try to get it right today.'

'Were you in love before?'

'No. And I never even thought I was. I knew it wasn't love, but I thought it would be okay. I thought there was no such thing.'

'What happened?'

'Lasted about a year. I got fed up. He was bewildered. Didn't know what to do. Didn't know what was wrong and couldn't understand why I was going when I said there was nothing wrong. He interfered with my drinking, that was all. I couldn't drink the way I wanted. I was drinking with the brakes on. Jesus, that's awful.'

'What about the doings and the baby you lost?'

'They were part of it, of course, but drinking made me controllable. As long as there was drink at the end it was okay; I'd put up with anything to get a drink. If someone had said that to me at the time I'd've been highly indignant, but I can see it was true. If he gave me a doing, I could let go; I could drink the way I wanted to all along. If he hammered me I had an excuse. It was his fault. Don't look at me like that; I know it doesn't make sense. Why must everything make sense. Some things are just unreasonable and make no sense at all. This is a contradiction, Andy; another contradiction. My life is full of them. Just when you think you've got it, along comes something else. You're going to have to accept the contradictions. Recognise it doesn't make sense and you'll get on fine.'

'I wasn't thinking that. I don't have a problem with contradictions. Folk have often told me one thing and done another. I was thinking about my own marriage. I know it's over. She's settled and back with the guy she was going with before she married me and I don't mind. But there's something else and I don't know what it is; there's something not quite right there. I'll tell you later. It's not important.'

She touched his leg and kissed him with her tongue protruding slightly. She was crying.

'What is it?'

'You.'

'What about me?'

'You and your life. Trying to sort out things you don't understand.'

'I understand some of it.'

'Like what? Like that you don't know what's wrong with you, so when anybody asks you say, Nothing, hoping it'll fool them and they'll go away.'

'It isn't that. Ever read *Don Quixote*?'

'No.'

'I read it in the jail. It's about this preposterous old man who has an insane belief in himself, against all odds. Everyone around him, the reader, his servant, know he's crazy, but he keeps on believing in himself and trusting what he thinks. I've often thought I could do with some of that.'

'What you need to believe is that something worthwhile could happen to you, or even to someone from your background. Do you know, when I got sober and started feeling good I didn't think that I deserved it.'

'I know it has to do with me and what's inside and not taking second best. Everybody tells you, Molière, Descartes, Voltaire, the lot; a clear line of preposterous egotists. But it isn't just that. It's all we've got. Ourselves. If we don't believe in ourselves we're nothing. Which is why I hate the patronising nonsense you get, especially in the arts. This play, opera, whatever, is not you and has nothing to do with you and you won't understand it, so we'll cut out the boring bits, put in a drunk man and make it accessible, easy to understand. Cyrano, the Cid, Quixote, Commedia, the basis of European literature is about a man who says I am as good as you, not because of my birth, my wealth or position, or what I know, what I believe or what I can do, but because of my potential. I can be what I want to be. I am uncontainable.'

'Even you?'

'I know the theory, Myra. That's all. The rest is hard.'

She looked at his face and thought he was going to cry. He tried a smile instead.

They sat in silence for a long time. Shades of traffic drifted into the room, the occasional shuffle of a man and his dog, car horns from Woodlands Road.

Eventually he reached forward and played with the strands of her hair, kissing the top of her head every now and then, reaching down to rub her stomach with the palm of his hand. She had a packet of tissues.

'I knew it would be like this,' she said and blew her nose. 'What are you going to do?'

'I thought we might go to bed.'

'I don't mean now. I mean, generally.'

'With my life? University I think, I don't know. I want to know if the Open University stuff's any good. I've got to find out what's needed to go full time.'

'What'll you study?'

'I thought about history, English, that sort of thing. I don't know what I'll do when I've finished, or even if I'll finish, but it would keep me active until I decide.'

'What was the Open University course like?'

'Terrific. I didn't start until a couple of years ago. They might give me credits or something and let me go to university with what I've got. I did the Humanities course, concentrating on English and history. I wrote about Glasgow.'

'You still haven't let me see your essays.'

'I meant to. I must have forgot. Why did you ask what I was going to do?'

'I don't know. Well, that's not really true. I want to start nursing. I've applied for psychiatric nursing. It's going to be difficult. Some of these people play God, turning alkies into social drinkers and so on. I might need to revise my attitude before I start. But the reason I asked about you was that I've got us a house.'

'What do you mean?'

'Along the road; West Princes Street, two rooms, kitchen and bathroom, fully furnished. I'm moving in at the end of the week and I don't want you near the place.'

'I was thinking of going walking at the weekend.'

'Good.'

'What's this house?'

'I've been coming and going about it for long enough. I had my settlement from the divorce in the building society doing nothing. A woman I know is getting married, so she's selling her house and furniture. She offered it to me and the deal obviously benefits everybody. I gave in my notice to the landlord when I met you. Coincidence, really. I'm fed up living in the basement. This flat's gorgeous. It's on the top floor, on a corner with one of those corner windows. You'll love it.'

'What do you mean, us?'

'I thought it would be a good idea to give you a set of keys and we could see how it goes. Obviously, you could keep this place on until we were sure. It's a new start for both of us.'

'Do I have a say in this?'

'That was meant to be a suggestion. I want to know what you think.'

'Would you like to get married?'

'Is this a proposal?'

'I don't know.'

'Davie and Lorna think you're wonderful. They phoned to tell me.'

'Are you really moving in at the weekend?'

'Saturday morning. Davie's bringing a van. He's coming for my stuff. I'm spending Saturday and Sunday getting used to my new house and I thought you might like to come for dinner on Sunday night.'

'Are you working tomorrow?'

'Day off.'

'Fancy coming up to the Social with me?'

'I want to go to bed with you first.'

They did not go to the Social Security Office. Too many people had their benefit stopped because of their honesty: unable to take a job if offered, was the official reason.

Andy went on his own. Myra began packing up at Huntly Gardens.

The repeated appointment system, the hostile and incompetent staff were evidence of a bureaucracy surviving by and for itself. The only people who did not know this were those who never dealt with it. There were a repeated number of forms to be completed, letters to be written and long delays.

There was the matter of his revised housing benefit. If there was a change in his circumstances, he would need a new benefit to comply with the changes, was what they said. First the housing and then the Social. They were interchangeable, the same attitude, the same trick questions.

The new office in Maryhill Road had glass doors with numbers and a loudspeaker system. His clerk told him to wait and went to chat to a girl in the office. He watched them and thought of the barmen, bus drivers, taxi drivers, waiters, those who serve the public and come to dislike their customers.

Afterwards he went back to the Social Security Office. A man was shouting because his benefit had not arrived. 'I'm fed up being lied to,' he said. 'This is the fourth time you have told me my money's in the post.'

He told Myra later how much he admired the small man with the greasy hair, the unshaven man with dirty fingernails. Andy was conscious of not saying what he wanted to say because of their power, because counter clerks could make it awkward. He was aware of having to take the attitude, the queues and the system. To complain was to ensure punishment. The man who was told his benefit cheque was in the post would have to appeal more than once.

This was at night, in bed again talking. He had gone to the Mitchell, finished at nine, met Myra when she finished in the café and walked back to West End Park Street.

He was doing an essay. The problem with researching a piece based on newspaper cuttings is that today's newspapers can hardly be believed, so are we to suppose they were ever any different? Anyone with any experience of the press tells how distorted the newspaper account was. Poverty has always had an interesting relationship with art; now it was having a relationship with media, especially television. Television stories always happen at night. We seldom see the homeless and what they have to contend with during the day. Night-time was dangerous and slightly sexy. Good people stay at home at night.

How accurate was this picture? Most poverty is not lived on the streets. Most poverty is endured indoors in housing schemes and bedsit flats, in housing benefit and Social Security offices. Most poverty is relentless, ugly and boring. Poverty would not make good television.

*

'Tell me again,' said Granny. 'Tell me how you gave him a doing.'

They were waiting for Grandpa to come back from the pub. He told the story of the boy with impetigo.

'Was he bleeding?'

'Just a wee bit.'

'Did he cry?'

'He was crying. There were snotters and everything.'

'Did you kick him?'

'I kicked him in the privates.'

'Was it sore?'

'He screamed.'

'Good. Was it for your mother you did it? Did you do it because he was lying?'

'No. I did it because he was telling the truth. I did it for my daddy.'

'That's right. You did it because your daddy deserved a better wife than that, sure you did.'

'That's right.'

'I know it's right. By the way, your mother's coming to see you.'

Malky never came to the house. He waited with a cup of tea in the Lido Café at Saracen Cross.

He remembered his mother in a pink or lilac suit, with a matching hat and handbag. His sister wore floral dresses, her hair in pigtails or bunches when she was little, with ribbons to match the tone of her dress, yellow ribbons, blue, green or red ribbons. Her hair was cut when she was eleven, short, clipped around her ears, it made her face look pinched, thin and hungry.

'That wean could do wi a feed,' said Granny. 'Stand up and

let us have a look at you. My God, look at the legs on her, like matchsticks. It's a bowl of soup you're needing, a good bowl of soup that'll stick to your ribs.'

'How have you been, Mrs Paterson, and how's your husband?' His mother's tone was formal when she spoke to his grandmother, as though she was speaking on the telephone. Grandpa was never there when they called.

'I want this boy back here for five o'clock. He has his tea to get. I feed him.'

His sister often sobbed. His mother seemed perplexed, but she stuck it out and left when Granny dismissed her.

Once, just before Christmas, as she was going, his mother left an envelope on the kitchen table. 'I want you to get something for yourself and your husband, Mrs Paterson. I'll see to Andrew's present as usual.'

Granny's face turned white and she started to shake; she could not control herself. First her hands; when she tried to grip them, they shook the more. She stared at his mother, straining forward, like sightless eyes trying to see.

'If I was a man I'd kill you,' she said. 'Here and now, in front of your children, I would cut your throat. Do you think I would take your prostitute's leavings? How dare you insult me. We may be poor, but we're never so poor that we need to whore ourselves out for Christmas.'

She grabbed his sister, twisting the child's hair around in her hands. 'Do you know what a prostitute is? Do you know what a prostitute does? Ask your mother. Ask her. She'll tell you. Then ask her where she gets her money. Ask her how she manages to keep you. Ask her. Go on, ask her.'

Eileen started to sob, grabbing the air as her head was twisted back and she stared at the ceiling.

'The child knows. That child already knows about her mother. She'll hear what goes on in the bedroom and she'll maybe even see it. Get out of here, the pair of you. She'll end up the same as you, but the boy'll be all right so long as he's with me. I'll look after him, along with everything else I've got to do.'

He sat at the window, the smell of petrol rising from the street, watching his mother tug his crying sister along Bardowie Street to Saracen Cross. His Granny started cleaning the house. After washing the floor, she wrung the dishcloth into the bucket. 'I'm imagining this is your mother's neck,' she said.

For the first time he thought he had a worm inside him.

*

Myra woke early on Saturday morning. Showered and dressed, she pulled the duvet off the bed. 'Get up, you lazy bastard,' she said. 'Breakfast's ready.'

Myra was sitting by the kitchen table with a mug of tea. Andy did not always waken immediately. Jail had made him a heavy sleeper.

'I thought you said breakfast was ready.'

'I lied. There's tea in the pot. I'm going out to get the breakfast stuff in a minute.'

They were sitting on opposite sides of the kitchen table, her bare feet on top of his, reading the paper, breakfast finished, when Davie arrived.

'Did I disturb anything?'

'Not at all. Want a cup of tea?'

'Wouldn't mind. I've brought the stuff, Andy.'

'Great. Let's see it.'

'You two chatter about your manly things while I make the sandwiches. And you can pour your own tea.'

'I've brought the Ordnance Survey and there's a couple of the wee Pathfinder maps as well. Look at this. They tell you where the bloody stones are. And that's the book, son. All you need. Wish it was me.'

'Have you got the key?'

'Next door. They know you're coming. He said he'd phone this morning.'

'Where is it on here?'

'There it is: Gallin, just beyond Meggernie Castle. And you know about crossing the hill beside Ben Lawyers? Either that or you go up the glen from Fortingall.'

There was enough food for a weekend. Myra made sandwiches and a flask of coffee. 'We won't be here when you get back,' she said. 'Have a lovely time and come back safely.'

'I'm only going away for a night.'

'You have the keys and the new address?'

'It's all here. I said to Davie, he and Lorna should try to come down sometime during the week.'

'Fine. You arrange it. They can go to your place. You can feed the kids and babysit while we go out and have a nice time. Drive safely, darling.'

Outside the city, on the road to Aberfoyle, doing seventy miles an hour, he deliberately slowed. He hadn't driven so fast in the Beetle and realised this was the influence of Myra's careful driving. He put in a tape of the Mozart Serenade for Thirteen Wind Instruments, wound down the window and ate the jelly babies she had left in the car.

This was his first time outside the city. Driving towards the forest and the mountains, with clouds scattering above the windshield, the elegant music and invention, Andy felt a desperate joy.

He turned right at the Rob Roy Motel, passed the Lake of

Menteith, left at the bend, past Loch Rusky, through the woods, left again and along to Callander.

For no reason he stopped. He later said it was because he wanted to see someplace other than Glasgow, which was the only place he'd been since coming out of jail, but at the time was not so certain.

Callander is a monument to consumerism. The place depressed him. What looked like a disused church had been converted into the Rob Roy Centre, with a ludicrous three-coloured painting of a warlike Highlander. It looked pathetic, like a bluff hand at brag. They knew they had nothing but would brazen it out, attracting folk who knew no better.

There was an arts and crafts fair in the Rob Roy Centre. Solemn-faced people, most of the men had beards, stood behind stalls selling wood or ceramics, a few oils and some knitting. The newspapers said small businesses would regenerate the economy.

A young girl served his tea. She was around fourteen and very self-conscious. She gave him a plate with a scone, butter and jam, included in the price of the ticket, and asked if he was enjoying the fair.

'I've just arrived,' he said.

'Are you a visitor?'

'Passing through on my way to Glen Lyon.'

'Where's that?'

'In the middle of Perthshire.'

'It's lovely there. I hope you enjoy it. And I'm sure you'll find something to your liking at the fair.'

There was a trickle of cars leaving Callander, elderly couples with the Saturday shopping. In a mile or two he had the road to himself, with Ben Ledi rising left and the generous Loch Lubnaig. The road skirts Strathyre and Balquhidder and from

Lochearnhead climbs through Glen Ogle, with the Creag MacRanaich viaducts, which carried the railway across a landscape where few folk had walked, running along the side of the hill. Descending towards Glen Dochart he saw the Lawyers hills and the last movement of the Shostakovich Concerto for Piano and Trumpet carried him round the corner towards Killin; not as bad as Callander, but definitely heading in that direction.

Beyond Killin and above Loch Tay, the single-tracked road crossed the Lochan na Lairige pass. He wanted to stop round every corner. Behind the shieling remains at the horeshoe peaks of the Tarmachen Hills and again at the ridge behind Allt Bail a' Mhuilinn, which runs into the Lyon, he knew at last he was ready to die and desperate to live.

Over Bridge of Balgie, through the estate; the key was waiting and the house was cold. He lit the sitting-room fire and the Raeburn in the kitchen, had some soup and within an hour, as he was leaving, the house was warm. He had left Glasgow three hours ago; it was now a little over one o'clock.

A stream from Cam Chreag passed the side of his house. He crossed the bridge, walked up Gallin Brae to the Top Road, crossed the bridge before Moar Farm and set off climbing Creag Dubh. He stuck to the sheep paths, moving down the glen through woods and bracken. He didn't care. The joy was to be there.

He came across an ants' nest. On the surface, they appeared and disappeared like bubbles on a pot of boiling water, at times barely distinguishable amongst the movement. He watched for about five minutes, the way he watched bees on a flower or flies on a window-sill. Then, without knowing why, he smashed his foot into the side of the nest. It was more resilient than he thought and dented slightly at the bottom. The ants did not scatter, neither did they show any sign of panic. They simply started to rebuild their home. He wondered how they carried the grass, the colour of flame or a jaundiced face, the colour of his grandfather's eyes when he was blind.

He climbed the wood through patches of sunshine, his head wet with perspiration, his shirt sticking to his back and the tops of his legs sore. He was breathing heavily, stopping often, climbing slowly, rising though a ripple of whitish cloud, which was always behind, lifting and threatening to catch him. He was always thinking, When I get to this bit I'll be all right, it'll be clear; when he arrived, clouds were waiting. What he presumed to be the top was a plateau of grass and rocks, veined with sheep tracks. This is how people get lost, he thought. This is how it happens. They think they're all right and carry on, even though the mist is down, they take no heed. They believe they will be okay, because this is what happens to other people, not to them. Yet there was no other way to go. He could not descend. He carried on walking along the top, crossed a burn or two, with rocks and rowans, dipping to small and noisy waterfalls and suddenly the mist was over. He could see up the glen, Loch Lyon sparking in the distance, patches of water across the valley, the castle and estate and on the verge of the wood, the smoke still rising from the fires he'd lit, the awesome sweep of landscape.

It was now well after four o'clock. He sometimes walked and sometimes ran along the top, looking for a descent, when he came at last to a dip in the hill, a hanging valley at about 2000 feet where he could descend and climb the thousand feet or so to the ripple of peaks on the other side. The cloud was waiting. To the right and behind him was clear. Through the rising cloud he saw a rainbow, half imagined at first, a rainbow that seemed to be something else, a pale and lucid, colourless rainbow, white, a purer white against the white of the cloud, with a strand of azure flickering in and out of the rainbow like a line of mayflies. As he moved he saw there was nothing to stop the rising rainbow. It came from a hollow, with no ground beneath it, so the rainbow became a circle, a white circle against a white background, with a shimmering azure centre. There, in the middle, was his own reflection, his own shadow a light grey with a white and azure aura in the middle of the circular rainbow. He raised his right arm, waved and the left arm in the middle of the rainbow waved back. He stood staring at the figure till they all disappeared into the wind and the horseshoe of the glen lay where he and his rainbow used to be.

She had an answering machine. He phoned from the shop at Bridge of Balgie: 'I'm sorry there's no one here at the moment, but if you'd care to leave your name and number, I'll get back to you as soon as I can,' she said.

'It's me. I saw a rainbow and had some soup. I ate all your sandwiches and drank the coffee. Thanks for the jelly babies. I've also managed to make myself some spaghetti and this is just to let you know I'm all right. I've got the bottle in my bed and I'm going to snuggle up with a good book. I know it's only nine o'clock, but I feel quite tired. I miss you and keep seeing things I want you to see. Where the hell are you? Night-night.'

He got up when he wakened, just after six. Standing at the window with a cup of coffee, highland cattle in a field on the edge of the river, a herd of half a dozen deer tiptoed from the woods beside the stream, drinking, every now and then turning back to the woods or into the wind. Above them, a shape he thought was a crow spiralled in the sky, rising steadily, finding the thermal to take it down the glen. He thought it was a buzzard, or maybe an eagle, then, in one magnificent glide and swoop, it was gone and the last of the deer bounced into the woods.

He climbed on the other side of the glen, up the road towards the dam and the village of Lochs, submerged when Lochs Giorra and Daimh were joined. He climbed Stuchd an Lochain, unsure if the wind alone had watered his eye as he looked across at the Lawyers hills, the humps of Carn Mairg, to the top of the glen, the Wall of Rannoch and the Orchy hills beyond.

On the road going home, the house resting, key returned, he turned right at Glen Dochart, drove to Crianlarich, Glen Orchy and Glen Coe where it started to rain. He pulled into a lay-by, wound back the seat and slept, woken in the dark with a sore neck by the splash and rumble of a lorry and trailer. He drove back the way he came, then down Glen Falloch and Loch Lomond-side, staying awake with the windows down, the Prokofiev Seventh Symphony, the Rasumovskys and Kubelík conducting the *Glagolitic Mass*.

He came into Glasgow along Great Western Road, turned down Park Road, along Woodlands Road, round West End Park Street and then he was home. One a.m. He fumbled with the entry system key and ran to the top. She had a new brass nameplate above the old pull bell. Her doors had been stripped and varnished, everything was restored or preserved, cornices, handles and the glass front door.

He dumped his stuff and fumbled around the strange, dark house. As he came out the kitchen, Myra said, from the room opposite: 'If your name's Andy Paterson, where the hell have you been?'

He sat on the bed and yawned. 'Terrific,' said Myra.

'I have had a wonderful time.'

'What do you mean you saw a rainbow?'

'It was circular. Pale blue and white.'

'Your feet are cold. Do you like the house?'

'Love it.'

'How can you tell in the dark?'

'Do you always go to bed with your knickers on?'

'Depends. Only if I think it would be appreciated.'

'Move your arm round.'

Monday night and she went to her meeting. Andy worked in the Mitchell Library.

He had tried to phone Fenian McGuire and was told to call back three times. He phoned his home at half past eight.

'I hear you've been quite persistent.'

'I thought I'd let you know I was back in Glasgow.'

'Where did you go?'

'Glen Lyon.'

'Where's that?'

'Perthshire.'

'Nice part of the world that. What were you doing there?'

'Hillwalking.'

'I don't think I could get up a hill if you paid me.'

'You don't know what you're missing.'

McGuire coughed. 'That's they fags. I'll need to chuck them. Does the name Mickey Ryan mean anything to you?'

'No.'

'Mickey's a wee rascal and I wouldnae trust him as far as I could kick my Auntie Bridie down Buchanan Street with my bare feet.'

'This sounds a terrific tip-off. I cannae say I wasnae warned and I'll no ask you to defend me.'

'Code of conduct, son. You know what it's like yourself. Mickey likes to play wee games. He thinks he's a hard man and has occasionally been known to talk out the side of his mouth like James Cagney, but that's as far as it goes. He's as hard as your mother's bosom and has a house full of second prizes. Now, don't interrupt; Mickey sometimes does a wee bit work for me, this and that, nothing fancy, cash on the nail; he's a fucken pest. I've had a word with him and he's prepared to spend a wee while talking to you. He runs a taxi out of the Anderston Bus Station, Holm Street. Know it? I won't ask how. When you find him, get in his taxi and ask him to take you to Cranhill. Got it?'

'You're some operator, Fenian. This is sensational.'

'He'll ask if you want to go on the motorway and you'll say you want to go whatever way Mr McGuire goes. He will ask, Which Mr McGuire's that? And you'll say, Mr Gerard McGuire; he's a friend of mine.'

'Is that your name, Gerard?'

'Gerard Patrick Austin Aloysius; my parents were Irish of the Roman Catholic faith.'

'I'm running out of money. That's the pips.'

'By the way, talking of money: if Mickey Ryan asks you for anything, tell him to see me. Okay?'

'Tell me something, why are you being so nice to me?'

'Everybody deserves a wee break.'

The line went dead and the three ten pence pieces clunked into the machine.

He followed the grid, up the hill to Blythswood Square and down towards Holm Street, by the Anderston Bus Station, one of the buildings which destroyed the grid, a place where people get lost.

Women stood in doorways and along the pavement, standing singly or in groups of two and three with their knees bent, unconsciously tugging at the front of their skirts, smoking, ducking down as the cars went past to smile or nod at the driver. A young girl, pretty and nicely made up, her hair frizzed and gelled, wearing a long coat, her hands in the pockets, turned her head to the side as he passed and opened the coat. She was wearing a very short skirt. At exactly that moment, she turned, caught his eye and nodded her head. It was done by looking. In the rear view mirror he saw she was talking to a man in a raincoat.

Some looked like children, dressed in fashionably dark clothes, smiling and nodding into the cars. Young men in shell suits and trainers, jeans and leather jackets, hung around, singly. They looked tired and he wondered if it was safe to park, what would happen if he walked about. He followed the traffic. A policeman and policewoman were talking to a girl. They looked inside her Safeway carrier bag. Next time round she nodded. Third time round she was gone.

He parked opposite the taxi rank. 'I'm looking for Mickey Ryan,' he asked a driver.

'Havnae seen him.'

'Do you know if he's working tonight?'

'Ask somebody else. I'm first in the rank.'

'You'll know him,' said a driver. 'He always uses this rank, except when he picks up a fare in town or works from another rank.'

'What hours does he work?'

'Varies. Mind you, he usually works nights, though I've seen him down here during the day. Depends.'

'How will I know him?'

'He's a wee guy, about that size. He's got a rough voice.'

'Thanks.'

'Nae bother, son. If I see him I'll tell him you were asking for him.'

Beside the rank and at a few points in the Anderston Centre, plants were growing through the tarmac.

A young man with a mountain bike was talking to three girls. It was obviously a deal. A younger man from the shadows grabbed a girl's arm and flung her out onto the street.

'That's for fucken after,' he said.

'Don't fucken shove us, right. Just don't shove us.' When she passed Andy, she smiled: 'Looking for business, darling?'

He followed the grid to Charing Cross and home, turning again to drive across the Kingston Bridge, with the litter of interpasses and roads ending in the sky. He was driving along Victoria Road before he realised where he was going. He was driving to Allison Street and could not say why.

That was enough. He left the car outside Myra's flat and walked round to West End Park Street. He lay on the bed, listening to the Antal Dorati recording of Respighi's *Ancient Airs and Dances*, trying to think.

Now they knew most of each other's secrets. At first they whispered in the dark, then things would spill into conversation.

Myra showed him the forms before she applied for her psychiatric nursing course and by the time he was accepted for Strathclyde University, she knew the courses, options and semester system. She gave him *Middlemarch* and *To The Lighthouse*. 'They were on your list,' she said. 'Best of luck, especially with that one. Never fancied it myself. Too precious.'

She took him to see her parents. He loved the idea of lots of relatives, cousins he had never met, sisters and brothers in law, nieces and nephews. Something he imagined as appropriate to other people, something he wanted, but never thought possible for himself.

'What about you?' she said. 'You must have a family.' He told her things he never thought he would be able to tell, school, his father, mother, Cathie and a little of Margaret.

'That's an odd one,' she said as though he had not told her the truth.

'I don't understand it either,' he said.

'I wish I'd met your Granny,' she said, lying in bed.

'It's the innocence of that generation,' he said. 'Her favourite phrase was, Away and raffle your doughnut, and I'm sure she never thought of it in any context other than its literal meaning. Same as she spoke of guys as being Mammy's boys, He'll no leave his Mammy, she said and the guy was an absolute queen. I don't think it embarrassed her, I think she couldn't see it.'

'But imagine her having a fancy man.'

'I don't know that's what he was.'

'Andy represents the side of the family who has always kept in touch,' said Orlando. 'We sometimes see a little of Joe, but nothing at all of Eileen. This is distressing, but only to be expected in families. Not that I have much experience, you understand. My own family, such as they were, scattered and I kept in touch with no one. Years of wandering from place to place have left me with very little to carry. Andrew's grandmother was my salvation, as she was to many a soul in this city.'

She met Joe in the Halt Bar, turning up for the last hour when he and Andy went for a drink.

'I wondered what had kept him from his weekly session,' said Joe.

Later he told Andy: 'Not long now. My tank is swelling. Maybe I'll move into your place when you move in with Myra.'

'Why don't you do it now?'

'I don't know. Can't afford it, but I think it also has something to do with what you're used to. I can't really imagine living in a bedsit at my age. This past wee while hasn't been too bad.'

'Do you think you'll ever go?'

'I hope so. I'm stagnating where I am. I've become a non-person. I dread the idea of going on holiday with her and don't mention Christmas. Otherwise, it's tolerable.'

Myra wore a new dress to meet Eileen, who was tense and polite. Myra brought a box of chocolates which lay unopened on the display cabinet. Neither woman talked for the first twenty minutes. Eileen went to the kitchen to finish with the food. Myra asked if she wanted a hand; Eileen said she would manage. Joe followed Eileen into the kitchen. Myra and Andy looked at each other. They both made a face and smiled.

'We'll have the coffee next door,' said Eileen, when the meal was finished.

'She means in the sitting room,' said Joe. 'She does not mean we are going to the house next door for a cup of coffee. It would take three weeks' notice in writing for their dug to bite you, but the son's in trouble again, driving a stolen car, joy-riding.'

Everyone laughed except Eileen. Myra began gathering the dishes. 'Just leave them,' said Eileen. 'I'll do them later.'

'I'll help you clear the table,' Myra said and carried on with what she was doing.

When they came into the sitting room, Eileen looked uncomfortable, as though she was in another house, or Myra had taken over this one. She poured herself coffee and sat on the edge of her seat, looking at whoever was talking, saying nothing.

The afternoon went slowly. Joe and Andy talked about

football, the World Cup gubbings and the good-natured fans. On the edge, Myra picked her way through a conversation. 'Have you lived here long?' she asked. 'It's a lovely house. Have you always had the same neighbours?'

They did the washing-up together and Myra helped to make the tea. They left around seven o'clock. Eileen told Myra it was nice to meet her and hoped she would see her again soon.

'Come over sometime with Andy,' she said, 'one night during the week. We can have a blether while they're at the pub.'

'It's a start,' said Myra. She was almost asleep, her head against the side window.

'I'm a bit cynical about it all, especially Eileen. There's a lot of ground to be made up there.'

'I asked about your mother. Hope you didn't mind.'

'What did she say?'

'I told Eileen you wanted to see your mum. She said she'd arrange it.'

They drove in silence, her hand on his knee. 'You okay?' she asked at the close.

'I don't know.'

'Was I wrong to mention it?'

'Not at all. It's just a bit sudden. I can't believe this is going on. I can't believe I'm dealing with it. Look at me, look at my life. Jesus. None of it makes sense, none of it. I thought I'd worked it out in jail. I'd plenty time and I tried to get it done; did what I could, looked at things for what they were and tried to change them, I really did. And now there's my mother. Jesus Christ. I haven't seen her in years. She could be dead for all I knew.'

'Do you want to see her?'

'I don't know. I'm not sure I can handle it. Does this make sense to you?'

'I'll think about it.'

'So will I. Can I borrow the car?'

'What for?'

'I don't know. A drive. I can sometimes think when I'm driving.'

He drove to Allison Street, parked in Westmorland Street and walked past his window on the opposite side of the street. He'd recognise the curtains anywhere.

A drunk came down from Victoria Road and fumbled with the close key. Andy went in at his back. There was no entry system when he lived there.

He knocked on the door. A wee girl asked, 'Do you want to see my Daddy? Mammy, it's a man.'

'You'd better come in,' she said.

He stepped over a tricycle in the hall. There was Lego on the sitting-room floor, fluffy toys and games. The mother was wearing a skirt and blouse, her hair piled on top of her head.

'I'm no long in,' she said. 'Wait a minute.'

She switched on the video. Pluto ran from Mickey Mouse. The child sat in front of the television wearing her nightdress.

'They're dead dear them, but they're worth it. Weans love them. It's the only thing that'll keep her quiet. She'll watch it for hours, twice a day sometimes. When she's seen that, she'll go to bed. She should be in bed now by rights, but it was a babysitter and she wouldnae go doon.' She lit a cigarette. 'What was it you wanted? He's no here any mair. I'm on my own, thank fuck.'

'I was wondering about the house.'

'What about it?'

'I used to live here and my wife sold it while I was in jail.'

'That's why he's no here. Six year he got. Screwing shops. I tellt him, but he widnae listen. Six year.'

'Have you had the house long?'

'We bought it about a year ago off a woman and a man. I don't mind their name right, but I've got an address for them.'

She wrote the address on a piece of paper. Thorntonhall. Andy had never heard of the place.

'Come on, Kelly,' she said. 'That's nearly finished and it's half past ten. Bedtime.' The child did not move.

'I'd better be going.'

'She'll be going doon in a minute. Do you no want a cup of tea?'

'I'd better get back.'

'Maybe we'll see you again. I'll get somebody to watch the wean. My number's on the paper.'

'Fine. Thanks very much.'

'Right, Kelly Wallace. That's it.'

Driving back he thought of something Charlie Sloan had told him: 'I was offered my nookie more when I was married than at any time before or since.'

'That's because you were married for thirty years, you stupid old bastard,' said Eddie Coyne.

'Not at all. Women like married men. They're a challenge.'

'How would you have liked it if your wife was doing what you were doing?'

'A woman's place is in the home.'

'Was that why you killed her? Did she have a wee fancy man?'

'There's that to it as well, of course.'

A bungalow in Bishopbriggs; neat and indistinguishable from the others.

Rose, his mother, opened the door. She was wearing a straight, yellow striped dress with a collar and a belt. Her hair was greyish, short and tightly permed. Make-up gave her mouth the appearance of having been drawn onto her face.

The sitting room was warm. The gas fire glowed at miser rate. A coffee table with Queen Anne legs stood in front of the sofa. There was a pot of tea, two china cups, saucers and plates, cutlery, biscuits and a plate of small trimmed brown bread sandwiches. There was a posy of flowers and no books in the room.

They drank tea. His mother wanted to know where he lived, was sorry he was not working but glad to hear he was going to university. She was interested in his course. He asked how she was and his mother sighed.

'I think I saw you at poor Malcolm's funeral,' she said. 'God rest him. He was very ill towards the end. Cancer.'

'I saw him in hospital.'

'So you did. It's a terrible disease. You'd think they'd be able to do something about it these days, wouldn't you, with all the technology they've got. I saw him at his best and I saw him at his worst. I saw him in nice restaurants and his days at the races, which bored me, of course, but you have to let men have these sorts of pleasures, haven't you. Otherwise it's as if they're in jail. They become restless. I heard you were in the jail. A husband killed and a son in the jail. What a life.'

There was silence. He finished his tea and had nothing to say. The only noise was the hiss of the fire and the rasp of nylon when his mother crossed her legs.

'More tea?'

'No thanks. This is very awkward for me.'

'Why's that, Andrew?'

'I feel you're a stranger.'

'We haven't seen a lot of each other, certainly; but I am your mother.'

'There have been times when I've needed a mother, times when I would have done anything to have had a mother to talk to.'

'I was always here.'

'I've never felt we were emotionally close. I was bewildered, thrown into the deep end and told to get on with it.'

'Sometimes that's the best way.'

'Do you think so? Do you think that's best for a child, for your child, not any old child, your child, mother; do you think that was the best way for your child to be?'

'Your grandmother and I did not get on.'

'I remember. I remember the last time you came to see us.'

'I don't wish to discuss it.'

'Why not?'

'No point in raking over old coals, opening old sores. Best to let these things heal.'

'But they haven't healed. If they had healed you would be able to talk about them. They haven't healed for me either. That's why I'm here, to try to begin a process that can let us get to know each other. Do you know that I've hated you for years.'

'That's not a very nice thing to say to your mother.'

'I didn't hate you, I hated what I thought you were and I hated what I was told you were. I hated the fact that you left me.'

'I couldn't leave your grandmother with nothing. She had lost a son, so I gave her mine.'

'Shut up and listen.'

'You shouldn't have come if that's the way you're going to carry on.'

'I'm trying to tell you I'm sorry. I love you. I worked it out in jail. I love you and I don't care about Granny or what she said. I am sorry for what she did, it must have hurt you very much.'

'Would you like some more tea, Andrew?'

'No, thanks. I've met a girl and we're going to get married.'

'I believe you were married before. What happened there? Did that break up?'

'It broke up when I was in jail.'

'Of course. No woman wants a criminal for a husband.'

'You had a murderer.'

'I think you had better go.'

'Sorry.'

'You've said quite enough. I think you had better go.'

It was raining. He drove to the top of the road, turned towards Glasgow, punched the steering wheel and screamed.

*

You learn how to jail, to serve your time and be a criminal. You learn ways of breaking the law, of getting by, ways of waiting until the big one comes; how to work a cheque scam, how to break into cars, rob hotel rooms, burgle houses and shoplift. You hear stories of the real cons, who squandered their money on women, drink and gambling and got caught because they were careless or because it was their turn to get caught.

Every prisoner is fascinated by the law and its intricacies. Many study law, some study religion; politics is a popular subject. Many take an Open University course and go to university to finish their degrees when they come out.

Charlie Sloan read books on natural history: 'There are a group of people, a tribe living on an island in the South Pacific who haven't worked out the connection between shagging and childbirth,' he said. 'They think weans come from the stars and the gods.'

'Don't talk daft,' said Eddie Coyne. 'If a guy came up to me and asked where babies came from, I'd tell him a stork brought them. They thought he was a social worker and took a len o him.'

'Not at all,' said Charlie. 'It's in the book. I'll show you.'

There was Eddie Coyne, Charlie Sloan and Andy, three beds in a row. They hung around together. Eddie was interested in guns and weaponry.

A couple of days later, Andy asked Charlie to show him the book about the naïve Indians.

'Not today,' he said. 'I don't feel well. It's my wife's birthday. She was a good woman and I was terribly fond of her.'

'I'm sorry, Charlie.'

'No, it's all right, son. I don't talk about it, because I don't like to remind myself what the last few years were like. She wasn't herself. Some days she was all right, then she'd change, like that.' He snapped his fingers. 'She knew she was doing it, knew what was happening. She was well aware of what was going on. She went to the doctor. He told her to pull herself together. The papers said I was The Henpecked Killer. I wasnae henpecked. She changed, that was all, she changed. Now when I think of her I think of the way she was afore that. I think of when she was a girl. A year to do and then I'm out. I dread it. I don't know what I'll do. I've nowhere to go.'

*

He dialled the Polisman's number: no reply.

Sheila worried about the neighbours, yet she let him sleep with her. Twice. But someone's stains had sent him to jail.

Fenian McGuire had little or nothing to do with the case, he had withdrawn his services. As far as Andy knew he had no reason to know when he was getting out. 'Thought it would be about now,' he'd said.

He dialled again. The Polisman answered. Andy replaced the receiver.

He dialled Fenian's number. 'He isn't here,' his wife said. 'He won't be back till Friday. He's away on business.'

He drove to the house. The Polisman's car was in the garage. Andy waited in Myra's car, watching the house. A light was on in the downstairs sitting room, sometimes the hall and sometimes the kitchen. He walked past the house. The Polisman was downstairs on his own, watching television. By the time Andy got back to the car, the curtains were drawn.

He did not know why he was there. What would he say if the Polisman caught him? He turned the ignition. Nothing; he pulled the choke and the car started. He was about to move off when a taxi passed. It stopped at the Polisman's house. A woman, not the Polisman's wife, a woman other than Sheila, ran up the drive. The Polisman opened the door. Ten minutes later a light went on in the spare bedroom window.

Again, he phoned Fenian's wife. 'Sorry to bother you, Mrs McGuire. I wonder if you could tell me how I can contact your husband. It's very important.'

'He's at the Peebles Hydro.'

The drive took about an hour. They were sitting by the fire, with brandy, coffee and chocolate mints on a silverish tray.

'I think you and I should have a wee talk,' said Andy. Sheila stood up; with her shoulders back, she carefully walked to the toilet.

Fenian sighed. 'What brings you down here? Just passing? Were you in the area?'

'It didn't add up,' said Andy. 'Your little secret is safe with me, because it guarantees my freedom. At least some of the problem's solved. Which leaves the matter of the Polisman, who was well out of order and needs sorted out.'

Sheila was back, her make-up adjusted. She lit a cigarette and stared at the fire. She looked older, the little lines around her eyes were more defined. Her hair had been done, a quasi-platinum blonded look to quell the impact of approaching grey.

'Can we get you a drink?' said Fenian. 'Or maybe you'd like some coffee? Nice wee reunion this; made more pleasant by its surprise. The thing is, I am sorry to say you've got it wrong again. Sheila and I met when I interviewed her for your trial.'

'That'll be right. She knows as well as I do it wasn't me that was there the night the Polisman found the evidence on her bed.'

Shelia lit another cigarette. 'What are you talking about? My husband knew nothing about you. What gives you the idea I'd want him to know about that? It had nothing to do with you going to jail. That was coincidence, pure and simple. You were jailed because drugs were found in your house.'

'Which your husband planted because you told him I was screwing you. I wondered why you did that. Was it to save someone else, like Mr McGuire here?'

'Don't be daft. I told you, my husband never knew about you and me, unless you told him.'

'You'll never prove he set you up, even if he did, which I don't believe,' said Fenian. 'It's an interesting theory, but, as I say, quite wrong. Have you seen Mickey Ryan?'

'I'm not sure Mickey Ryan exists.'

'You'll be sure when you meet him.'

'What is this Mickey Ryan shite anyway?'

'I have a wee theory about what happened to you. I believe and always did believe you knew nothing about the cargo that was found in your house; not that it proves anything. It's only a theory and not as far fetched as your idea.'

'I'm going upstairs,' said Shelia. 'I won't be long.'

Fenian looked at Andy and smiled. 'Can I get you anything?'

'I'm fine.'

'Listen, son. Forget it. I don't know; honestly, I don't. I met her when I defended her man and we see each other from time to time. I don't believe her man set you up because he doesn't do that. I don't think it would occur to him. Look at the state he's in; hassling folk to pay their Poll Tax and getting chased by a bunch of women. Drugs is big business. Talk to Mickey, he'll show you a bit of it; the obvious side, the sort of thing anybody would see if they cared to look. I'll ask around and see what I can do.'

'So this is coincidence? Me and the Polisman's wife, you and the Polisman's wife, the Polisman and somebody else?'

'They're not the first. I think they let each other get on with it. I don't know why. You'd think it would be easier to separate. Not that I fancy that much. Her mother likes me. Her man's a polis and I'm a lawyer. She wants her daughter to get on.'

'Does her mother know you're a Catholic lawyer with a wife who goes to chapel and a whole squad o weans?'

'Sorry it's been a wasted journey. Nice seeing you, son. Off to bed says Sleepyhead, Time for work, says Slow. We'll grease the pan, says Hungry Nan, And eat before we go. Drive safely.'

He knew she was angry. The light was on. It was after one o'clock when he rang the entry bell.

'Where the hell have you been?'

'Peebles.'

'In my car?'

'Yeah.'

'Tell me you're kidding. What do you think you're going to do now? Move in here and use the car to run around in? You'll be asking me to make sure your birds are fed next.'

'It isn't like that.'

'What's it like, Andy?'

'I went down to Peebles to see McGuire.'

'I don't care why you went to Peebles. For some daft reason I expected you to be here tonight. Probably because you said you were coming. I had your supper cooked. When eight o'clock came and you didn't show, I phoned your digs. It's been an interesting night emotionally. I can't take this, Andy. You could have phoned. I deserved a bloody phone call. Whatever's going on, you'll have to work it out for yourself. I don't want your past hanging over me. Leave the car keys here, please.'

A driver said Mickey Ryan was working. 'Christ knows where he is but, comes and goes, know what I mean. If I see him I'll tell him.'

An hour later Mickey was at the end of the rank. He looked lost, with a pointed face and sleeky black hair.

'It's okay,' he said. 'I know who you are. Mr McGuire told me. Is it true yous call him Fenian?'

'So I believe.'

'Does he no mind?'

'I think he likes it.'

'Has he always liked being called Fenian?'

'I think so.'

'How long have you known him?'

'Too long.'

'He said you met him at the casino, is that right?'

'Yeah.'

'And then he defended you?'

'No, he was going to defend me. He withdrew from the case. I got someone else. Fenian was already involved in another case about the policeman who arrested me.'

'Was it drugs?'

'Someone tried to get him for wrongful arrest, but he got off. I was sent down and Fenian has always felt responsible. Can I ask you some questions now?'

'Nae bother.'

'What was that all about?'

'I just wanted to know.'

'Know what?'

'He told me to tell you something and I don't know why he told me.'

'Are you any wiser?'

'No.'

'Then why don't you tell me and if I know what's going on I'll tell you.'

'What did he say?'

'About what?'

'Me. What did he say about me?'

'He said you thought you were a hard man, that you sometimes talked out the side of your mouth like James Cagney, that you were a wee rascal and I wisnae to give you any money.'

'I wouldnae've asked you for money anyway. He squared me up.'

'If that's the interview over, you can tell me what it is.'

'What what is?'

'What Fenian told you to tell me.'

'Smoke?'

'No thanks.'

He lit his cigarette. 'There's two runs we get, two distance runs that come off the rank. The first is a city tour sort of run. A guy gets the bus in from the airport and wants to see a bit of the city. Some of them have got guide books and everything. We take them round some of the well-known buildings, City Chambers, up to the Cathedral, onto the motorway passing Martyr's School and a nice view of the city, coming off the motorway at Kelvinside for the Art School, past the Hatrack and the St Vincent Street Church and back to the rank at Anderston Bus Station. So far, so good?'

'I'm listening.'

'You might have gathered, the lassies around here are prostitutes. Most of them have AIDS. They have a better chance here than in a massage parlour. No desk money and more customers. Funny, intit, aa the women that work in massage parlours tell you they're behind the desk, doing the towels and answering the telephone. You never meet any of the whores. They lassies here are drug addicts, most of them. One or two maybe aren't, but those that arenae addicts pretty soon become addicts if they're down here long enough. Feel no pain. Heroin.

'Any heroin you get here is seven per cent pure, no more. Seven per cent heroin, ninety-three per cent icing sugar, cleaning powder, stuff like that. Some of these lassies are on two grammes a day at eighty or a hundred quid a gramme, £160 a day minimum, just to get by, as well as your ponce and all the extras. No wonder they're shabby. I can assure you, every one of them, every fucken one lives in squalor. If they're down here to help out with the kids and family, they're better off than the addicts.'

'How come you know so much?'

'That's what I'm about to tell you. There's another run, twice a night. Ask yourself: what the fuck is a taxi driver doing at the Anderston Bus Station at two in the morning? We know where to go when the bingo comes out, when the bingo goes in, which halls run a wee bit late, when the hospital visiting times are across the city and so on. So if a taxi driver is standing at the Anderston Bus Station at two o'clock in the morning, he has to be waiting for a fare.

'We call it the drug run. I could show you where it goes, more or less, there are a few variations, but not too many. It goes to Possil, Springburn, Cranhill, Ruchazie, Gorbals and Easterhouse every night. The drivers love it, thirty or forty quid a time for the fare. All the lassies chip in, well, the young ones, the older women tend not to be addicts. They send a couple for the stuff and when they come back there's a big share-out. They take it to that wee drop-in centre they have, The Health and Beauty Sauna in Holm Street. They get free Durex and needles there, a cup of tea.

'Very few take the kind of drugs we're talking about. Very few. They wouldnae turn it down, but it's inconvenient. They're no really interested in the kind of stuff that was found in your place. Jellies is the thing these days. Jelly Babies. Pills. Mostly sleeping pills, painkillers, two or three pounds each and they take them like sweeties. A few ampoules and a hot cup of tea and that's them all right for an hour or two. I was talking to one lassie. She took a hundred. She said she didnae mean to. I took her up to the Royal. She got something from one of these guys with the bikes, do you know about them? They're the runners. They have cell phones: 0800 numbers are difficult to tap. You phone them up, put in your order and down they come, like a take-away. There's shooters down here too, by the way. If you think this happens by accident, think again. It's big business, carefully controlled.

'This is how it works. The kids get employment schemes that pay rubbish wages. They feel exploited. Someone says, and this is schoolkids I'm talking about, Away and get us a wee roll, and gives the kid a fiver. The kid comes back and is told to keep the change. Next thing, the kids find punters for the dealer and so it goes. The dealers go to the main dealer, get their whack. The dealer tells them how much he wants back and the rest is profit.

'I never made any kind of special study of this. Every driver knows the run. It happens every night at least once, twice on the busy nights, say Tuesday, Thursday and Friday. If the taxi drivers know, the polis must know.

'The lassies try it on with the drivers. They need the money. Wee Andy shagged one of them instead of taking the fiver fare. They were aa wantin in his taxi after that, asking when he was on and everything. The only thing the money's for is the drugs. They'll try anything to get you going so they'll save the £3 or £4 for the fare. You can get anything you want. Drivers always take the dosh but.

'There's unmarked squad cars down here every night, taking numbers. If you're down a lot, say a couple of times a week and if, especially if, you go round more than three times, your number's taken and recorded. The polis know the regular punters as well as the lassies. They know who goes with whom, who's only looking and who's a punter. I'd say half of them come here to look, especially women; car loads of them, men and women, come down here to look at the whores. It's a shame, they say. God love them; young lassies.

'I've got my work to get back to. So, if you don't mind, I'll leave you to it. Does it make sense to you?'

Andy sighed. 'I'm not too sure.'

'Why would a polis want to set you up? They know who the dealers are.'

'Thanks.'

'Nae bother.'

'I was set up, though.'

'So you say.'

'There's something of the Calvinist about you. For someone who says he's not too interested in women, you haven't been exactly celibate.'

'I become interested in women, obviously. But I don't go around chasing them.'

'No wonder Myra's fed up. It has nothing to do with her car. That is a symptom, not the cause. Don't come here complaining of her and what she's done. Sort it out.'

'I might have known better than come to you for sympathy.'

Orlando sighed. He looked neater and sprightlier. There was a new rhythm in his voice. He smiled more. The rhythm had to do with ease and comfort. When he came back with the tea, Andy watched his movements.

'How is everybody?'

'I have no idea how everybody is, pretty miserable I should think, given the state of the world.'

'How's Bernadette O'Hara?'

'I don't see too much of her, though Mrs Esplin was telling me Bernadette's daughter has got herself involved with the money lenders, not the legitimate money lenders, rather the illegitimate money lenders: borrow a fiver on the Saturday, pay back seven by the Friday; if you can't pay it becomes eight and so on. Thousands of per cent interest. She was caught operating some sort of cheque card fraud, selling things around the doors. She came here once or twice with the sort of items in which I have no interest: microwave ovens, television sets. The girl is seeing a social worker, of course, having been given a nine months' suspended sentence. Mrs Esplin is none too healthy either. She is taking tranquillisers, she tells me, worried about her son who is a drug addict. He steals money from her purse, stole her television set and her man's clothes, a suit and coat, I believe. Mrs Esplin admits to taking 100-milligramme tranquillisers four times a day, sleeping pills as well, so what is she actually taking? This came up when she told me her son stole them. You can apparently sell them; quite profitable, I believe.'

He dipped a digestive biscuit into his tea and looked out the window.

'There was a young lad, twenty-three or twenty-four, hung himself in that building last week. He had a sign on his chest. It said, The People Here Are Animals. What would your Granny have made of that? I heard two women talking about it in the butcher's. They said, He was aye funny that boy. There was something odd about him. He never had a girlfriend.'

He took another biscuit. 'And did I tell you we have new neighbours. A family across the way. Mother and child. A young girl. The child is about eighteen months. Poor thing. The girl looks as if she knows every penny that's in her purse.'

Orlando opened the window and the smell from the street, summer dust pitted with rain, came into the room. Someone was shouting, selling papers.

'How's Joe?'

'Haven't seen him for a week or two.'

The last time Andy saw Joe, things were awkward. 'I'm not going to take your place right away,' he said while Myra was in the lavatory. 'Tracy's pregnant, which puts a different complexion on things for the time being. Thomas, the financial adviser, got the bullet; and he's in debt, for clothes and cell phones, appearance money.'

'What about your wee tank?'

'Gone, more or less. I've had to help them out.'

When Myra came back, he bought them a drink and left. 'I said I'd pick up a wee cot. I'm going to do it up for them. They don't know yet.'

Orlando sighed. 'Is everything okay with Joe?' he asked.

'Tracy's pregnant.'

Orlando looked out the window. They sat in silence till Geordie came home with a new poem.

William was my friend.
I have not seen him for a long time
And am lonely.
When I see floods on television
I wonder if he has drowned.
When I see riots
I wonder if he's dead.
Has he been bombed
In a disaster
Or caught in an earthquake
In another life?
I have other friends
But no one like William
Who needed looking after.
If he came back
We would have a wonderful party.

When he phoned she started to cry.

'What's wrong?'

'Nothing. Come over,' she said.

She had obviously been crying, had washed her face and started crying again when she opened the door.

'I can't handle this,' she said. 'I simply cannot deal with it. I have no emotional experience to draw on. Any time there was something I couldn't handle, I got drunk. I have tried to thole this out and can't. The number of times I have almost called you, picked up the telephone, dialled it even, then put the receiver back at the last minute. A day at a time, I tell myself. I won't do it today. Why not? I want to. Why not do it then? Because I want you to know you were wrong and to tell me you know you were wrong.'

'I told you.'

'I know you did, but it isn't enough. I know it's all I'm going to get and I don't want any more, but there should be something more. Another thing I've been telling myself is that we grow from experiences like this. I told my head I could do without you. Can't.'

'Here.'

'I don't want a hankie. I want you to listen. I tried to read *Don Quixote*. Couldn't. I got as far as the bit where he strips to his shirt and turns somersaults because he thinks he's in love. I started to cry. I wanted to know you were okay. What have you brought me?'

'My essays. You always wanted to see them.'

'You are like a wee boy sometimes, sitting there with your hair combed showing me your homework. Jesus Christ. Give us them over. I'll read them just now. It'll take my mind off myself. You make the tea.'

She tucked her legs beneath herself and sat on the sofa. He caught a glimpse as he closed the door and knew it would be so. There would be times when she would return to the mind unbidden, sitting on the sofa with the William Morris print, the lamp by the table, a green and a dark blue cushion behind her, wearing jeans and a black woollen shirt with short sleeves, red socks and a red ribbon tying the back of her hair, a small gold watch on her left wrist and a bangle on her right, wearing no make-up, reading the A4-sized typing paper which she held in her left hand, twirling a strand of hair with her right forefinger, her right elbow leaning on the sofa arm. Years from now she would sit this way. She would not age. She was immortal. He started to cry. Thinking it was silly, he wiped his face, but the tears would not stop. He was sobbing when she came into the kitchen. 'Baby,' she said, holding him tightly, crying now herself. 'Oh, Andy darling. My wee baby.'

Two hours later they were still talking: 'We have to keep trying,' she said. 'With your mother, with ourselves, with Eileen, we have to keep trying; Joe, Orlando, everybody, everything, we have to keep trying. Sounds really simple, but it isn't. The only people who decry it are those who can't do it. We have to keep on going for what we want.'

'Can I tell you a secret?'

She kissed his neck.

'Something Orlando said reminded me of it. I hadn't actually forgotten, but it seems to have a deeper significance. When I was in Barlinnie, before I got sent to Dungavel, there was a young lad in there, younger than me, maybe eighteen or nineteen, a nice lad, good looking. He was sharing a cell with two really hardened cons and they were screwing him. They called him sweetheart and stuff like that. They offered him out for tobacco and he would have to go. He told the screws and they did nothing. He had three months to go on his sentence, it had something to do with drugs, I don't know what; anyway, he had three months to go when he stabbed himself to get out the cell. He was taken to the prison hospital. He hung himself when he found out he would have to spend the last five or six weeks of his sentence in the same cell with the same guys. I hardly knew him. I don't think I ever spoke to him. I heard about it, of course. I can't get him out my mind. I don't want to forget him. Somebody has to remember him. I wish I knew who his parents were. I'd go and see them. I don't know what I'd say, but I'd say something.'

He was crying again. 'The guy in the next bed to me died. Wee Eddie Coyne got peritonitis when his appendix burst. He complained about the pain, the screw never believed him and that was it. You learn to live with the system, the jail hierarchy, give and take, doing the screws' work for them, not seeing what's going on; when there's a stabbing everybody's in the lavvy. It's a bit like here actually, a bit like the real world.'

They fell asleep on the sofa in front of the fire and sometime in the night moved through to the bedroom where they wakened after ten.

'Was this your day off?'

'No, I'm going in for lunches.'

'And are you doing a meeting tonight?'

'I think so.'

'I've made my mind up, Myra. I'm going to see Fenian. I might be late. Don't worry. I don't know when I'll be back. I need him to confirm something for me. Can I borrow the car?'

She smiled. 'So long as you give us a lift to work.'

Fenian McGuire squeezed brown sauce onto his bacon roll. They were in the Grosvenor Café.

'Can I have another bacon roll, dear? They're good them. Want another?' Andy nodded. 'Two, dear. And two more cappuccinos.' Fenian finished his coffee.

'The more I look at it, the simpler it becomes,' he said. He wiped his mouth and fingers with a napkin. 'Quite simple really. I had a word with my client and he confirmed as much as he could, unofficially, of course. I think he wants to set the record straight. Perhaps Sheila told him something, I don't know. Thanks very much, dear. There's the bill there, just add it on. Do we pay at the desk?'

They ate the rolls in silence, wiped their mouths and fingers. Fenian lit a cigarette and sighed. 'Nothing like it,' he said. 'Nothing like it. Simple fare.'

'Am I right then? Was that what happened? I'm not asking you to break confidences. I just need to know and you're the only one who can tell me.'

'This is all I know and I shouldnae even be telling you this. My client did not plant the evidence in your house on the night you were arrested. He was acting on information received, a tip-off, from an unnamed source. A woman, I believe. When pressed, and he cannot confirm this, my client believes the call came from your ever-loving wife, Margaret Paterson by name. He interviewed your wife at some length at the time of your arrest and clearly remembers thinking how similar the voices were at the time. This belief was further confirmed in my client's mind when he learned the said Margaret Paterson was now living with Frankie Shaw. Shaw is a well-known dealer. We did a little checking, my client and I. Frankie Shaw went into jail about six months before you were married and came out about a year before you were arrested. There is good reason to suspect your wife visited Mr Shaw while he was in the jail and you being a waiter with irregular hours would hardly notice what the little woman at home was up to. Shaw, by the way, is presently *persona non grata* in certain quarters. This is because he embezzled the funds. He did it in much the same way as the bunch of crooks who were involved in the Guinness take-over swindle did it. He took the money. It was as subtle as that. He also thought he would get away with it and so far has managed to avoid retribution, but he is definitely being hunted and there is talk of a gang war. That's press patter, of course, but it could be nasty, so I would advise you to stay away from your ex-wife, her man, their car, cat, dog and the fine home in Thortonhall, which he bought with the profits he earned with his business flair, acumen and entrepreneurial skills.'

'Thanks.'

'Nae bother. What you have to work out, for your own peace of mind, is whether or not she was holding for him or if you were simply planted. Could be coincidence. I don't know. Anyway, I have to go. Mickey Ryan was asking for you.'

'Fenian.'

'What?'

'Thanks.'

'Nae bother.

'I mean it.'

'I'll get this. Give us a ring. We'll go down to the casino one of these nights and have a wee flutter. I always liked your style in these matters.'

'I've kind of given it up.'

'Then don't let me tempt you. Give us a ring anyway. I always like to hear from students.'

He found the house without much trouble. It was on top of a hill, a single-storey bungalow with a four-car garage, a field and paddock for three or four horses, stone lions on either side of the front door. There was a small copse beyond the field.

He drove to East Kilbride, went to the cinema, saw *The Hunt for Red October* and came out around ten o'clock. He looked up the phone book and dialled the number. There was no reply.

He drove towards Glasgow, bought a two-gallon petrol can, a bottle of ginger beer, paper tissues and a box of matches. He filled the can at a station near Uddingston, drove along the motorway, turned towards Clarkston and waited. He dialled the number again. No reply.

He drove to Thorntonhall. The house was dark. He parked behind the copse and at five past two drank a little ginger beer, pouring the rest into the hedgerow. He walked across the field to the house. It was heavily furnished and definitely empty. He came back through the field, filled the bottle with petrol, stuffed tissues in the bottleneck and started the car. With the engine running he returned to the house.

He lit the paper and counted ten, threw the bottle in a downstairs window to the back of the house. There was the sound of breaking glass, then nothing. He walked away and as he turned he saw the flame, the little light behind the curtain, then the explosion.

He ran to the car and drove to the city, dumping the stuff in a Pollokshaws bin while he walked around to clear his head.

He was back in the bedroom at five past three. He moved the clock to ten past one, nudging Myra as he leaned across the bed to put it back at her side.

'What time is it?'

'Back of one.'

'What were you doing?'

'Checking the alarm.'

'We don't need the alarm. Tomorrow's Saturday.'

'Give us it here then.'

She passed him the clock. He altered the time, put the clock on the floor to his side of the bed, got under the duvet and snuggled in.

'What's this you've got on?'

'Waste of time. I'm too tired. Did I tell you, I've been offered a place in psychie training? The letter must have come at lunchtime.'

'That's great.'

'Good, i'n't it.'

'We'll go out and celebrate tomorrow night.'

'I want to go to the pictures. There's that film with Sean Connery.'

'Do you fancy him?'

'Every woman in the world fancies Sean Connery. And Davie phoned. He wants to know if you're going to the game. I don't know what game. You've to phone him. Don't, Andy; I'm too tired. How did you get on?'

'Fine.'

'That's good.'

He cooried at her back as she pressed towards him.

Later in the night he wakened. From somewhere below came the sound of music, piano and fiddle, so faint at first he thought he was dreaming. It stopped and started and was finally lost in Myra's breathing.

Just a small city sound in the dark.

Also by Carl MacDougall and available from Minerva

Stone Over Water

'Apparently the life and reminiscences of Angus McPhail, but it soon becomes apparent that Carl MacDougall's real subject is Scotland and what it means to be Scots. As his name implies, Angus is the child of failure . . . While his adoptive brother tries to save Scotland for socialism by robbing banks, Angus, representing the bastard majority, is happier working for number one. Not that he *is* happy. Having alienated a succession of women by his dour self-absorption, he finally ends up in a cosily incestuous relationship with his adoptive sister . . . Despite its lightness of touch, this is a novel of complexity and ambition, hilarious, moving and thought-provoking'
Observer

'This novel . . . sets Carl MacDougall firmly among the pantheon of Kelman, Gray and Archie Hind . . . sparkling and exhilarating in many places; wise and, above all, entertaining'
Iain Crichton Smith, *Scotland on Sunday*

'Carl is a hero of mine . . . a great storyteller' Billy Connolly

'An exceptional first novel' *Scotsman*